AF407296

The Salt and the Salve

Traci Tucker

1

Jillian hating camping—in Florida, anyway, in any month other than February. She hated how her skin felt after being outside all day, sticky and itchy; hated how her hair looked when it dried naturally, dishwater blond waves every which way, in no logical order except wrong; hated feeling so exposed at night. Anyone could just walk right up. Anything could, too.

She grew up in Florida in a house on a dirt road. With no air conditioning and nearly no pest control, it was always hot and sweaty and buggy. Any time a car raced down the road fast enough to stir it up, the dry sandy dirt floated through the open jalousies. She had had enough of that experience and had invested a lot of time and energy into putting it behind her.

She recalled their last camping trip in March. Zach, their five-year-old son, was snuggled on his side on his air mattress in the tent, sound asleep. His perfectly round cherubic face looked so peaceful, but his soft dark blonde hair was a bit matted to his forehead with sweat. Peter sat by the fire, beer in hand, silent, while she cleaned up the campsite for the night.

Peter loved camping—maybe just one example of how their relationship, their marriage, frustrated her. Maybe it brought back some fond childhood memories or made him feel manly somehow. It couldn't have been putting up the tent (which Jillian was better at). Maybe it was making a fire (which she tried not to get involved with). Maybe it was just as simple as not having to shower or shave or having a valid excuse for drinking lots of beer. Like he needed one. Maybe it gave him some hope that they would have sex on the air mattress in the hot, stuffy tent, like they used to years ago.

They had packed up and left for home early that Sunday, instead of later in the afternoon. She remembered that she was feeling pretty content that morning, even though she had let Peter make all the decisions, as usual. It might have been one of the last peaceful moments of their marriage, but she didn't know that then.

2

On a warm, humid Friday evening a month later, Jillian's life was turned upside down at a conference center on Clearwater Beach.

It was a typical beach hotel with pastel decor and palm trees, always a little warmer inside than most hotels because of the numerous doors to the beach opening and closing so often. After three days of lectures and learning, she joined her coworkers and peers to celebrate and release the tension (or boredom).

As the sun set over the Gulf of Mexico, the crowd under the white tent thinned from a few dozen to twenty, ten, then just a handful, all completely drunk and tousled from being on the beach in the salty sea air all evening. It had even rained for a few brief moments, but Jillian was so drunk she didn't care if it had poofed all the straight out of her hair. People were slurring their words and tripping in the wet sand and starting to get too personal with one another.

"So, you're still married, right, Jillian?" Guy, one of the junior account executives, posed. He was handsome, attractive, younger than Jillian—maybe around thirty, while she would be forty in a few years, although she was often taken for years younger.

"Yes, I believe I am," she replied, trying to focus, wondering in her stupor why he was asking. "You?"

"Most of the time." He chuckled. "Happy?"

"I try not to think about it," she said.

"Me, too. I wonder, though, if I shouldn't just try to have some fun." He looked at Jillian from the corners of his eyes, grinning.

"Whaddyou mean, fun?" she laughed, looking him over. He was handsome, that was for sure. Nice teeth (crucial), tan, deep brown eyes, short sandy hair. Nice build.

"Guy, shut up! You don't even know what you're talking about," some woman said from behind him. "You wouldn't cheat."

"How do you know what I would or wouldn't do?" Guy said. "Why not? Lots of people do. Some say it helps. I have a kid, after all. I want to be there," he said.

"Can't cheat. It's not right," Jillian said. "It's lying."

She had never cheated. Even when she knew that a relationship was over, she never cheated, never even thought about another man, until it was officially done.

"Whatever. I'm going to get another drink," Guy said, tottering off.

Jillian was wasted and staggering, too. She couldn't focus. But her drink was empty, so she made her way inside to the elevator to go up to the bar. A man jumped in behind her, from nowhere, drink in hand. She immediately recognized Ethan Chase, with his dimpled smile and lilting laugh. They worked in the same building, for different advertising agencies. Where he'd been all night, she had no idea. She didn't recall seeing him all day, in fact.

"Hey, hey, Jillian! Where you off to?" he said, giggling—drunk too.

"Bar, time for a refill!" She said showing him her empty cup.

"Yep! Me, too!" He punched a button on the panel.

Being past the point of no return, meaning she was too drunk to know it was past time to stop drinking, she said, "Let's go!" and leaned into him, smiling, giggling with him.

The next thing she remembered was being in a hotel room, half naked, with Ethan, who was more than half naked. He jumped on the bed and Jillian was on top of him in a flash, kissing his neck while he laughed, running his hand up her thigh to her hip, telling her how good she felt. As they engaged, it struck her that he had the same crooked smile on his face—and eyes closed—that Peter had when they screwed. Shit. She rolled her eyes.

"You've done this before," Jillian said.

"Had sex?" He laughed.

"No, cheated," she said.

"No, I haven't," he said, without a change in his expression. "Have you?"

"No," she said, and kissed him.

They were both so drunk they couldn't complete the act. After a few lame attempts, they finally conceded and said they would save it for next time.

3

She was sick with a hangover all weekend after "The Incident" with Ethan, as she came to call it. She couldn't look Peter in the eye, but couldn't give herself away, either. She was practically silent, doing her best to focus on Zach, feeling sick to her stomach, wondering silently what the hell was going on, and avoiding Peter as much as possible.

She knew serious trouble was brewing Sunday morning when she looked in the mirror and counted the number of years it would be until Zach was eighteen. She could stay married to Peter until Zach was eighteen. She should stay until he was eighteen. But when she counted the years and realized that she would be fifty years old, she burst into tears. Divorce, which she had never used within the context of her own marriage, loomed large.

That evening, after Zach was in bed, she sat on the couch to watch "Grey's Anatomy," scratching their gray tabby cat, Friday, behind the ears.

Peter planted himself in front of her and, looking her right in the eye, said," Did you cheat on me?"

"No." She stared right back at him. She felt the adrenaline rush through her as she lied to his face. Friday jumped down and ran out of the room. She hoped she wouldn't blush as she tried to push her guilt further down into her gut. She had no idea why he would be suspicious, and it was highly unusual for him to be so confrontational. He was too much of an emotional coward. Even then, she could tell he was nervous by the way he held his shoulders a little too high, and how he stood ramrod straight. He gave himself away. Maybe she had too, somehow.

As soon as she said no, he tapped his front teeth with his right index finger—another tell that he was uncomfortable. "OK," he said, and walked out of the room without another word.

6

Jillian had been rationalizing with herself for months, years probably, making excuses for her discontent, thinking she could change things, trying to get Peter to work with her, then trying to improve their relationship without his cooperation by reading books and experimenting with the words she used, the approaches she took with him, trying to adjust her own attitude. She could fix it, right? Even if he wouldn't help, she could fix things. She could learn, change. She could affect things.

Within the first few years of their fifteen-year relationship, she realized she didn't enjoy sex with him, but she did what she was supposed to do. Correction: She realized she didn't enjoy sex. She didn't think it was isolated to sex with him. She thought she had a chemical, hormonal, or other biological problem that kept her from physically desiring him. She didn't want to have sex. She believed she didn't want to have sex with anyone. She didn't have fantasies. She didn't take care of herself (often). And she didn't cheat. She didn't do anything to have her needs met because she didn't have any needs.

She didn't understand what had changed. After holding off until she was nineteen to lose her virginity (accidentally, at that), she had been a very sexual woman during her college years, sometimes to the point of promiscuity.

She had changed. At some point, something in her had shifted. She finally screwed up the courage to ask her OB-GYN and PCP about it when Zach was around six months old. They both said everything seemed fine physically and that she should talk to someone.

Peter had never been great at initiating sex. Really, he wasn't great at initiating anything if she thought about it. She had asked him out the first time, after they had worked together and flirted for months. It had taken him five years to ask her to marry him. She didn't know if he was insecure or what, but they had numerous but brief conversations—arguments even—about sex and their lack of it. He said he wished she were more assertive. She wished he were, and not just with her. He fancied himself a writer; and he was decent at it, professionally. But he never did more than he was asked, and he never strove for more responsibility than he was given.

Once she asked him what was stopping him from initiating sex when she had never said no, had never turned him away. He couldn't come up with an answer. She never really figured out what the issue was, but eventually realized that she just did not want him. She didn't find him to be sexy or appealing even any longer. Perhaps he sensed it. Perhaps he knew it even before she did. Maybe that was why he'd given up, only going for it when they were camping, in a hotel, or trying to get pregnant.

Maybe she had been gone from their relationship for longer than she realized. Or admitted.

None of that helped her understand why "The Incident with Ethan" had happened—other than their drunken states—or what might be coming next.

One thing she did know was that she wanted to find out what Ethan remembered, why he had let it happen, and how he felt now. She didn't know him well enough to know why he might have cheated on his wife. Maybe he was separated. Maybe he was a Player or some sort of predator.

They had been working in the same building for a couple of years, but he was with a different advertising agency a floor up. They had worked with some clients together and exchanged gossip in the deli in their building at lunch occasionally but had never talked much about their personal lives. She knew he was married and had a couple of young kids, and that was about it. She had no idea how he would react to her when they saw each other next. She didn't know if she would blush from embarrassment—easy to recognize on her fair skin—or fidget with her hair, as she sometimes did when she was nervous. She guessed she would just have to wait and find out.

4

Jillian was at her desk Monday morning when her office phone rang. Her stomach, still not quite right, lurched when she saw his name on her caller ID. She knew it would be best to get it over with but was nervous about talking with him.

"Can you go to lunch today?" he asked.

"Sure. Noon good?"

"Yep. Not in the building though. We should go somewhere so we can talk. Do you mind driving?"

"Sure. I'll pick you up out front," she said. That was interesting. Why would he want her to drive? Was he being paranoid, worried that her scent might linger in his car and cause suspicion?

Jillian was antsy all morning, anxious to find out what he was thinking. It sure made it hard to concentrate, but she did her best. She didn't know how she was going to play it but decided to let him take the lead and she would follow. If he wanted to have some more "fun," maybe she would go for it. If he was remorseful, she would chalk it up to too much drink and let it go.

Noon finally arrived and she waited outside One Metro, their office building, in her black Camry, engine running to cool it down inside. It was a typical Tampa spring day. Hot already, for sure, but the sky was crystal blue with only a few puffs of white cloud here and there. No matter how much she complained about the hot, sticky Florida heat, she would still take it any day over freezing cold and snow.

He finally pushed through the glass doors at almost ten after twelve wearing his usual suit pants and dress shirt—gray and white today—both a little too big. No tie. Dress shoes. He was tall, over six feet. Thin but fit. His build was like Peter's, but his coloring was totally different. While Peter's thick, pin-straight hair was dark brown, almost black, Ethan's was the color of the wet sand on Clearwater Beach that night, and he constantly had his hands in it. It had a bit of wave at the ends, cut short over the ears but longer in back and over his light hazel eyes. Clear, tan skin, always perfectly shaven.

He looked at her through the windshield as he approached, rolled his eyes, and sighed to exhibit his ready-made excuse for being late, that his morning had been hectic. He opened the passenger-side door and slid inside.

"Crazy morning. Sorry you had to wait. How are you doing?" he said as he buckled up, then turned to her, stiffly.

"I'm good. No problem. How are you?" she asked as she shifted into drive and headed out of the parking lot and toward a nearby neighborhood with several restaurants and shops.

"I'm not sure exactly. Nervous, for one thing. Confused about what happened," he replied.

Her heart pounded in her chest. She was trying to control her breathing, forcing herself to take slower, steadier breaths. She was nervous. After all, she had never had a conversation with a man she had slept with about how he felt about cheating on his wife with her, how she felt about cheating on her husband with him, and whether one night was going to turn into something more. Uncharted territory, for sure. She had no idea how to handle it; no idea how to handle him.

"Well, I don't know exactly why it happened, but I don't think I regret it," she ventured.

Was that enough to send him the message that she was in for some more if he was? God, was she ready and willing to have an affair? She was confusing herself. She wasn't even sure what she really wanted. She kept her eyes on the road ahead, glad that she didn't have to look at him.

"I don't know why, either, but I feel terrible. I owe you an apology. I'm sorry," he said.

OK, so he didn't say he didn't regret it, meaning he did. It was a mistake.

They didn't say much else, but parked, walked to a deli, ordered Cuban sandwiches, inspected the counter, the ground, anything to avoid looking at each other, while they waited for their sandwiches to be pressed, then found a table and tried to eat a few bites. Jillian didn't even like Cubans but that was what Ethan had ordered and she ordered the same, so she didn't have to think about it.

"I'm not really that hungry," she tried. "I don't know if I'm still hung over, or what, but nothing really tastes quite right." Anything to get some conversation going and dispel the awkwardness.

"I haven't been eating well myself," he said. It was becoming obvious to her that he was completely uncomfortable and didn't want to be there, as if she were going to say something too loudly or that what happened between them would be apparent to anyone who cared to look.

She was disappointed. But she wasn't ready, or didn't know how, to do anything else about it.

As they sat at the table, both unsure how to act or what to say, a couple of project managers from One Metro walked in and waved at them. They smiled and waved back, then looked back at each other, and Jillian wondered if they made Ethan nervous.

"Ready to go?" he asked. Apparently, they did.

"Sure," she said, and rewrapped her mostly uneaten sandwich in its thick white butcher paper, being careful not to give herself a paper cut.

They got up, threw everything in the trash, and started to walk back to the car.

"At least maybe it will help us work together better, right?" she asked, forcing a smile, bumping his arm with her elbow. Anything to lighten the mood.

"Sure, of course it will," he replied unconvincingly, staring at the ground, walking with his hands in his pockets, shoulders drooping.

They rode back in silence, parted with the usual courtesies, and that was that. A total bust. She tried to put it out of her mind. She had plenty else to think about, considering this was probably the final sign that her marriage was over.

A couple of weeks earlier, she had met Megan, one of her college roommates, for lunch at the mall food court. Megan was in town from D.C. for only a day and a half for a business meeting, but she managed to squeeze Jillian in.

Megan and Chad had the perfect life. Chad was an academic, had his doctorate in education, had high ideals. Megan had been a CPA and worked full-time in a professional capacity, but then they'd adopted a daughter, so now Megan worked part-time from home and did the whole wife-and-mother thing. She brewed tea every morning, worked out every day, carpooled to day care and preschool, made well-balanced meals, and kept their well-balanced life in order.

Jillian didn't think Megan ever liked or respected Peter, but she liked and respected Jillian, so she never said much. They tried to hang out as couples before the kids came along, but Jillian could tell Megan didn't care to be around Peter and that maybe Chad didn't like him, either.

Megan—all five-foot-three, preppy-dressed hundred pounds of her, pale skin she was proud of, her reddish-brown hair in a long bob—had supported Jillian through the whole "Are Peter and I Ever Going to Get Married" era (five years), including the "Should I Leave Him Because He Won't Commit" dilemma. (She should have.) Megan was one of Jillian's bridesmaids. She felt she should have been the matron of honor instead of Chrissie, Peter's sister.

(She should have.) She was there through Jillian's pregnancy even though she hadn't been able to get pregnant herself. She was the very first visitor to the hospital after Zach was born.

Then Chad got an offer from a firm in the capital and off they went. They didn't get to catch up nearly as often as they liked anymore, with their families and careers. Jillian missed her terribly.

Megan ate her salad while Jillian had pizza, and they gabbed as fast as they could about everyone they knew because that's how they always talked. Usually, they would have three or four stories going on at once, everything spilling out, laughing, skipping forward and backward. No matter how long it had been since their last visit, it was always the same. And then she asked how things were with Peter. Jillian complained about the usual things, and they commiserated for a while.

"Do you think you'll get through it?" Megan asked.

"Of course we will. After all, I do still love the guy." Then Jillian stopped as if she'd walked into a wall. Her jaw dropped open as she felt herself get sucked out of her body and up toward the rafters like in one of those freaky movies where the dead person's soul is floating above, looking down on their own body. As the words echoed in her head, she recognized with her own ears what was lacking: conviction. For the first time, when she said she loved Peter, she knew that it wasn't true.

And it was just a few weeks later that she got naked with Ethan before giving Peter a clue, before truly even admitting to herself, that she was on her way out.

When Jillian realized she didn't love someone anymore, it seemed surreal to her that she once did. She wondered if it was real, true, genuine, or just some illusion. Had she talked herself into it? Can a person do such a thing? Can you want so much to feel something that you convince yourself that you do through simple focus and attention and obsession with that feeling? Can you make yourself believe in something, believe that the feeling means something, with no evidence to work with other than what you feel? If you can, does the diminishing of that feeling, that love—losing the feeling of it, or not believing in it anymore—just mean that you stopped trying?

She had stopped trying with Peter. She realized that she didn't want to try—try so *hard*—any longer. She couldn't. It wasn't making a difference, and she was so tired! She knew, when she finally allowed herself to ask the ultimate question and to honestly answer, that the answer was no. No, she didn't love him anymore. She wasn't in love with him. And she didn't want to try to be or pretend to be for a moment longer.

Her internal debate raged on as she sat in her Herman Miller Aeron chair at her cherry desk in her fifth-floor office staring out at Port Tampa. Her eyes roamed over the port buildings with their puffing smoke smudging the clear blue sky.

She wondered if she just expected too much from Peter, from their marriage, if the fairytale romances of books and movies had deluded her into believing she could have everything. She had read every John Gray book published and several others on similar subjects and conducted research online. She went to counseling, tried talking with Peter about what she felt. She kept trying, trying everything she knew how to do, to connect with him, to get some spark of feeling or passion back between them, to make him understand how she felt (shut down, rejected, unwanted). He didn't care to listen. She even wrote him a letter a couple years into their marriage, a long letter about how neglected she felt, that she was upset about his increasing visits to porn sites and finding pictures in her own bathroom of gorgeous nude or nearly nude women staring up at her from their glossy magazine pages, while he was uninterested in having sex with her.

"Peter, do you want to go get naked?" she once attempted. "I already took care of that today," he'd replied. She never asked again.

It all made her feel inadequate. She didn't feel wanted or needed. She handed the letter to him after dinner one night and waited three days for him to say something, anything, about it. She finally, tentatively, asked him. They were watching television, and she intently waited for a break so she wouldn't interrupt his show, god forbid.

"Have you read my letter?" she asked, trying to sound nonchalant about it. But her heart was pumping blood through her veins so fiercely she could hear it, see it beating in her chest through her T-shirt.

"Yeah," he replied, without even looking at her, while he changed the channel with the remote.

"And … ?" she asked, really wanting to talk, but afraid to push too hard, in case he pushed back.

"I don't know what you want me to say. I figure if you wanted to talk, we would talk instead of writing," he replied.

Jillian was stunned. She stared at him, having no idea how to react, respond.

"Well, how do you feel about it?" she managed.

"You said what you wanted to say." He still hadn't even looked at her. She got up and left the room, and the letter was never mentioned again.

She should have taken heed, as she'd done when a similar scene had played out with Mike, a guy from her hometown she dated her sophomore year in college, to whom she was even engaged for a few months, despite knowing she would never marry him for myriad reasons.

Mike was most definitely blue-collar, just like Jillian's father. But he was blond and beefy, instead of dark-haired and slight like her dad. Blue eyes, boyish face, muscular. But with the same work ethic and same family values. Respect your parents and work hard at whatever you do.

Jillian met Mike at a party that he and his roommate had at their duplex, the last on a dead-end street with more sand than grass in the yard, lots of potholes in the street, and plenty of cats and dogs wandering around. She had come home from college for the weekend and was hanging out with some high school friends. Mike hit on her, and they ended up making out on his couch. She doubted anyone even noticed. The place was about six hundred square feet, and seventy or eighty people were crowded inside and spilling out through the open front and back doors. The windows were open, too, the music loud, people drinking, smoking, yelling, laughing, wrestling, belching, dancing.

They started sleeping together. It was Jillian's first sexual relationship. That guy she had lost her virginity to was a basketball player at her college who didn't even know her name; they hooked up at a fraternity party.

Mike and Jillian had a lot of fun, but his feelings for her were stronger than hers for him.

He would ride his motorcycle the forty miles from home to her dorm, and they would spend the weekend in a Super 8 near campus. Sometimes they'd hang out in her dorm lobby with her dorm mates and watch television.

A couple of months into their relationship, he was leaving after one of those weekends and they walked out to his bike in the crowded dorm parking lot overlooking the lake. They hugged and kissed and talked about the next weekend.

"So, I'll see you next Friday night, OK? I'll leave right after work," he said, holding her hand.

"OK. See you then," she said, smiling. She was anxious for him to leave. She had a huge research paper to finish.

He hugged her for longer than usual. "I love you," he whispered in her ear.

She squeezed him tighter, surprised, but not ready to return the sentiment.

He finally pulled away, looked her in the eye, smiled, and turned to get his helmet.

"Be careful, OK?" she said, smiling.

"Of course. I'll call you when I get home," he said.

When she did eventually tell him she loved him, too, she still wasn't sure she did. It was just easier than facing him after he said it to her, which happened more and more frequently—at the end of every phone call, whenever they said goodbye, sometimes after sex. It was becoming uncomfortable for her, so, she said it, and that made it easier. For a while.

Just a few weeks after she had finally told Mike she loved him, she and his roommate's girlfriend were cleaning up the kitchen one Sunday afternoon. (Well, the kitchen was about four feet of counter with a fridge on one end, a stove on the other, and a sink in the middle, with a small table and two chairs pushed up against the opposite wall.) They'd had an epic party the night before and the place was wrecked.

"So, you two are pretty serious, huh?" Sonia asked in her thick southern accent. She was a large girl, maybe twenty years old, about six feet tall and 220 pounds, large-breasted, big blond hair, big toothy smile.

"I guess. Not really," Jillian said, unwilling to commit.

"Well, Mike is, that's for sure," she said, smirking.

"Why do you say that? What do you mean?" Jillian asked.

Sonia stopped scrubbing the chili pot and turned to look at Jillian as she dried a bowl. "I'm not supposed to say anything, but maybe you can guess," she said.

What was she was talking about? Sonia cocked her head and raised an eyebrow at Jillian, apparently annoyed that she wasn't catching on.

Jillian shook her head, puzzled. "Sonia. What? Can't you just clue me in?"

She opened her eyes wider, pushing her face toward Jillian's, like Jillian was being totally dense. "Hello? Surprise? Serious question?"

"Wha…? Oh…my…god. No. He's not. Please tell him not to. I'm not ready," Jillian begged. She was horrified. He couldn't.

He did. A few weeks later, they were in his waterbed, which took up practically his whole bedroom, and he unceremoniously leaned over, opened a dresser drawer—banging it into the base of the bed—pulled out a ring box, smiled, and asked her to marry him. She said yes. God, how do you say no? That would be quite uncomfortable and confrontational, and doing what might be right at the expense of someone else's feelings wasn't her style, no matter how high the price might be later. Who thought that far ahead?

A couple of months later they argued about wedding plans. Jillian had been sitting on the floor in the duplex, tearing pages out of bridal magazines for things she liked—dresses, flowers, color schemes, China patterns, you name it. Mike picked up the pile and started to look through it, occasionally commenting. The first gift-type item he came across was a pair of frosted glass Waterford candlesticks shaped like doves. He asked, "What are these for?"

"Oh, I love those, so I thought maybe we could put them on our registry."

"Registry? What registry?" he asked, laughing.

"Our gift registry. You know, where we go into the store and pick out what we want so people can send us wedding gifts?" Jillian laughed, too.

His smile vanished. "We are not telling our family and friends what to buy us. No way in hell we are having a registry. How rude!" He was mad! Jillian was shocked! Everyone had a registry! How could you not have one? She told him as much.

"We are not having one. No way. End of story," he said.

What could she say?

She laid awake next to him most of the night, wondering how to talk to him, trying unsuccessfully to wake him a few times. She was seriously annoyed that he had just shut her down like that, that he had decided like some sort of dictator.

She tried again the next morning to talk about it, and he blew her off, saying it was passed. She decided that, to say what she felt she needed to say, without being diverted or distracted by his denials or defensiveness, and without getting so entangled in her own emotion and insecurity that she couldn't get it out, she had to write it down. It wasn't that she wanted to be able to speak and be heard without response; it was that she wanted to be heard. Writing was the best way she knew how to accomplish that. She expected a response, a reaction. She wanted nothing more.

She wrote, and she sent, and she waited for a reply.

"Let's talk about your letter," Mike said at his place the next weekend. Jillian was immediately nervous but happy that he wanted to discuss it, that he had read it and knew how she felt.

She sat at the tiny kitchen table, and he got down on one knee next to her, letter in hand.

"If we're going to be husband and wife, we have to talk to each other. Don't ever write a letter to me again."

As he was talking, he tore the letter to shreds, right in front of her face, slowly and neatly. He was in complete control, steady, as if he'd planned it out. To him, she supposed he was sending the message that he wanted to talk, not write. To Jillian, he was dismissing her feelings, her opinions, telling her he didn't care about them, that they didn't matter, that she didn't matter. He shut down the best form of communication she had at the time for her true feelings. If they were going to share, it was to be on his terms. As the pieces of her letter fell to the floor, so did any feeling she had for him and any hope or chance of them staying together. Those pieces would not be reassembled. He tore her up and shut her down, so she checked out.

She supposed the same thing happened with Peter. How she felt didn't matter to him, so why bother trying to tell him? He either didn't care or didn't know what to do about it, so it was pointless, and she was at a loss as to how else to communicate with him.

She was happy to see Zach that evening. Peter disappeared before she even changed her clothes. She and Zach had dinner and played Matchbox cars and, as she watched him in the bathtub, thoughts in her head kept spinning.

She thought about how she first realized she was alone, that she had only herself to count on, when she was about ten years old. Not that she knew what that meant at the time. But she realized, while her parents, who had adopted her as an infant, would keep a roof over her head, clothes on her back, and food in her stomach, that was about all she was going to get. She was in the sixth grade the first time her mother betrayed her, and Jillian never trusted her again.

She had received a little love letter from a boy at school whose family lived a couple of houses down from Jillian's grandparents, her mother's parents—just a few blocks down, but in the paved-road part of their small town. Jillian was excited to get one from this particular boy, especially since so many of the other girls in her class were "going with" boys, even if that only meant note-writing and couple-skates at the roller rink on Saturday afternoons.

Jillian showed it to her mother, proud of it. She thought her mom would be excited, too. Her mother didn't react much, but first chance she got, she told Jillian's grandmother, who then told the boy's mother, her neighbor. So humiliating.

Jillian was introspective and shy as a child, still was, which was often misinterpreted as standoffishness, snobbishness, or coldness. Ironic, because that was the exact opposite of how she saw herself. Self-analysis along with low self-confidence was a difficult combination for a child with out-of-touch parents. She was unsure of herself, and she knew it. She criticized herself for it. And there was no one to correct her negative self-perceptions.

Her father believed in constructive criticism, which to a child—well, probably to just about everyone, really—is just plain criticism. But she now had the perspective to understand that his criticism led to her attention to detail, focus, and effort to always do better, more, and a striving for perfection that, of course, can never be reached. In fourth grade, her color-pencil sketch of Martin Luther King Jr. won second place in the elementary school art fair, even beating out the sixth graders! Her dad said, "Good! But why didn't you color in the background?"

Her parents were decidedly not introspective, insightful, sensitive, encouraging, or able to provide any kind of emotional support. Jillian learned two things about emotions from her parents: anger and withdrawal. Yell, curse, call names (her mom), or retreat into deaf-, dumb-, and blindness (her dad), not speaking and pretending not to see or hear anyone you don't want to. Yes, he did that, as if he were some precocious six-year-old.

Her Dad never spanked her, or her three-years-younger sister; he preferred to smack them across the face, usually smacking Jillian because of some smart remark. Her sarcasm was her defense.

"Jesus, I can't stand that damn bitch," her mom was saying one afternoon when Jillian walked in from school. She must have been fourteen or fifteen. Her mom was sweating bullets in the Florida heat and humidity due to the lack of A/C in the house, standing over the kitchen sink, staring through the jalousies into the back yard.

"He can go to hell, damn bitch," she kept saying. "God! I can't take it! Damn!" she swore, getting louder. Lord only knew what had happened this time.

"Mom, women are bitches. Men are bastards," Jillian said, chuckling, trying to disarm her, and feeling a little shot of adrenaline at saying curse words to her mother. If she calmed down, Jillian could let go of some of the tension that had sprung up as soon as she'd walked into the house.

"I know, but he is a bitch. A damn bitch. I can't stand it. I can't take it!" she yelled, working herself further into her fury. She limped from Multiple Sclerosis, and her balance was awful. Sometimes she would get so mad, whipping herself around, she would trip herself and fall over, like a wide, branchless oak, without enough coordination or muscle control to even try to catch herself. The one time she had managed to get her hands behind her in time, she'd broken both wrists.

"Well call him a bastard, then!" Jillian had tried. She hated it when they fought, which was regularly. She always felt it was her fault somehow, like she'd done something to set them off, or that she should do more to facilitate a truce.

"God! I hate this place! I can't stand him, bitch! What is his problem anyway? He can go to hell! He can get the hell out! I can't take that stupid bitch!" she ranted, one hand on her hip, the other hip leaned up against the counter in front of the sink.

Jillian finally just stared at the back of her head, letting the contempt she felt start to seep through her eyes. She sighed and said, "Yeah, stupid bitch," and left the room. Her mom was too into her own rage to even notice.

She once said to Jillian, when Jillian was in high school and in the middle of exams, that if she had a knife in her hand Jillian would be dead. Jillian made honor roll anyway.

And Jillian was living back home with them when she and Peter started dating, having moved back in after she lost her third job after college. It was the late 80s, who had a job? One time, her mom asked if Jillian would be home after work that night for dinner.

"Nope. Peter and I have plans because it's our six-month anniversary," Jillian answered smiling, expecting her to say "how nice" or some other polite but lame response.

Instead, she leaned her fat ass against the stove, planted a hand on her hip, and barked, "So what?"

She might as well have punched Jillian in the gut.

A couple months later Peter asked Jillian to move in with him. She couldn't pack fast enough.

23

Jillian got Zach out of the tub. He was so adorable with his round, little belly and wet hair dripping with bath water, starting to shiver. She wrapped him up in a towel, dried his hair, and gently brushed his teeth (which he disliked because it "tickled"), then carried him into his room and got his pajamas on. As she watched her beautiful, innocent little boy concentrating on picking out a bedtime book, she vowed to always respect his feelings and never make him feel like he was alone, invisible, or responsible for anyone else's choices or feelings.

5

Jillian and Peter had barely spoken since she got back from the conference. They just kept going through the motions of their everyday life over the next few weeks—Peter working at home and picking Zach up from school, Jillian taking Zach to school in the morning and going to the office, then coming home in the evening to take over Zach-duty.

Their role reversal began when Zach was a newborn. The week before Jillian had to go back to work after maternity leave, they had still made no decision regarding childcare. They both had full-time office jobs, both in marketing. Peter was a writer in the marketing department at a Fortune 500 company, and Jillian was already a managing executive at Sagency, the advertising agency. When they realized they had to decide, they felt they would be more comfortable if one of them were taking care of Zach. Jillian's job was more stable, and she made more money; Peter had been through three jobs in their eight years together. Peter would ask his boss if he could try working from home full-time so he could take care of Zach. His boss agreed, and the pattern was set. She had to hand it to Peter, despite everything he always seemed to take good care of Zach in those early years. She never worried about whether Zach was safe.

In the weeks after the conference, she was still trying to sort things out in her head, figure out what she was doing, what she really wanted, and why. It was over that period of silence and introspection, and observing Peter with a cold, detached eye, that she started to realize how much disdain she truly felt for him. He kept his distance, accepting the silence, and did not approach her, either from hope it would pass or fear that if he started a dialogue, it would turn out to be Pandora's Box he had opened. The more he let her pull away from him, the less she felt for him.

Not a good time to be away from home, but Jillian and Ethan both happened to be giving presentations to a prospective client in Orlando. The whole group had dinner in the Marriott. Jillian had no appetite, hadn't since "The Incident." She picked at her food.

"Not eating?" Ethan asked—the first words she'd heard from his mouth since their lunch.

"Not feeling well," she replied quietly, ensuring that the client didn't overhear.

No reply.

After dinner, the client suggested going to the bar. Jillian did not want to go but was obliged to. She was the last one out, and Ethan held the door for her and hung back. She turned to wait for him, everyone else a few steps ahead of them.

"Are you OK? Why aren't you feeling well?" he asked.

"I'm really fine. A lot going on. I'm not pregnant or anything, if that's why you're asking." She chuckled.

He froze for a split second, and then asked, "Hey, can I borrow your cell? It's my mom's birthday and my phone won't pick up a signal in here," he said.

"Sure," she said, handing it to him.

The group ordered drinks in the bar and continued chatting about politics, sports, the weather, the usual. Ethan walked in twenty minutes later and handed her the phone. "Thanks a lot," he said, and ordered a drink.

Half an hour later, after having practically ignored her the whole time, he excused himself, saying goodnight. She followed soon after and called him through the hotel operator.

"So, your place or mine?" she asked when he answered. Ha. She had had too much to drink (again) to be so bold.

"Neither. That's just not going to happen," he replied coldly.

"OK, so let's talk. You will talk to me, won't you?" she pressed. She thought if she could get him to her room, she could get something started.

He paused. "I really don't want to walk back through the lobby."

"Meaning what? Why?" she asked.

"I just don't want to run into anyone, have them wondering what I'm up to," he lied. What an excuse.

"Oh for god's sake. Whatever." She hung up on him. Then called him back.

"Why are you lying to me? Who cares who sees you? We just need to talk. I need to talk about what happened, Ethan, because you are the only one I can talk to about it." She was practically begging. Not good.

He sighed. "OK. Where are you?" He sounded defeated. Definitely not good.

She gave him her room number and just a few minutes later he was there, dressed very like the way Peter usually dressed, she noted mentally, in clothes that were ill fitting and unflattering, right down to worn leather deck shoes, ugh. She dismissed the parallel, pushing the warning signals out of the way in favor of her intentions.

He sat in the chair by the bed and Jillian, dramatically, sat on the floor in front him and pulled her knees up under her chin, locking her hands in front of her shins.

"Should I sit down there, too?" he asked, chuckling a bit.

"No, sit where you want," she replied.

She didn't try to seduce him. She didn't embarrass herself in that way, but the alcohol had kicked in, and her vampire emotions, the ones full of intensity and drama that suck the life out of whomever they're aimed at—most frequently herself—were on full charge.

"Thanks to you and what happened, I know what direction my life has to take now," she said. "I've done a lot of soul searching and have realized that my marriage is over." Oh, how was that for dramatic? How could he resist?

"I don't really want to be the cause of the end of anyone's marriage," he said.

"You didn't cause it, Ethan. But what happened between us woke me up, reminded me I am a woman," she said, still sitting on the floor in front of him.

"Of course you are," he replied.

She kept throwing out lures, trying to get him into a real conversation, make some connection, but got nowhere.

"Are you happily married?" she asked, looking up at him, leaning back on her hands.

"Yes. Yes, I am," he answered. "Kelly and I have been to counseling more than once, and I'm not so sure it helped, but yes, yes I am," he said.

"If you're happily married, then I must've been the one to initiate things that night, because I am not. I'm sorry. I'm sorry I did that, and I hope you will forgive me. There really was no intent, it just happened. I didn't plan it."

"I know. You couldn't have. I appreciate that, and I don't hold grudges, anyway, so we're good." Then he stood up and said he needed to go. "I need to put all of this insanity behind me."

And he walked out, leaving her unmoved from her spot on the floor.

6

Back in the office the following Monday, a soft knock on her door brought her out of her head and away from her client review.

"Miss Jillian?" Candace, her administrative assistant, addressed Jillian in her Southern style. She was staring at Jillian with a questioning look on her soft, round face. "Jillian, are you all right?" she asked as she took a step forward, her perfectly manicured brows crinkling together in concern. Then she put her hands on her ample hips. "Is there someone I need to take care of for you?" she asked, then smiled.

Jillian smiled back. Candace had been with her for the past three years. While she was a smart worker with a serious work ethic, she was a little rough around the edges. But she was good at what she did, and she was fiercely loyal to Jillian for some reason she couldn't fathom.

"No, Candace, I don't need you to take anyone out, but thank you for offering."

"Are you sure you're OK?" she asked again.

Jillian picked up the Magic 8 Ball on her desk, shook it, turned it up, and waited for the sign. She smiled again and turned the window toward Candace, though she wouldn't be able to read it from ten feet away.

"Absolutely. See? Says so."

"OK," she replied, sounding unconvinced. "I just wanted to let you know that your car is still in detailing, but it will be ready for you by five for sure, and I'll have your dry cleaning put in the back when it arrives," she said, knowing Jillian would be agitated if she couldn't rush right out to get home to Zach.

"Thanks a lot, Candace. I appreciate it. I don't have anything else," she said, smiling, then turned back to her laptop.

"Yes ma'am!" she said in her accent, and turned to leave.

Jillian checked her email but focused for only a minute before her thoughts wandered yet again. She had never wanted to be divorced. Who did? She never planned to be. She never considered it to be an option. Divorce was for people who were weak, abused, or selfish—not for her.

She was strong, independent, smart, committed, loyal. There was just one little catch. She was weak. She was abused. She was selfish.

She was weak in the sense that she let Peter call too many of the shots. She was abused because he took advantage of that. She was selfish because she woke up one morning and decided it was over. She refused to be oppressed any longer.

Jillian had worked with Monica at Sagency for years. Since the company moved into One Metro, their offices were much closer, and because they were about the same age, with few other women at their level, became friendlier. Some of their coworkers teased them because they often unintentionally showed up to work wearing coordinating outfits. Between that and their similar coloring—dark blonde hair and fair skin (her eyes blue instead of gray like Jillian's, though)—they were sometimes called the "Twins."

Jillian had started sharing more with her over the last couple of years, starting when she and Peter were trying to have a second child. Monica was very easy to talk to, open, honest, and nonjudgmental. Jillian had so needed some support, to vent and to share, and Peter certainly wasn't offering any of that.

The first year after Zach was born was difficult. Zach was an active, happy little baby, but did not like to sleep through the night and ate constantly. He weighed nine pounds at birth, and at times Jillian thought he was trying to grow into adulthood in his first year. His first few months, he didn't sleep for more than a couple hours at a time. It slowly stretched into longer and longer periods, but he didn't start regularly sleeping through the night until he was ten months old.

Peter was against any kind of routine, probably because it made him commit to something. And Jillian was too tired to argue about it.

With a bent toward mild depression and anxiety to begin with, postpartum was no joy for Jillian. She didn't have deep depression; she wasn't in fear of hurting Zach or herself. But she was sad and overly emotional. She had anxiety dreams almost every night. She and Peter went to counseling for the first time when Zach was about a year old. It didn't help much. Jillian suggested they go to a counselor specializing in sex, since they'd had sex twice since Zach was born. Peter didn't want to go.

And so they swept it all back under the rug and moved on. After all, they had this beautiful, radiant, happy little boy to take care of. Did they really need each other?

Peter finally brought up the subject of another child when Zach was two.

The whole conversation, less than fifty words, took place during Zach's dinner at the kitchen table. Jillian and Zach were about finished—he with spaghetti sauce all over his adorable round little face but full and happy, Jillian not so much of either—when Peter came in to get his third Budweiser from the refrigerator. They didn't eat together because Peter had to get his six-pack appetizer in before he ate.

"So, are we going to have another one or not?" he said without preamble. His right index finger tapped his front teeth.

"Do you want to?" she asked, looking at him in surprise, but thrilled.

"Yeah, do you?"

"Yes!"

"OK. Good, let's go for it," he said, and left the kitchen.

The next morning, she scheduled a doctor's appointment and went off the Pill. She knew she would get pregnant right away, as she had with Zach.

The following week the doctor gave her the go-ahead. Jillian worked on the calendar, and she and Peter started sneaking into the bedroom for very unsatisfying quickies (except for the fact that they were quick) when she was ovulating, while Zach watched Barney or the Teletubbies.

After the first cycle, her breasts were tender, a sure sign she was pregnant. She knew she was, that they had nailed it the first time; a relief, since they wouldn't have to continue to have sex. She told Peter she thought she was pregnant, even though an early pregnancy test from the drugstore was negative. He wasn't as certain as she was.

He was right. She got her period two days later. She was shocked. She wondered if she had been and it hadn't taken, since it was so unusual for her to have breast tenderness.

They followed the same process the next month. And the next. Nothing.

She went back to the doctor, who ordered blood work and tests to check Jillian's fallopian tubes, and who suggested Peter get tested as well.

Jillian had the test done, which consisted of having a balloon inserted into her vagina and inflated, then dye injected, for an x-ray. None of it seriously painful, but certainly uncomfortable.

Whatever the doctor said to do, she did right away.

It took Peter six months to take in a semen sample for analysis.

They spent another six months waiting while he was supposed to take vitamin supplements and stop drinking alcohol to improve his sperm, neither of which he seriously committed himself to, but that Jillian certainly could not do for him (like everything else).

They ultimately went to a specialist they didn't like, then another they did, and committed to in vitro fertilization. Again, Jillian was certain it would work the first time. She was fertile, she knew she was. All the tests said she was fine. Peter had issues with both mobility and motility. IVF would find some of his few happy sperms and inject them into her happy eggs, then they would be injected into her happy uterus, and everyone would be happy.

Not. Jillian started the drug therapy. One, two, sometimes three injections a day. Two short needles she could give herself in her thigh or abdomen. Man, the first time she gave herself a shot, she was sweating like she'd just run a marathon. But she did it herself, and she didn't whine about it. She didn't need anyone to hold her hand. No one was volunteering to, anyway, so why ask? Peter didn't even bother to come into the room with her.

The third shot was difficult. It was a two-inch needle that had to go right into her ass, a hard angle. Peter would give her that shot. He was proud of himself for doing it. He had an issue with blood, needles, doctors, hospitals. He once left Jillian alone in the ER when she'd had some complications after having her gall bladder removed, because he thought he was going to faint. He could give her a shot! No matter Jillian was the one taking that thing right in the ass.

One night, they were really on edge with each other. They'd been through the routine several times. She had to get the shot at the same time every night, and yet Peter continued to force her to come and ask him if he would administer it instead of just showing up. Jillian felt like she was totally on her own, like the whole thing had been her idea, and he was just playing along, like he was doing her a favor. She resented that she had to ask, but she went out to the family room and interrupted his TV show and said, "Are you going to give me my shot tonight or what?"

"I'll be right there," he said tersely, without looking up.

"Thanks," she said, and walked back to the master bathroom at the other end of their ranch-style house.

"Don't worry! I'll bring the ice!" he yelled sarcastically.

The extraction was the most difficult and painful part for Jillian. The doctor had to go in through her vagina with a micro needle and vacuum to puncture her ovaries and suck out the eggs, rending them from her body. But they had to bring Peter's contribution to this process with them. When he had the nerve to ask her to get on her knees and "help him out" with his own extraction—quite a different experience from Jillian's—she did, even though it disgusted her, repulsed her, made her gag. She tried to hide it, the resentment growing, because she knew it was the only way she would get pregnant again, the only way of repeating the happiest time of her life, the only time in her existence that she hadn't felt alone.

Three cycles they went through. Twenty thousand dollars' worth of chemicals and shots and hormones and doctors' visits and tests and samples and extractions and insertions and visiting the blastocysts at the doctor's office, watching the cells multiply. Implantation and bed rest and mood swings and night sweats and nightmares from all the chemicals, and ultimately her own flesh and blood and hope, hope, hope flushed down the toilet. She said goodbye to numbers one and two; then three and four; then five, six, seven, and eight. Her could-be babies. Peter did hold her hand on the way home from the doctor's office each time after getting negative pregnancy results, but they never talked about it. They just moved on. He never asked her if she was OK. She never asked him either. But she mourned on her own. She cried alone in the bathroom or silently in bed at night so he wouldn't hear.

She did continue to hope that the next time would work. Things would get better. You never know what is going to happen, and she still had enough curiosity and hope that she wanted to be around for tomorrow. It would all work out. Of course, it would all work out.

Monica was there for her through all that time. When Jillian realized how serious the rift between her and Peter was—no one knew yet about "The Incident" with Ethan—and she needed to hear the words aloud, needed someone to react to them, she went to Monica. She hadn't cried with her over the could-be babies, but

Jillian had kept her informed of each step of the process, and Monica was as supportive as she could be. Jillian called and asked Monica if she had time for Happy Hour, as they called it. It was really time at work, usually in Monica's office, late in the afternoon, when it was too early to leave but when their brains were fried from too much thinking and needed a break.

Jillian was nervous. She hadn't voiced her fears, or anxiety, or thoughts, whatever they were, to anyone, yet. She knew saying it all out loud, sending the words out into the Universe, would make it real. She needed to make it real. She was sick of hearing her own voice knocking around inside her skull. She needed someone else's perspective.

She asked if she could close the door when she got to Monica's office. "Of course," she replied.

Jillian sat down. Monica watched her, concerned.

"What's going on?" she finally asked.

"I think my marriage is in serious trouble," Jillian said. She was conspicuously and suspiciously dry-eyed.

"What? Why do you say that?" She was obviously concerned.

"I've realized that I don't love him anymore, that I am not in love with him, and I don't want to be married to him," Jillian stated.

Very strange. Very anti-histrionic of her. Very un-Jillian like, at least with everyone besides Peter. She was freaking herself out that she wasn't freaking out. The little vampire was acting calm and cool. She was either in shock or already completely over the drama of it.

"Have you talked to him? You need to talk to him, tell him what's going on," she offered.

"You're right. I do. I will," and Jillian got up and left her office, feeling queerly lighthearted.

She had decided, solved the problem after not even knowing what the problem was. She had endured years of having a sense, a nagging, a tickling in her brain, but had ignored it, pushed it down and away because the implications of acknowledging it were overwhelming. She had handed him the power to shut her down, even if it was unintentional on his part. So much of her had become closed off that she was a shell at home, a body going through the motions with her spirit locked inside, sometimes silently screaming, sometimes exhausted into silence.

7

When she got back from Orlando to his credit Peter tried to hold her hand, to kiss her. She let him, of course; he was still her husband. But it embarrassed and revolted her. She dropped his hand as quickly as she could, and certainly didn't return his kisses. She wouldn't even meet his eyes.

Still, he said nothing. She started to feel mildly sorry for him. His emotions were so suppressed, he was impotent to do much about the situation.

The night after her confession to Monica, she marched out to the family room, where he was watching TV with a beer in his hand. (Where else would he be?)

She perched on the edge of the navy-blue leather recliner, waiting for a commercial. He hadn't looked over at her.

"We need to talk," she said when a commercial came on, her body as taut as a rubber band stretched and ready to fire.

"OK," he replied. Shockingly, he turned off the television and turned to look at her. He suspected it was serious.

"I know I've been distant lately. I need some space. I'm not happy. I need some time to figure things out, and I hope you will give me that," she said smoothly, staring right at him.

He looked at her like a deer in the headlights and freaked.

"What? You want a divorce?" he asked, sounding incredulous, leaning forward on the couch, head turned to glare at her.

"I don't know," she lied. She couldn't put that out there so quickly.

And then she could barely hear his voice. She was in a tunnel, his voice dimming, her blood pounding in her temples, her chest, her eyes, her ears becoming the center of the Universe. She was trembling a bit from being so tense, but she was dry-eyed from shock, detachment, terror, or all the above.

She had felt the same way when she and Peter went skydiving one year for his birthday. They tried to go the day before, but the weather kept them from going up, though they had completed all the training (a whole hour's worth, to jump out of a plane at 15,000 feet!) and signed all the paperwork agreeing that if they plunged to their deaths, it wasn't the company's fault. They returned the next day, and the weather was beautiful. Great. Just great.

They waited their turn. Peter was bouncing with excitement, highly unusual for him. Jillian was calm, highly unusual for her. They'd had numerous arguments over their opposing perspectives, his being that getting excited or anticipating good things only led to disappointment. Better to not expect good things and therefore not be disappointed, but occasionally pleasantly surprised. Jillian felt that she would much rather be happy and hopeful about the future, looking forward to things and occasionally be let down, than to be so pessimistic. He argued that he was a realist, not a pessimist. In her book, they were the same thing.

It had taken her a long time to figure it out, but she knew that hope and expectation were two different things. Hope means you want it to happen and are excited about the possibility of it, whether it's world peace or that the neighbor will come by with your Girl Scout cookies when you're craving a Thin Mint. Expectation means you're planning on it happening. Expectation is why Megan doesn't play the lottery. She expects to win, and when she doesn't, she's pissed.

Jillian played the lottery. She hoped to win. She wished, with all she had, that she would win. She wanted to win. But she didn't expect to. (Some might say that's why she didn't.) And when she didn't win—which was every time she played (twice a week for drawings on Wednesday and Saturday nights, which she bought two weeks in advance, four plays at a time, which just proved she didn't expect to win)—was she a bit let down? Sure. But she waited for the next draw and checked her numbers online the next morning and hoped that maybe next time they would come up, or at least a few of them. So, was she really expecting not to win? Was she sending the Universe the wrong message by buying multiples? Or, maybe she just hoped to win more than once? Ha.

She didn't think Peter had hope or even understood what it was. Since having positive expectations was too disappointing, too risky, he couldn't allow himself those, either.

The plane came in and they met with the instructors, preparing to jump tandem by being hooked to them in four places—at each shoulder and hip—and shuffled to the plane.

Jillian was the first to enter, which meant she'd be the last to exit. On the floor of the empty cargo plane, they each sat in between their partner's knees with the next person between theirs, stacked like so many Pringles in dark green jumpsuits. The tin can circled up, up, up to the designated height, each of them watching the instructors' altimeters as they rose higher and higher, and getting more and more nervous, having failed to realize how far up and away fifteen thousand feet really was.

They all stood at once sort of, awkwardly struggling up while still snapped together. The door was opened, and wind roared through the space. Each pair approached the vacuum and disappeared, the rest of the teams shuffling up a few feet toward their turn. They didn't even jump, really. They just leaned forward (or got pushed). Approach the door, look out into nothing, lean forward, and start gasping for air like a jumping fish that has mistakenly landed in some surprised fisherman's boat.

Jillian didn't have a sense of falling. They were at too high an altitude for that. She felt like she was standing in front of a giant fan, pressure, pushing. No sensation of the Earth flying up at her or of hurtling toward it. She did keep looking down at it, though, and her instructor, on her back, kept pulling her head up with two fingers on her forehead. Jumpers are supposed to look at the horizon, with arms and legs spread eagle, so that they don't start tumbling, from which recovery is difficult (hence the whole release-of-responsibility paperwork, in case you tumble because you couldn't look at the damn horizon).

Then he pulled the chute. It jerked them up—to a stop, really—and Jillian was in agony! The straps between her legs were so tight they were cutting into her, attempting to separate her legs from her pelvis. She couldn't adjust things from there, so she tried to enjoy the fall, but failed.

They finally alit, pulling down hard on the chute handles as they neared the ground, so the chute lifted them up and plopped them down right on their feet. Peter was already out of his chute, running over to her, yelling how great it was, and wasn't that just amazing, and did she hear him yell, he fell through a cloud blah blah blah. She barely heard him. She felt robotic. Shock. Detachment. She wasn't there.

That was the only way she had managed to do it, to get herself to lean out of that plane: to not feel it. To not feel the fear, the anxiety, the distress, the panic. She shut it off, went through the motions emotionlessly.

When Peter reacted to her careful request for time by raving on and on, she felt the same way. Distant. Elsewhere. Well, raved on, but his rant was over in less than ten minutes, talker that he was.

"Should I just start packing up those books in a box, it's all over? The last fifteen years, wasted! Man, I am going to be so fucked up over this." He didn't expect any kind of reply from her. He held his head in his hands.

"Is there anything I can do?" he finally asked, turning his head back to look at her.

"I don't think so," she replied, looking up briefly, then back at the floor.

He got up. "I can't take this. I'm going to bed," he stated, and left the room.

Well, that wasn't so hard after all. She was quite relieved. She slept on the couch that night. He came out some time during the night and asked her again if she'd cheated on him, to which she answered no, for the last time, no. And she realized that she was now a cheater and a liar. He only made it worse when he said he was sorry, that he wouldn't ask again. He went back to bed.

The next day Jillian was floating on air. She burst into Monica's office first thing and, without waiting to close the door or even take note of whether she might be on speaker (thank goodness she wasn't) announced, "I did it! I talked to him!"

She swiveled around in her chair and Jillian leaned on her desk with her knuckles, too antsy to sit.

"And?" she asked.

"And, it's over! I think we're going to get divorced!"

"Wow, that was fast. What happened? What did he say?" she asked, puzzled.

Jillian related the whole non-event. As she did, she became more certain they would get divorced, that she would finally be free of him, and a burden was lifted, one she hadn't even fully realized she was carrying until the past few weeks. She was overjoyed.

"Jilly, just take it easy. Don't rush into anything, OK? Why don't you take a couple of days off?" she asked.

"Are you crazy? And do what? Go where? Home to my loving husband? Besides, there's too much going on here," she said.

"I know, but we'll keep moving even if you're not here. We'll survive a few days. Don't you need some time to think?" she said.

"No! That's all I've been doing, thinking! I am sick of it! I'm fine! I need to be here," she said, and took a deep breath and finally sat down. "Did you have a chance to talk to Ethan about the referrals?" she asked, diverting Monica.

"Yeah, but just for a minute. I think if we can get Delta to work with Ethan and his team—which he said he'd work on—we can gain some momentum," she said and sighed. She was still eyeing Jillian but didn't push the issue. Monica knew Jillian would talk to her in her own time.

'Delta' was the nickname they'd given to their team of insiders working informally to create a referral partnership with Ethan's agency, Black&Gray. They wanted to refocus their lines of business, their specialties, become more of a boutique agency. This would require referring some of their current clients to Black&Gray. In turn, Ethan's firm would send Sagency their clients who fit the new model. The team felt it would be better for the efficiency and long-term growth of the company. The traditionalists, of course, were against it for the typical public reason that it would mean lost business and lost opportunities, but it was really because they might have to give up some of their egos and empires.

Jack, Sagency's CEO, was content to let them make waves without truly supporting or endorsing their position, so they were attempting to build critical mass internally until the scales tipped in their favor. They ran reports, conducted research, revised job descriptions, talked to other agencies with a structure like what was envisioned, created spreadsheets on efficiencies, and talked to the creatives about how they would work in such an environment.

If Sagency restructured in this way, it would send a block of clients to Black&Gray, swapping them for a pool of their clients that fit Sagency's model, and both agencies would benefit. Jillian was nervous about trying to involve Ethan in the effort, wondering if he'd think she had an ulterior motive. But she did have another reason, one that made her even more nervous: she wanted to spend more time with him. She tried to convince herself that talking with him about Delta just made the most sense, since they were familiar and friendly (friendlier than they cared to admit), but she was also creating a legitimate reason to be around him more often.

Jillian had a meeting to get to, so she told Monica she would try to catch up with Ethan, too, and she practically skipped down the hallway. Little did she know that the glee she was feeling would be very short-lived, like fireworks that burn out after a few moments, leaving only fast-fading images on our retinas, some puffs of smoke, and a lingering acrid odor.

After the meeting, she walked past the glass-walled boardroom to Jack's mahogany office, with its gorgeous view of downtown Tampa, the Port, and the Aquarium. He was leaning back in his black leather chair with his feet up on his desk, crossed, reading glasses perched on the tip of his nose, the Tampa Tribune open in front of him. Hard at work, as usual.

"Have a few minutes?" she asked, standing in the doorway.

"Of course! I always have time for my favorite people!" he said in his booming voice, rising and moving toward his conference table. She followed him over and took a seat.

"What's up?" he asked, sitting at the end of the table, leaning back, hands pushed into the arms of the chair.

"Well, Peter and I are… I was hoping you could refer me to a good divorce attorney," she said, wondering how much he would ask about before he gave her a name. She also knew that as soon as she told him, the whole building would know. Though one of his favorite phrases was "between you, me, and the fencepost," the fencepost frequently meant just about everyone he took into his confidence, which was, well, just about everyone. He gossiped more than any woman she had ever met, herself included, which was saying something. So much for stereotypes.

"Oh no! What happened? I mean, it's none of my business, but…" He leaned forward and put his hands over hers on the polished table. "Are you OK?"

"Yes, yes, I'm OK. Nothing dramatic happened, we just need to go our separate ways, and I need an attorney's advice," she explained. She didn't want to get into too many details but didn't know how to evade very well, either.

"OK. If you need anything, though, please just let me know. And I do know a good divorce attorney. I'll get her number for you before you go," he said, taking his hands off hers and leaning back again into his chair.

"Thank you, I really appreciate that. I am just not sure what the right process is and need some guidance, so that would be helpful. I want to move out, but I'm not sure about what my rights are, and…"

"Oh, don't do that!" he interrupted, leaning forward again. "At least not until you talk to the attorney. I would guess you need to stay there to protect yourself. You let him move out," he said, pointing his finger at her as he said it.

"Oh, I'm sure he will do nothing of the sort. He won't be doing me any favors. It will be a battle every step of the way," she said, unsure of why she was so certain of that.

"Why, this wasn't his idea?"

"No. At least I don't think he wants a divorce. It's just, well, pretty much trying to get him to do anything I want is a battle." She dropped her eyes.

Jack rose from his chair. "Let me get her number for you."

"Thank you. I really appreciate that." She got up, too, so that she could bolt as soon as he handed the post-it to her, probably to head straight to the ladies' room for a few deep breaths.

He handed her the yellow sticky. "Here you go. Call her now and schedule an appointment, and don't do anything, don't go anywhere, until you talk to her," he insisted.

"Will do. Thanks so much," she said and turned to go.

"Jillian, are you sure you're OK?" he asked.

"I'm sure I will be," she said, forced a smile, and stepped out.

8

A few days later, Jack stopped by Jillian's office on his "rounds," as he called them, and sat down.

"What's going on? Did you have your consult yet?"

"Yes, and you were right. I can't move out. Great. She was helpful, though, and we're going to get things started. Thanks again for the referral," she offered.

"Well, again, if you need anything, let me know."

"Of course. What's the status of the Heights Project?" she asked to change the subject. They chatted for a few minutes about that, and he left to continue his rounds.

She had met with the attorney, Helen, given her an overview of the situation, and put her on retainer. She said they would start with a standard Marital Settlement Agreement, including a custody schedule, and see how far they would get. She told Jillian not to move out of the house, either alone or with Zach, as it could work against her. She'd been sequestered. She sure didn't want to go anywhere without her baby boy. She just dreaded continuing to be around Peter.

The evening before, Jillian had walked into the den and told Peter she wanted to talk about how to share time with Zach.

"Let's just keep it the same as it is now," she said. "You pick him up from school and keep him during the day while I'm at work. I'll pick him up after work and keep him overnight, take him to school the next morning. We'll alternate weekends," she added.

After all, that was what they did. As soon as Jillian would walk in from work, sometime between 5:15 and 5:45 usually, Peter would almost immediately disappear into his office while she and Zach had dinner, played, had his bath, played some more, watched maybe thirty minutes of television or a video, did some reading, then bedtime. She still stayed with him every night in his room until he fell asleep. Sometimes that took ten minutes, sometimes longer. Sometimes she fell asleep with him.

"No, I don't know. Let's see what the lawyers say," he said.

"That's what we do! Why does that have to change?" she said, frustrated. She thought it was a very reasonable and workable plan with as little change from their current routine as possible. They'd just have separate residences.

"Because that means he'll be in three different places every day!" he argued. Jillian was baffled.

"And? What's the difference? Lots of kids do that. They go to school, they go to after-school care, then they go home. Same thing," she said, shaking her head.

He refused, turning back to his computer. "Let's let the lawyers work it out."

She walked out.

She bought an air mattress and put it in Zach's room. She felt too exposed sleeping on the couch and refused to sleep with Peter in the master bedroom, which he was not leaving. Peter then moved the air mattress to the spare room, saying he didn't want to "confuse Zach." She was a gypsy in her own home.

That room, the one that was to be the nursery, the one that was painted bright yellow and had the crib and all the baby furniture and toys in it—everything Zach was done with that they'd been keeping for Baby Number Two, the baby they couldn't conceive before and now never would try for again—became her room. She guessed that sometimes things do happen for a reason, if only one can wait long enough for that reason to be revealed and are deft enough to connect the dots.

"You'll never believe what he did last night," Jillian told Monica at their regular Wednesday lunch a couple weeks later. They fanned themselves to cool down after walking a few blocks to the sandwich shop in the humid July heat. Jillian didn't know how she would survive without Monica. She was filling her in on what was happening, reporting Peter's latest ridiculous actions, like the night he kicked her closed bedroom door, muttering, or his seemingly innocent remarks made to Zach that were really digs at her, in his typical passive-aggressive style. Monica was learning the truths about Jillian's marriage as she doled the details out to her like a jellybean trail in the woods, not intentionally holding anything back but leading herself, analyzing, discovering as they talked. Monica followed, sometimes suggesting, sometimes holding her hand, never judging, just listening, and helping and being a true friend and confidante.

"Sometimes his actions are so transparent, I can't believe he can tolerate himself. We were at the kitchen counter, Zach eating dinner. 'I read Men Are from Mars, Women Are from Venus,' Peter says. That book collected dust on his nightstand for two years after I asked him to read it. Then, he says, 'It's amazing how dead on it is about some things. I highlighted a bunch of stuff. I hope you don't mind.' I had no idea what to say. Was it some lame attempt to connect? 'Too little too late?' he says. I still didn't say anything. What the hell was I supposed to say? Then, get this, he says, 'I talked to my mom today. She said that my dad doesn't want anything from you for his birthday, and that she'd like you to only contact them in case of emergency regarding Zach or me.' Zing! Then he walked out! Can you believe that asshole?" She was still incredulous.

"Oh my god," Monica said. "What a jerk. Was he always like that? It's like he can't even deal with anything, deal with what's going on."

"Yeah, no shit! Yes, he was always like that. He can't deal, you're right. It's like he's just on the surface, and just because he thinks something you're supposed to know where he is, read his fucking mind."

"Do you think you were just a utility to him?" she asked. Boy, she hadn't heard it described so succinctly before.

"I was definitely useful as 'the wife.' Never his wife, his love, his soul mate, but the one who took care of the bills, and sending cards, and buying gifts. Someone who did the dishes and the laundry. Someone to keep the other side of the bed warm. Sometimes more like a roommate than a partner—someone to grocery shop with, fight over the television with, negotiate chores with…" she trailed off. She realized what she really was describing, or what she really felt like, was that she was the maid, or the babysitter, or both. No rights, no opinions. Subservient.

"Weren't you in love at some point?" she asked.

"I suppose. I did think I loved him. But I don't think he ever felt I was someone he wanted to take care of, learn about, or just spend time with. I guess he loved me in his own way, needed me in some way. But not in the ways I needed him to."

"Were you in a daze when you married him? The Jillian I know wouldn't put up with that, wouldn't have accepted that, wouldn't stay in that kind of situation. You are such a strong person, so independent, so capable. I just can't picture why the two of you would be together, why you would stay with him." She seemed genuinely puzzled.

"No, I wasn't in a daze. I just had different priorities. And I wanted to get married; it was time. We had been together for five years. Though I always knew something was missing between us, I never defined it. Now I know what it was: respect. Or empathy. Caring. Valuing. Willingness. He doesn't seem to care at all about what I want or need or what his role might be in fulfilling my hopes or dreams."

Tempe, a new sales executive, walked up and asked if she could join them.

"Of course!" said Monica, sliding her lunch bag over to make room.

"I'm not interrupting anything, am I? You ladies look a bit intense," Tempe said.

"Nope; all good. So how are things going so far?" Jillian asked.

"Well, good! Interesting! There sure is a lot going on around here. Anything you two ladies would like to fill me in on?" She smiled.

Tempe was in their same age range with thick, straight blond hair, very little makeup, nicely built, attractive.

She'd just started with Sagency a couple weeks earlier, and Jillian liked her immediately. During the first meeting they were in together, Jillian had watched Tempe's eyes slightly squint, her eyebrows barely wrinkle, her head cock just a tad, almost completely controlled but not quite, all at the same times that Jillian's eyes were squinting, her eyebrows were wrinkling, her head was cocking, at the insane, inane conversations and decisions being made around them. Tempe had asked a lot of questions—questions that Jillian had asked long ago, the answers to which she supposed Tempe wouldn't like any more than she had, and that, she supposed, she would eventually stop asking, too, though they might still infuriate her.

"What did you think of the meeting last Thursday?" Jillian asked, wondering if she would speak up or play it safe.

"Um, seems to me already that I'd like to see some changes, but since I don't know what the processes or politics are around here, I think I'll wait until after at least my first month to make those recommendations," she said, chuckling, unpacking her leftovers.

Monica and Jillian peered at each other with smirks, barely able to contain their glee. Tempe was a Delta candidate, no doubt about it.

"Well, I think you need to join us for happy hour Friday," Jillian said, smiling, and looking at Monica, who was nodding her wavy-blond-haired head in agreement.

After that day, Monica and Jillian knew they had a new ally. Tempe would soon become one of Jillian's dearest friends, someone who helped her immeasurably over the next few years, someone she would ultimately claim as a true sister, as she had Monica.

And after that day, Peter's entire family, the ones who had professed to love Jillian as their own daughter and sister, the flesh-and-blood mother of their kin, completely shut her out. Not one of them contacted her to get her side of the story, to find out if she was OK, if she needed anything, to yell at her or throw accusations, or try to convince her to change her mind. Nothing. Jillian sent Chrissie an email telling her she hoped they could talk about it one day, and her cold reply stated that Peter had asked her not to be in contact with her and she had to respect his wishes. She wasn't just divorcing Peter; she was divorcing his whole clan.

9

At the next Delta meeting and lunch with Ethan and Monica, Ethan sat next to Jillian at the little tile-top café table, so they were thigh to thigh. She tried to pay attention to what Monica was saying across the table. The sleeves of Ethan's white dress shirt were partially rolled up, allowing the blond hair on his freckly tanned arm to peek out. She realized she was staring right at it, she didn't know for how long, and at his hand, the one that had slid up her thigh, his left hand, the one sporting his gold wedding band. They sat close enough that she could feel the heat of his body (or was it her own?). She was so nervous, excited, distracted, terrified by his nearness that her whole body was trembling. She couldn't hear anything Monica was saying, only the racing of her own blood. She tried to take deep breaths to steady herself, but at one point felt that if he were to turn and look right into her eyes again, as he'd done a couple times already, if his breath were to warm her skin again when he laughed, if he leaned in and whispered in her ear one more time about the "dork club" sitting a couple of tables away, or oh, god forbid, if he were to touch her, she would simply burst into flame.

She was in big trouble. She had no idea how long she would be able to control herself.

They hadn't spent much time together since "The Incident," but when they did have the occasional joint conference or meeting together, she was looking at him, listening to him from a different perspective, studying him. In the meeting—almost three hours long—her mind kept wandering. There was so much she didn't know about him. She tried to imagine what he was like as a husband, a father, a son. She had never even thought about him outside of their working relationship before they crashed into each other that night. Who was this person? Who was this man, this derailing pebble on the train track of her life?

The more she tried to figure him out from afar, and the further her home life deteriorated, the more she was drawn to him, or at least the person she imagined him to be. The more she thought about Ethan, the more she was compelled to think of him, as if thoughts of him were some sort of addictive drug that had hold of her, one thought leading to another, to another, to another...What was the interest there, anyway?

The next day she had an email from him with a referral, the exact type they were discussing in Delta. Jillian was surprised that he would proceed with it, since there were no official agreements in place yet and not likely to be for quite a while. But, before she had time to rethink it, she typed a reply: "Hey, thanks! Have any big plans tomorrow? Have time for lunch? Any time to acknowledge we had sex? That it happened? That you were there? That you didn't stop me, and I didn't stop you? That you were smiling and willing and talked about the next time we would be together? Then you totally blew me off? Any time to acknowledge I exist while my life is falling apart?"

She erased all but the first two questions. And she still hesitated to send those. She held the pointer over the Send button for a long time, weighing, waiting. Why didn't she just call him instead?

Because she didn't want to put him on the spot? She rolled her eyes at herself. That was not it. It was really because she was a coward. She was terrified that he would shut her down. At least if she sent him an email, they could both gracefully pretend she never sent it, or he had never received it. Stomach in knots.

Send. Puke.

He hadn't replied by nine the next morning, so she sent him a follow-up: "Let me know if you are going to ignore me so I won't be expecting an acknowledgement all day." She waited ten minutes before she sent that one, nearly hyperventilating while trying to decide. Five minutes after she sent it her phone rang.

"Hey," he said. "I have somewhat of a crisis going on up here this morning, but we should do lunch early next week, OK?"

"Fine," she said, and hung up. Now she was mad. Hurt and rejected. Asshole.

He called back about an hour later. "I can get out for lunch today, after all. Can you go around 11:30?"

"Sure. Meet you out front." Still annoyed.

He called again at 11:05. "I have another emergency. I'm going to the hospital to meet my mom; a friend of hers has had a heart attack," he explained.

"OK, fine. Hope she's OK." Did she buy it? Not really. She rolled her eyes at herself again. So typical of her to accept being yanked around. She was so annoyed at that point, though, that it was probably for the best. She felt one of her dark-and-twisty moods setting in.

As the weeks wore on and the humid summer heat finally began to abate, they were settled into a new routine at home. Jillian would arrive home by 5:30 every day; Peter would have Zach's dinner on; she would change quickly and take over with Zach. Peter had asked if they could start alternating giving Zach his bath and putting him to bed, and Jillian had agreed, not knowing how or why to say no, though she was suspicious of the request. She would finish Zach's dinner with him and, on Peter's nights off, he would disappear into his office or the master bedroom. Or, more and more frequently, he would take off in his truck. Sometimes he would be gone fifteen minutes, sometimes a few hours. She had no idea where he went, nor did she really care. He could leave and never come back, as far as she was concerned.

She was still sleeping on the air mattress in the spare room; she did not make a request to alternate use of the master bedroom. She was doing her best not to care, to keep everything inside, especially at work. The people she worked with, worked for, and who worked for her needed to have confidence in her. She needed to be strong, professional. It was hard enough being a female executive; she certainly couldn't show emotion at the office. She did wish that someone would occasionally ask her how she was doing, as some demonstration that they gave a shit, yet she was unwilling to let them see that she wasn't OK. They could ask, you know? It wasn't like they were in the dark about her situation. Did they just not know what to say? Was she invisible to them, too? Ethan didn't even ask! Ugh.

The whole thing was starting to wear on her: impatience at trying to keep the divorce process moving, the tension from Peter, trying to protect and act "normal" around Zach, trying to push Delta forward without making too many enemies, not to mention doing her job every day, and not having any way to release the stress except by drinking—which really made everything worse, not better. It was piling up.

Most of the time she tried to be the person people expected her to be: effervescent—as someone had once described her, a description she adored—and occasionally sarcastic. She smiled, laughed, spoke professionally, intelligently. She continued to do her job well, not really knowing where she was drawing the strength from each day. What else was she supposed to do? Walk around crying, bawling, screaming, bleeding? Curl up in a ball under her desk, humming and rocking herself? Yeah, that would go over well.

She sat down at her desk and turned to the window. It was a bright, sunny, Florida day. Too sunny to suit her mood, for sure. Tempe walked in, ready for lunch, and as soon as she looked at Jillian, tears streamed down Jillian's face.

"What in the world is going on?" Tempe asked.

Jillian couldn't answer. She just barely shook her head.

"Do you want me to close the door?" Jillian nodded, still unable to speak, knowing if she tried, she might very well wail.

"Zach OK?" Tempe asked as she closed the door. Jillian nodded, her hand over her mouth to try to keep her lips from trembling. She hated the way she looked when she cried, her eyes and nose turning red, tears smearing her makeup, eyes puffing, nose running.

"Did you just quit?"

Jillian looked up at her then, chuckling a bit, and shook her head again, her hand still to her mouth.

Tempe was deftly distracting Jillian, allowing her to recover, regain control. Jillian wanted to tell her what the tears were about, if only to tell someone, anyone at all. She needed some perspective.

Tempe had told Jillian and Monica that her own divorce was almost final, that she had two kids, a boy about Zach's age and a girl, a couple years older. She was more than a year into her process, but they were living apart. Seems they were a bit more amiable than Jillian and Peter. Jillian had grilled her about the process and about how her kids were handling it. Tempe had willingly obliged, and they had a frank conversation about the stress, the emotion, the anxiety of the whole thing, and trying to stay sane for the kids' sakes.

"I had an indiscretion with someone a few months ago. I can't tell you the whole story because one, you really don't want to know …"

Tempe cocked her head, then pointedly pulled out a guest chair and sat down.

"… and two, because if the divorce gets ugly and we end up in court, it's best you don't know."

"That's a wise strategy."

"I think I have feelings for the guy, but…" Jillian couldn't say the words out loud, though she knew how to finish the sentence: he doesn't feel the same. "I know it's not real. I know it's just a distraction or projection or something to keep me from freaking out about the reality of my life. He can't even, like, ask me how things are going. He doesn't even give a shit!"

Jillian closed her eyes and rubbed her forehead with her fingertips. She was getting a serious headache.

Tempe made sure Jillian was finished talking, then started her analysis.

"It's a strength issue, Jillian; even though you weren't getting what you needed from Peter, you thought you were getting something. Now that you've realized you weren't, you're trying to fill the void. There's a vacuum, a big black hole, that you're trying to figure out how to deal with. Only when things are finished with Peter, and you're on your own and being self-reliant emotionally, will you find out whether what you want with this other guy is real or imagined.

"I've been there," Tempe continued. "I wanted a relationship with someone who was unavailable. We had dialogue after dialogue about it, and he told me directly more than once that nothing more was going to happen, that he was never going to leave her." She paused, shaking her head, to herself more than to Jillian. "I'm no angel, believe me," she said, realizing what she'd revealed. "I think I made up so much in my own mind because of what I thought I wanted, that I turned things that didn't really mean anything into what I wanted them to mean. And if things really had gone the way I wanted, it would have led to a lot of destructive behavior. You'll get past this."

Jillian barely nodded her head, looking down at her lap.

"What you really need to do is just take care of yourself and Zach, and be on your own, and support yourself. Then, what is real, and what you really want, and need, will be positive and healing, not this hurtful mess it is now."

Jillian hoped to god she was right. The glee and relief she had initially felt had turned into sorrow. Nothing was going as she wanted it to, and she was frustrated, tired, and just plain disgusted. She had to keep it all inside most hours of the day—at work, with Zach—and by the time she shut herself in the nursery at night, the only thing she had the energy left to do was cry. And cry. And cry. Until she fell asleep.

She might have cried over the end of her marriage, or the loss of love between her and Peter. But those things had been gone for so long that there was nothing left to cry for.

She cried for her son, but only because she never wanted him to have divorced parents. She knew he would survive that and probably be better for it. The primary reason she had allowed herself to move forward with the divorce was that she wanted to be the best mother to Zach that she could possibly be, and she knew she couldn't do that married to his father.

She cried because she was sick of dealing with Peter every day, living in the same house with him—killing her with his looks, judging her with his body language, controlling her by using the conditioning that had been put into place over more than fourteen years. She wanted to be away from his snarls, barks, slams, snores, smells. Away from his clothes on the floor, whiskers in the sink, dishes on the counter, piss in the toilet, shoes by the door. *Away away away.*

And she started crying for the man who tipped the scale, the last bit of water that caused her cup, or bowl, or bucket, or ocean of unhappiness to overflow beyond the point of containment. She thought about asking him to tell her something about himself that he knew she wouldn't like so she could talk herself out of what she was talking herself into, but she was afraid the thing he would choose to tell her was that he had cheated on his wife.

That night, she went to bed (well, to her air mattress) alone and cried herself to sleep again—another night in a long trend. She cried because it was this meaningless tryst that had made her realize how wrong her life was, her marriage was, her decisions had been, and that made her realize she wanted to live, and she wanted to be close to someone, close to a man. That she wanted to be in love and to make love. That she had passion and desire. That she was a real woman, and she was alive and had choices. This man she barely knew had kissed her back to life and then abandoned her, too.

She was watching television in the recliner the next night after putting Zach to bed when Peter pounced.

She heard him come out of his office and head to the kitchen; she hoped he was just coming out for another beer. But he stepped out into the family room, in front of her.

"Hey, light a fire under your attorney," he ordered.

She looked up at him, every muscle taut, but felt like laughing. He was such an asshole. He just couldn't even get out of his own way.

"What? What do you mean?" she asked.

"Get things moving," he said, then tapped his tooth.

"I thought you didn't even want this," she countered.

"I do now. Get it going!" he practically shouted and stomped out of the room without waiting for a response.

Well, well. She grunted, then smiled. Un-fucking-believable.

Honestly, she was frustrated with her attorney, too. She had to call all the time to find out what was going on, the status of things, when the next deadline was. When she called the next day, the office staff offered their usual lame excuses, lackadaisical responses, and hazy answers. No urgency there. And Peter's attorney offered no help, always waiting until the day a response was due to provide it. Maybe Peter was the one who should "light a fire."

Every time they established a new deadline for a reply to the revised Marital Settlement Agreement, Jillian would count the days, hoping the next one would reveal some progress. They had only inched forward, and then there was yet another deadline. All delays, to what end she wasn't sure.

Meanwhile, thoughts of what her next step was going to be—what she was going to do once the divorce became reality—had started spinning in her head. So, she did something that may have helped her from coming completely undone—she started making lists. Where she could move, all the details that went with that, new bank accounts, updating her will—everything that she would need to take care of once she was emancipated and could start her new life. She had to stop the spinning in her Tasmanian devil brain, so she transferred the thoughts to lists on her laptop, where she knew they wouldn't burst into flame and turn to ash before they slipped away, only to slither back in the middle of the night. She started planning her "new life."

10

One Metro was having a lobby party, sponsored by the new building owner. Everyone was invited to the cool marble-and-glass two-story expanse for free beer, wine, and appetizers, in the hopes that friendly tenants made happy-and-content tenants who would renew their leases. Jillian went, hoping Ethan would show up. That was really the only reason she stayed, that and the free drinks.

Monica and Tempe decided they could stay a while, too, since the next day was Jillian's birthday. She emailed Peter that she would be home an hour late. Woohoo. Big celebration.

Monica and Jillian were pointing out different people they knew from around the building in case Tempe hadn't met them yet, while they sipped on beers, and then Tempe opened the door.

"So, Jillian, do you think you'll ever get married again? Or are you turned off by the whole thing?" she asked, peering at Jillian over the rim of her plastic cup as she took a sip of beer and scowled. She preferred cosmopolitans.

Jillian looked away. "I have to get out of this one first!" she laughed.

"True, but…"

"Do you?" Jillian interrupted.

"I hope so! The next time will be for love. Then, if I ever get married for a third time, it'll be for money!"

They all laughed.

"Well," Jillian said. "I don't know. Maybe. It's certainly not my first goal."

"You'll have feelings for someone else someday," Monica offered.

"I might, already," Jillian sighed. Ethan was the only man she had had sex with besides Peter in the last fifteen years, and it wasn't even good sex at that, yet every time she saw him her heart raced, and she felt flushed and just wanted to try it again with him.

"What?" she asked, clearly surprised.

"Oh, yeah," Jillian smirked.

"Oh, well. Good!" she said.

Jillian could tell Monica was puzzled and wanted to ask who it was, but she also didn't want to violate her "no prying" policy. Jillian took another drink of her beer. "I'm not saying who it is. I think it's just a crush or a rebound or something." Oh, how mysterious! The way Monica looked at her told her she was in trouble.

"What?" Jillian asked, trying to seem chagrined. "What's that look on your face?" Monica was clearly suspicious, wondering why Jillian would keep it from her when she told her everything else.

"Is it someone we know?" Monica stared at Jillian with one manicured eyebrow halfway up her forehead.

"Look, this guy…He played a brief—very brief—but crucial role in recent events that I never could have imagined before it happened. And now he's like, my hero or something. You know, like when the woman falls for the fireman who saves her from her burning bed, or the guy who falls for the social worker visiting his cancer-ridden wife, or the rape victim who thinks her therapist is god? Hero worship, or the Stockholm syndrome, or some shit like that. Right?" Monica and Tempe were both staring at Jillian, forgotten drinks in hand.

"He just happened to topple my house of cards. What happened when we crashed into each other,"—Jillian smirked—"and crash we did, set off a chain reaction that had been under construction for quite some time. He lit the match, so he gets the credit. Despite that what happened was not an admirable act of intention. But the real problem is that he just isn't interested in anything further."

"I don't know what to say," said Monica. "I'm sorry?"

Jillian had stumped her. How unusual. "There's nothing to say. I'm sure it will be fine, right? I'm sure I'll fall out of falling for him. It's just a matter of time. After all, I fell out of falling for Peter, right?" she smiled wryly.

"This someone else? This someone you're interested in, he's the indiscretion?" Tempe asked, finally taking another drink of her beer.

"Yes, one and the same," Jillian said.

Monica's eyes about popped out of her head. "Indiscretion? What indiscretion?" she asked.

"Yes, an indiscretion. A few months ago," Jillian said.

Monica looked at Tempe, then back at Jillian questioningly, like why in the hell Tempe knew and she didn't.

Jillian answered her silent question. "He's married." Sheesh, and she had only had two beers.

Monica choked on hers, eyes popping out even further. Tempe's cup stopped at her lips, but no choking from her.

"It is someone I know, isn't it?" Monica said accusingly, trying to recover, to process.

"I don't even believe it's real!" Jillian tried to justify. "It's got to be some kind of defensive maneuver, some kind of survival mechanism kicking in, you know? That to get through this hell I am in with Peter, I need something else to hold onto, something to believe in, that there's something better, something right, someone out there for me, waiting. It's just imaginary to help me get through, give me some hope, you know?"

She was rambling again, starting to sound nuts even to herself. She still hadn't told a soul it was Ethan, and it was eating her alive. She wasn't usually one for keeping secrets.

"You have to believe it's going to be worth it. It is! You have something, someone better waiting. You're smart, beautiful, intelligent, warm, caring, successful. You're independent. You'll figure it all out. And you're going to make some man, the right man, very happy, and he's going to be a very lucky guy," Tempe counseled, taking another sip of her beer.

"Well that is wonderful of you to say, but where is he?" Jillian laughed. "It ain't this guy!"

"Jillian! You still haven't answered me!" said Monica, jumping back in and refusing to let her off the hook.

"I'll defer, so I don't have to lie." Jillian hoped Monica wouldn't press her, even though she was bursting to tell her. She really wanted to, if for no other reason than to gain some perspective on the whole thing, which she was lacking. A few glasses of beer or cheap wine always loosened her lips (and sometimes a few other parts of her anatomy) anyway.

"I really do feel like I need to tell someone about it, so if you two think you can handle it, I'll tell you. But you can't tell another living soul! And if I do tell you, you might eventually have to lie about it to other people! Do you still want to know?"

"YES!" they cried in unison. They looked at each other in surprise, and all three of them burst out laughing. Then they looked back at Jillian expectantly. Guess there would be no wriggling out of it now.

She moved in closer to them and lowered her voice, conspiratorially. "The conference in April? Right before I decided Peter and I were through? Ethan Chase. We did it, kind of," she said sheepishly, taking a quick drink of her beer instead of a deep breath.

"Holy shit!" Monica said, sloshing her beer onto the floor—quite the reaction for someone usually so calm and cool! Tempe was just staring at Jillian, but now both eyebrows had crawled up her forehead.

"We were both completely wasted and were both totally freaked out by it afterward, and nothing has happened since," she blurted, her right hand up like she was taking an oath.

"Well, I know how that happens! He sure is attractive!" Tempe said.

"So nothing's going on now?"

"No! I've tried talking with him, but he seems to be avoiding me," Jillian answered.

"You two had never hinted at anything before then?" Monica asked, trying to logic her way through this new piece of information.

"Nope. It was a total fluke, circumstance, as far as I know. Trouble is, now I don't know how to deal with him. I get anxious, nervous, whenever I'm around him, and that's not good. I need to be able to concentrate, communicate, especially now that he's in on Delta and has started making real referrals."

"Oh my god. You need to get a grip. He's still married, right? If he's not interested, you just need to avoid him," Tempe directed, as Monica nodded in agreement.

"I know that. I'm just finding that to be a struggle."

At times it was perfectly clear to her that the feelings she thought she had for Ethan were just an illusion, that as the sands in the hourglass of her marriage and relationship with Peter were running out, her feelings for Ethan were filling up. She was looking forward to seeing him, running into him in the elevator or the café. And when she did, her heart would race, and she would start to sweat.

But was it just a crush? An infatuation? Was it a yearning for just the feeling of being beside someone, of filling the emptiness in her heart, replacing what was lost with Peter, as Tempe had suggested? Was it just loneliness? Lust? Maybe desire for a true connection with someone she had a lucky hour with, hoping for more? Hoping what happened wasn't meaningless? Wishing it wasn't a fateful event that would change both of their paths, but in completely opposite ways? To Jillian, being the last sign her marriage was truly over, and to him, an augury that he wanted and needed to do something to save his own?

She was trying to keep her feelings to herself. She promised herself that when they were working together, that was all it would be. She would never expect anything from him, or act inappropriately, or expect him to act in any way other than professionally, as if they were nothing more than they seemed to be, like nothing ever happened between them and nothing ever would.

The three of them chatted a bit more, but Jillian's hour was up, so she thanked Tempe and Monica for staying and for supporting her, they wished her a happy birthday, and she drove the twelve minutes home to her house-prison.

11

Forrest, the agency's administrative executive, stopped at her office door. "Hello Jillian. Good day today?" he said with his fake, smug smile.

"Sure. How about you, Forrest?" she said, hoping he would keep moving.

"Great! Do you have a few minutes? Do you mind?" and he gestured toward the guest chair.

"Sure. What's up?" She kept turned toward her computer, hoping to send the message she didn't really have too much time but was being polite.

Forrest had been with the agency a couple of years and was tight with Jack. They went to church together, and Bible study, of all things. Forrest really irked her. Just his smugness, maybe, or the fact that he kissed Jack's ass all the time. He was also one of those old schoolers who was passive-aggressively opposing the Delta project, showing up for meetings and being polite so he could tell Jack he was participating, but talking to the other members of the team who opposed it every chance he got; and filling Jack's ears, she was sure. But of course, Jack did nothing about it.

"I heard that you're going through some personal issues," he started.

Good god. Where was this going? "Where did you hear that?" she asked, leaning back in her chair and lacing her fingers together in front of her.

He smiled and turned red. "Does that really matter?"

"No, as a matter of fact. Yes, I am going through some issues." She refused to look away from him, staring him right in the eyes. His faced turned even redder if that was possible.

"My wife and I went through a difficult time a while back. We got counseling from the church and recommitted ourselves and were able to save our marriage," he said smoothly, almost as if he'd rehearsed it.

"Good for you. That's great," she said with a small smile, lips pressed tightly together.

"We believe that marriage is forever, and that they all can and should be saved, and recommitted, even after times of doubt and trouble," he said, sounding even more rehearsed.

"Well, again, good for you, but you don't really know anything about my situation," she said. Not smiling now. Seriously?

"If you'd like the name and contact information of a counselor, or even if you'd like my wife and me to talk with you, we'd be happy to do that."

"Thank you for that. I'll keep it in mind, but I don't think this one can be salvaged," she said. Hint.

"They all can be. And they all should be. Good luck," he said as he stood up.

She watched in silent fury as he turned to leave. *Was he out of his fucking mind? Strolling in here like that, obviously judging me? And who told him, anyway? Jack, of course. Who else?*

"He can kiss my ass," she said as she recounted the incident to Tempe at lunch. Monica had a conference.

"Asshole. I bet he didn't really want to stay in his marriage but was too much of a coward to get out of it. So now, if he can keep others trapped in theirs, he doesn't feel so sorry for himself. Dick," Tempe said.

"I know! And did you hear what he was saying about the SoHo Project in the meeting? That's a perfect candidate for Delta, to refer upstairs, but he won't. And Jack won't tell him to, either. Everyone just does whatever the hell they want, and Jack lets them."

"Yep, you're right!" Tempe agreed. "I don't really get it. All the analysis says it makes the most sense. That our efficiencies will increase. That we'll gain new clients. That our sales team will be stronger. That our creative team will be stronger. Why are they fighting it so hard?"

"Because it wasn't their idea. Because they don't like change. Because we're the ones initiating it—strong, smart, beautiful women—and they resent us. And Jack won't get on board with it fully because he likes being everyone's bestie, and letting everyone do what they want, instead of what's best for the business, for our clients," Jillian seethed.

"Yeah, we're women, and even though Ethan is on our side, he's a young upstart compared to them, so they all feel threatened, even by him. A difficult situation," she said.

"I know. But I know in my heart it's the right thing to do, so I can't give up on it. Not yet."

"I'm with you. We just need to be smart about it, and careful," she continued.

"Yeah, how to do that is the big question."

They finished their lunches in silence.

Jillian did agree to go to therapy with Peter, at his request. Really, at his attorney's, since that was the only way they communicated. Peter wouldn't look her in the eye, and the house was filled with tension and hostility, cold war that it was, and Jillian hoped that maybe a therapist could help him accept things and want to move on and get it over with.

The therapist suggested they needed to communicate with each other verbally and gave them a strategy for doing so "safely," as she put it. They were supposed to pick two nights a week and a place to meet for five minutes, taking turns talking to each other. The rules were that one night it was one person's turn to talk, they were forbidden from using the word "you," and the other person couldn't say anything. The next time, the roles would be reversed.

Peter took the first turn. They sat in the dining room they rarely used, at the gorgeous cherry table with scrolled legwork that took them ages to decide on, in the chairs neither one of them wanted but had agreed to because neither would concede to the other's first choice.

"I think this is happening because your parents moved up north, your office moved, we moved, and you're shaken up. If you weren't making so much money, I don't think it would be happening at all."

He'd broken the rules and defeated the whole purpose.

He looked at her expectantly. The rules were that she wasn't allowed to respond, so she just stared back. Finally, she couldn't take it anymore. "Is that it? Are you finished?" she asked dully.

"I guess," he said, with a small shrug.

She got up and left the room, rolling her eyes as soon as they were turned away from him.

When it was Jillian's turn, she looked him in the eye and said, "I am going to counseling because I am trying to help. That is the only reason. We are not reconciling." He did not react in any way. She waited. He got up and left the room.

"Did you have your talks this week?" Dr. Clueless asked. She looked at Jillian first.

"I guess. Peter essentially broke all the rules and said some things that I would like him to explain," Jillian said calmly, though her heart was hammering in her chest.

It was true that her parents had moved up north, but she was relieved. She was hurt that they hadn't felt the need to stay close to their grandson, but it got her off the hook of having to spend time with them and worry about them. Sagency had moved into One Metro, into a place much nicer and newer, and she finally had the executive office space that she had earned two years before. The space they had before could not accommodate another office with

Jack and the rest of the executive team, so she was left out. And she and Peter had moved, too, from across the Bay, where they'd lived the last ten years, closer to her office, so she didn't have to commute over the bridge every day, and into a nice neighborhood in a great school district. And she was making great money, more than twice what Peter was making, not counting benefits. Shaken up about all of that? Maybe. But in a good way.

Peter replied before the therapist could say anything. "It's kind of hard to say I love you without saying the word *you*," he said, already defensive.

Jillian grunted, astonished. He really was delusional if he thought that was what he'd said to her. Dr. Sherlock-Fucking-Holmes said, "Jillian, I take it you have an issue with what Peter just said." *No, really? Jesus.*

Counseling was getting them nowhere. Jillian was too exasperated to believe that the process could work. She didn't want it to. She wanted it to be over. And Peter was living in his own little fantasy land as always, thinking everyone knew his intentions without him verbalizing them or acting upon them, then acting surprised when they didn't, and unable or unwilling to see anyone else's point of view.

She told Dr. Do-Little that she would call to schedule the next meeting. When she did call, she told her she had decided she wanted to go by herself and suggested she talk Peter into doing the same. She went to one session with her and tried to explain that he wasn't really trying to fix anything, that he was showing her no respect, never had, and never would, and a demonstration of that was that she was sleeping on an air mattress while he kept the master bedroom. The therapist said that was to be expected; for him to leave the room would mean he was conceding.

Bullshit. Jillian told her frankly that there would be no reconciliation, that the only reason she was even there was to try to help Peter move on. She asked Jillian if she couldn't slow things down a bit to give him more time to get used to the idea. Seriously? It had already been like, seven months! What the hell!?

The therapist called Peter and tried to talk him into coming in, but he bailed, saying the only reason to go was for the two of them to go together. Whatever.

Jillian's attorney still wouldn't let her move out of the house, and there had been hardly any progress with the Agreement, so Jillian fired her. She hired Tempe's attorney, who told Jillian the same things and that it would be at least six months before they were done, but that they should file with the court, putting it on their official timeline. Why Helen hadn't suggested that Jillian had no idea. Incompetence or apathy, she supposed. *Thanks, Jack, for the referral.*

Anthony, the new attorney, also said that Peter had the upper hand since he had been the one staying home with Zach. And, since Jillian had a higher income, she would probably pay child support and maybe even some alimony. Their role reversal was complete. Peter was the fucking Mr. Mom and Jillian was the sucker who worked her ass off every day and got screwed in the end because she was out earning a living, working hard to support her family. Anthony also suggested not rushing the process, since the situation was hostile, though silent, in hopes that Peter's ire would burn itself out and make a resolution more likely.

Jillian really didn't care. She didn't care about the money, the house, the furnishings, the IRAs; he could have it all. She wasn't going anywhere without Zach.

She was just so tired of being in that house, in that nursery, on that air mattress; of being in limbo; of waiting to escape, even though there was nowhere to run to, just things to run from.

Sometimes she just wanted someone to comfort her, a man who'd put his arms around her, smooth her hair, dry her tears, tell her everything was going to be all right, that it was going to be worth it. Someone besides Monica and Tempe she could trust to tell everything she was feeling: that she worried about Zach, that he wouldn't love or need her, that Peter would poison him against her or at least teach him through his own actions not to respect her (what she was leaving in order to counteract in the first place), that she wouldn't have what she needed to change that—most notably time—and that she wouldn't ever be able to leave the place that was making her sick before she grew to hate the man she used to love. But there was no one to do those things for her, no one to listen to the whole truth.

It was ironic, really. Initially, she wanted to be friends with Peter. She hoped that they could have a better relationship as co-parents than they'd had as husband and wife. She should have known better, should have predicted that, for all the reasons she was leaving him, he would not allow that to happen. Not that he wouldn't want to, but that he just was not capable of it.

If she had really thought about how it would be if they were going to have to live in the same house under those circumstances, she probably could have also predicted the silence, the sneers, the slams. They were terrible for each other when they were "in love." Why would she think, with all the hurt and heartache between them, that they would ever have been able to support each other?

She was also tired of the whole thing being about Peter and what he wanted and what he needed, and how he was incapable because he was a man, and how of course he would treat her the way he was because anything else would mean surrender, and she shouldn't take it personally.

Attorneys and therapists suggesting that she slow it down to give him time to adjust and accept it.

Are you fucking kidding me? She wanted to scream! Spend more of her life than she already had—the last fifteen years—trying to make everything OK for him? Trying to make sure he was hurt as little as possible? Trying to make sure he wasn't too uncomfortable? Being sorry she was hurting him? When the hell had he ever done the same for her? When had he ever put her first, ever given her the same consideration? Never. That was when.

Never. This was a man who allowed his wife, sick with bronchitis, and his toddler to use a sleeping bag on the floor while he, in perfect health, slept in the only bed in the room the one time they visited Jillian's grandparents together. Because he wouldn't be able to sleep otherwise. Really? They had no idea what they were asking.

Day by day, the life was being sucked out of her. Her hope for the future and fantasies of her life out from under him were the only things that kept her sane. She started another list, in addition to her lists of legal steps and moving plans: things she wanted to do with Zach that she didn't feel she had the freedom, time, or energy to do with him now, like cooking and playing games and going to movies and taking road trips.

"Well," she said in a particularly pissy tone one night to Megan on the phone, "I've decided that how Peter feels about this whole thing and how he's handling it is now his own problem. I am over it being mine. I have solved my problem. I am done," she exclaimed.

"So what do you mean, what are you going to do?" Megan asked.

"My attorney is going to file. That will put everything on the court's timetable, and both sides will be required to meet the deadlines. There will be a mandatory mediation. If it fails, we go to court and spend thousands more of our 'joint marital assets' on attorneys because Peter's too fucking stubborn or stupid or delusional or selfish to agree to do what a judge will just ultimately make us do anyway. I'm not changing my mind," she affirmed.

"Obviously, and I'm glad for that," she said.

"You know what's so fricking ironic? That nothing Peter and I ever had was ours when he talked about it to his mother or sister or buddy—until we were getting divorced. He hardly ever said *we* or *our* about anything when he was talking with his family or friends. In fact, remember when we were living together, and he went out and bought that house without me even seeing it? I was stunned. And one time we were at a car show with Chrissie and her husband? Peter handed our camera to Chrissie, when I was standing right next to her, and asked her to take a picture of him and Zach! Again, stunned. After she took the picture, I said, 'Now maybe you can take one of all three of us?' Peter grunted, like it was some fucking annoyance. So, yeah, now that we're· getting divorced, suddenly everything is *ours*. How fucking convenient for him."

"Well, of course! You have been the one working your ass off, moving up the ladder, getting recognition, gathering accolades, and his career's been going nowhere. I'm not saying that staying at home taking care of the kids and working is easy, but he is a man— or, a male, at least—and that's not a typical male role, so I'm sure he has issues with it," Megan said.

"I know. I just wish he would have told me what his issues were, instead of shutting me out and making me out to be the bad guy," Jillian said.

"That's not how he operates. You know that better than anyone. What else is going on?"

"Well, 'the guy'? He's really annoying me," Jillian said. She'd given her the short version on Ethan on their last call. "He's just not really responding to me at all, like he doesn't even give a shit about me. He seems to have gotten past what happened and is living his happy, perfect little life with his perfect little family like nothing ever happened. I'll email him and ask him to lunch or something, and most of the time he just doesn't even respond at all. Dick."

"He's just trying to protect himself, I'm sure, Jilly. It's pretty shitty of him to ignore you, but are you sure it's really him you're mad at? You're entitled to your feelings, of course, but it seems like Peter should be the target of most of your anger at this point."

She was right. Maybe it wasn't Ethan she was mad at after all, but Peter. Wasn't he guilty of all those same crimes: He wouldn't respond to her? He didn't give a shit? He didn't fight for her? She had tried to fix things; he didn't cooperate. She always had to go to him, to make things right, apologize, be the peacemaker, the love maker. It was always up to her. God, she was exhausted from all the effort.

She had made herself a promise based on Tempe's sage advice: Before she decided what she really wanted, she needed to be divorced, living on her own, and be by herself for a while. She promised to give herself some time before she decided anything for sure. Maybe something would change.

That was one more reason why she would get so upset when her Independence Day was postponed yet again. Every time a new draft of the Marital Settlement Agreement would go from her attorney's office to his, he had thirty days to respond. More waiting. Sometimes it would come back with no real changes from the last one he'd sent, all her compromises apparently unacceptable, but always the day before the deadline.

What was the rush, anyway? Ethan was still married and still uninterested. It was just that she felt such a weight on every day, every hour, every opportunity, as if every moment was a portent of the rest of her life, as if every day she lived was going to be her last, that if she didn't make something happen, she might live and die in limbo.

12

I asked Kate for help," she told Monica in her office the next day during happy hour, the first chance they'd had to talk all day.

Kate had been Jillian's assistant prior to Candace. She had straight brown hair with blonde streaks cut in a short bob, with long bangs over deep brown eyes that sparkled when she smiled. Sagency been her first professional job out of college; she was bright and personable, and Jillian could tell from the moment she met her that she'd like her and that she would do a great job for them. All of which turned out to be spot on. They became friends and occasionally spent some time together outside of the office. She was a very creative, helpful young woman, but Jillian could see a sadness in her eyes that she didn't understand. She seemed delicate, vulnerable, in some way that she couldn't quite peg, and that Kate wasn't willing to open up about. The only thing Jillian knew was that Kate's dad had an affair. No details other than that.

Kate disappeared one day about a year after she'd started the job. She just didn't show up. For days. When Jillian finally found out where she was and what had happened, Kate was in a rehab center hundreds of miles away. Her parents sent Jillian a letter telling her how much she meant to Kate, to be patient with her. She was. She missed her. But Kate apparently thought she had let Jillian down. She was ashamed. Jillian didn't care what happened; she just cared about Kate and wanted to help her, wanted to be there for her. Kate never let her. Over the next few months, Jillian sent her several notes and a birthday card with a silver chain with an angel charm on it, through Kate's parents. Kate sent a card back saying how much she appreciated the support and promised to call soon, when she was strong enough.

Several months later, Candace brought in the morning paper folded open to Kate's obituary. Jillian burst into sobs, and Candace quietly left her office, closing the door behind her. Jillian bawled her eyes out, laying her head on her desk for a long while. Finally, she pulled herself up, gathered her purse, took the back stairs out, and drove home.

She walked into the house and announced to Peter through her sobs, "Kate's dead!"

"Oh my god, are you serious? I'm so sorry," he said, but he made no effort to comfort her, just stood there looking at Jillian's tear-stained, freaked-out face.

Jillian locked herself in the bathroom and cried harder and for longer than she ever had in her life, which was something at the time, though it seemed later that it was just the dam breaking, a preamble for what would come over the next few years.

She thought she would suffocate; the sobs had come so hard and for so long. She didn't know how she could produce so many tears in one sitting, the moans emanating from somewhere inside were unrecognizable to her as her own.

She told Kate how sorry she was for not knowing what was going on, for not stepping in, for not getting her help earlier. She was so sorry she was gone, but she hoped Kate was at peace. She cried and cried and, when she could catch her breath long enough, whispered how sorry she was over and over.

She was devastated.

Monica sat quietly, knowing Jillian would share the story in her own time.

"I asked her for help. She is the only person I've been close to who is now on the other side, so I asked her to help me if she could," she explained, tears springing to her eyes as they always did when she talked about Kate. She looked at the floor as she spoke, knowing if she looked at Monica the tears would stream down her face. Monica was still quiet, but Jillian knew she understood what she meant; Monica's mother had passed away a few years earlier, and Jillian knew she missed her dearly.

"I told her I'm stuck—that I can't get this thing with Peter finished, that I can't get anything with Ethan started, and that I want to move on from both of them—and I don't know what to do. What should I do?"

That did it. Jillian's voice broke, her face squished up, and the tears started their stroll down her face.

"Jillian," Monica said softly, empathetically.

"This morning, I had a really strong sense that she answered me." She forced a smile through her tears. "And she told me Ethan is not for me. He is not the right man. Like I didn't already know that." Jillian rolled her eyes at herself. "And that I am doing the right thing, the right things, and to hang in there; this too shall pass. I'm grateful for her message," she said, sniffling, but starting to regain control.

"She is very wise. I would have to agree with her about all of that," Monica said quietly.

When Jillian finally looked up at Monica, she had tears in her eyes, too. She handed Jillian a tissue.

"I'm sorry. I didn't mean to…" Jillian looked at the floor again.

"Don't be silly. I'm worried about you."

Jillian looked up at her, nodded, rose, and left her office.

Back in her own office, as she was shutting down her laptop for the day, Jack strolled in and sat down in her guest chair. She'd worked for him for almost ten years. He was a very smart man, in his sixties, overweight since he'd had to stop running because of his knees, balding. She didn't find him to be very attractive, but he had an ebullient personality. Very self-assured. No one who had ever met him was neutral on their opinion of him. People loved him, or they didn't.

"Hey, Jillian. I know you're having a difficult time. Do you need anything at all?" he asked.

"Um, thank you, I appreciate that. It is difficult, but I've been doing my best to keep it away from the office. Am I doing OK with that?" She closed her laptop and wondered where he was going.

"You don't seem like yourself, that's all. And I just wanted to let you know that you can ask me for anything. We truly value you around here and want to make sure you're taken care of," he said.

"Thank you very much. I do appreciate it. I think I am OK at this point; I have good days and bad days, but I'm hanging in there. Please let me know right away if you think anything's slipping," she said, trying to keep it professional.

"Sure thing. Just let me know," he winked, rising, and turned to leave.

"Thanks, Jack," she said, still feeling uneasy. "Hey, have you looked at the new analysis on the restructure yet?"

He stopped and turned. "Yes, I have."

"Any thoughts?" she ventured.

"Sure. It looks good on paper. I think it probably makes a lot of sense."

"So we should keep working on it? You know there are a few people who are completely against it."

"Oh yes, I am well aware of that, and yes, I do want you to keep working on it, keep working on them. I'd like everyone to feel good about it."

Typical Jack. Even if they did get everyone on board, he still might axe it in the end, and typical to let them expend so much time and energy on it even if it was just an exercise in futility.

Keep them running, and ensure he has his fill of drama.

"OK. Will do. Thanks again." She wanted to throw something at him.

The next day, Friday, after an all-morning meeting that she barely had to participate in, she took a drive at lunch to try to get her shit together. She took I-275 south over Tampa Bay, over the Howard Frankland Bridge, over the sparkling blue water and under the sparkling blue sky, the most perfectly wrong backdrop for her mood.

Fridays sucked because the weekends meant two straight days of trying to spend time with Zach while avoiding Peter, and the tension of not knowing how he was going to treat her, react, respond to whatever was going on in the house-prison.

Her head buzzed the entire drive as tears streamed down her face. She kept hoping she would get over her infatuation with Ethan. She couldn't, though. She kept telling myself to, but she just wouldn't listen! What happened between them was all tangled up in her current state of affairs (or lack thereof), and she couldn't get closure anywhere. Maybe once she'd moved out of the house, or the divorce was final, her feelings about what happened with him would resolve themselves, too, as Tempe suggested. She hoped so.

But she still wanted to tell him what she wanted, what she needed. She didn't want to keep silent, as she had with Peter. Over time, she'd let Peter shut her down, topic by topic, subject by subject, feeling by feeling, until they couldn't even discuss the weather without bruising each other. Every discussion was a debate with him, a competition. To keep the peace, Jillian gave up. She didn't want to argue about everything. She didn't want to argue about anything.

Given the chance, and the courage, she wanted to lay everything out for Ethan.

But with Ethan, she couldn't operate from an open agenda, either. They worked together and they were trying to put the Delta deal together. She couldn't step over that professional line. Despite her lust for him, in her more rational moments, she was sure Kate's message was right, that they would not be right together, and that one day she would meet someone who would help her move on. Well, she wasn't so sure. But she liked to think so because that would have been her salvation. She couldn't picture him, who he would be. Until then, she needed her feelings for Ethan, however imagined and unrequited, to keep her going.

Given the chance, she would have laid everything out for Ethan, not only to unburden herself but to give him the opportunity to tell her how he felt about her. She just didn't have the courage or the energy to push any harder. She kept telling herself it was because she didn't want anything to negatively affect their working relationship. She preferred that he was as comfortable with her as he could be, considering. She didn't want to regret her actions later when she gained perspective. She knew she didn't need him. She knew he wasn't right for her. She knew she needed to move on. She told herself she would survive without him, without anyone, in her new life. All she needed was Zach.

And then, she considered an even deeper reason she was so mad about what happened. When it finally occurred to her, she couldn't believe it had taken her so long to figure out.

During the year after Zach was born, she decided that if something ever happened to Peter, she wouldn't bother with a relationship again. She didn't want the hassle of it, of meeting someone new, of trying to get to know him, of figuring out if she could trust him, all of that. She didn't want it. She didn't need it. She didn't need sex either, right? She would be quite content to be by herself and live her life the way she wanted to, without going through all that, without compromising. She had never lived by herself, and she regretted that she had never had the chance to find out how self-sufficient she could be or how she would handle herself. She thought maybe that was the only way she would ever really figure herself out—when she didn't have to "perform" for anyone but herself and the Universe.

And then the big collision with Ethan occurred. And what happened afterward. And now she fantasized about finding the perfect mate—the soul mate so many people talked about that she knew she didn't have, had never had, and never expected to find. She was tagging that desire on Ethan because she saw what his life was like (or what she thought it was like), and that was how she wanted her life to be. She was angry that she couldn't have that life, and she couldn't have him.

It felt so unfair. She might have been content to be alone if not for that one stupid drunken superficial incident that meant nothing to him, that meant nothing to her at the time, but that rocked her world, her beliefs, to the core. Everything she thought she knew was questioned, turned upside down, shaken out, dumped on the floor for examination. Perhaps she would have come to the same conclusions eventually anyway, but all it had done for her so far was cause heartache, wanting, loneliness, and, at times, a deep despair that she had never really had a strong sense of what she truly wanted out of life.

She always believed she should just handle life as it was dealt to her. She didn't really have a life plan, or five-year goals, or anything like that. She was just kind of like a leaf on the stream—or raging river—of life, following it along and adjusting as she went, dealing with bumps along the way, healing, not trying to avoid the pain. Not having expectations about what was to come and therefore not always trying to fit things into the plan, but always hoping for the best. Maybe that was why she was in the mess she was in.

For the first time, she could truly picture the kind of relationship she wanted to have, the kind of life she wanted to live, the things she wanted to offer her son. She didn't know if any of it would ever happen. Her fear changed from one of suffocating by staying married to Peter to one of failing to fulfill this new vision. She wanted to find a way to be happy and content in the moment, but also still hold onto hope for the life she wanted with the love of her life, if there was such a person.

Her impatience led her to seek out any means of finding out what the future would bring. When she thought she might be pregnant with Zach, she shook the Magic 8 Ball, and it had answered YES.

When she thought she was pregnant for the second time, it turned up LOOKS DOUBTFUL. She didn't believe it, but it turned out to be right.

Astrology, numerology, palmistry, psychics, the I Ching, you name it, she had dabbled in them all and still employed several methods regularly, including getting three different horoscopes and a tarot card reading daily via email. She was currently most fascinated with Oracle cards. She had drawn a card several times regarding Ethan, and three times in a row had drawn the Expect a Miracle card. When to expect it and what the possibilities were, of course, was not expounded on. At least something was left to the imagination and imagine she did.

She imagined that Kelly asked him for a divorce. Maybe Ethan would be devastated, unrecoverable. Why would she want a divorce from him? Maybe Kelly had an affair? Why? Was he too busy to give her what she needed? Was that the reason behind "The Incident," neglect? She sure knew what that was about. If he neglected her, he could, would likely, neglect her, too.

If they loved each other they would fight to stay together. They would ignore all the things that were less than perfect, shove them down so deep they could pretend they didn't exist. They could have the perfect life, the perfect marriage, the perfect spouse, partner, the perfect family, with the perfect home and perfect dog and perfect kids playing their perfect sports, and mom would be the perfect stay-at-home housewife taking care of everything including herself, so that she could look perfect. God. Disgusting. She hated them. She wanted to be them.

So where was the miracle? She truly hoped the miracle would be that she would not want Ethan any longer. She could think of only two ways for this to occur. Only two, because she tried talking herself out of wanting him in every other way she could think of, and she was obviously much better at talking herself into things than at talking herself out of them.

First possibility: He would do or say something, or she would hear something about him that she found completely appalling, repulsive, repelling. Like he beat his wife or his dog. Or he was wanted in three states for bank robbery. Or he was a child molester. Hell, she didn't know. None of those, of course, were even remotely possible.

The other option—and truly the one she hoped for, the one that would be the best outcome for Ethan and his family and ultimately for her (though she had a really hard time picturing it)—was that she would meet someone else. She just couldn't imagine who could tear her away.

13

Jillian tried to learn something new during those dark days: how to take gentle care of herself instead of always being so hard on herself. When she woke up in the middle of the night and couldn't fall back to sleep, she started talking to herself in her head the way she would talk to Zach.

Because there were no compromises, trades, nor discussions, Peter and Jillian had taken Zach trick-or-treating together. Zach looked so sweet in his little Pokémon costume, with Peter and Jillian walking on opposite sides of him and him looking back and forth between them, like he was surprised they were so close to each other. He wasn't a big fan of "scary," though. The neighbor's yard decorations at night—which he had seen only during the day and didn't like then—plus all the scary little creatures out for some candy, made him nervous. He'd had a hard time going to sleep, so Jillian sat with him on his bed, smoothing his hair, telling him it was all just pretend, that he should close his eyes. Eventually she lay down with him and fell asleep wrapped around him, as she had dozens of times before, with his little hand stretched back to rest on her arm, making sure she wasn't going anywhere.

She adopted and adapted this same ritual to mother herself: *It's OK, sweet pea. Give yourself a break. Get some rest, take care of yourself. You need your sleep. Don't think about that now. Just close your eyes, relax, and think peaceful, quiet thoughts. Save that for tomorrow. Calm, calm, quiet, quiet. Relax.*

And on and on until she fell asleep. Weird at first to talk to herself like that, like she was two different people. But it helped.

Sometimes she felt OK, but those moments were getting fewer and further between. Most of the time she felt tired, sad, and angry. She was full of anxiety, her body so taut with tension that her muscles ached. The air mattress didn't help. Tempe told her to go buy a bed but, just like sharing the master bedroom would be a concession by Peter, so would that be by her, that this was long term.

Jillian's face started breaking out, the rims of her eyes burned most of the time, probably from crying so much, and her deodorant stopped working. Sometimes she wondered if the situation would ever end, if the divorce would ever be final, if she would ever be able to move out without fear of what she was giving up and be able to move on. It was getting harder to remember her life before and harder to imagine what it would be like after. That limbo was her life.

In those last few weeks of rationalizing, bargaining with herself, before she realized it was over, she had thought about what would have happened if they just decided to stay married and live in the same house until Zach was eighteen, but to not really be married, meaning they were essentially emotionally and physically separated, living in separate rooms, but there for their son's sake. She thought it would be doable, acceptable, that she could manage it, she could live that way.

But Ethan had awakened her. And since that fantasy dragged on, her head was about to explode. She felt trapped, unable to move forward and unable to go back. She certainly could never go back.

It had nothing to do with pride or egotism or arrogance or being able to admit a mistake (something Peter could never do). She could not stand the thought of ever touching Peter, or him touching her, again. It repulsed her. She didn't want anything to do with it. At first, she tried talking herself into it; she did litmus tests with herself, imagining him walking over and kissing her, touching her back. It made her skin crawl. She'd come to think of him as her jailer, her captor, that he was holding her and Zach for ransom. She couldn't even look at him most of the time. The sound of his voice made her want to scream. Sometimes when he spoke—usually talking to Zach within earshot when it was "his turn" to take Zach and she had to sit on the sidelines—she would tell him to shut up over and over in her head, that he's so stupid, he's an idiot, what he says is just moronic.

Shut up shut up shut up.

Things at the office were becoming more and more stressful because of the Delta mission piled on top of her normal workload, and she was not as happy there as she usually was, either. Jack had started visiting nearly every day and quizzing her about her personal situation.

"How are things going at home? What's the status? Any progress?" he would ask, plopping down in her guest chair and grabbing a piece of chocolate out of her candy jar.

She would give him as brief a status update as she could manage, but she wondered why he was so interested. These questions sent up red flags that something was up with him. She enjoyed going to work if only to escape home, but she was now exhausted at work, too. She was stuck. Just stuck, everywhere she turned.

She cried on her way home from the office because she had to go home. She wanted to see Zach, but the stress and anxiety of being there with the man she was leaving was eating away at her guts and her head. Maybe her heart and soul, too. Her self-doubt and insecurities were fighting with the future, self-confident version that she was still searching for. The tension was wearing on her physically and mentally. She was drowning.

Peter's negativity had infected her. She wondered if they would ever come to a resolution or if she would give up and give Peter everything they had just to walk away with shared custody of Zach.

That would be OK. No baggage. No literal baggage anyway. Plenty, emotionally.

She kept reminding herself of the difference between hope and expectation. All along she hoped that Peter would do the right thing, the fair and just thing, what was best for their son and the future. That is also what she expected in the beginning. She was not sure exactly when that changed, but, at some point, she no longer expected that, though she continued to hope for it. Her friends kept hoping, too, for her sake, but she was discouraged. She was not hopeless, but she was discouraged. He was not a fair person. He was not just. He was not sympathetic or empathetic, just plain pathetic.

He couldn't find the way in his tiny petty selfish heart to put someone else's needs ahead of his own.

14

For Thanksgiving, Peter took Zach to the outlaws', and Jillian went to Tempe's for tacos. Her kids were with their father, too. The following Sunday, on their way to the car wash, Zach said, "Mom, Dad is drinking too much beer." She had to keep from gasping.

"What do you mean, sweetie?" she asked as she peered at him in the rearview mirror, strapped into his car seat. His little eyebrows were furrowed as he looked out the window.

"Well, he had two when we were playing, and he does that every night, and beer is not good for him, and he needs to not drink so much." He had a scowl on his round, little face.

"Did you say anything to him?" she asked. How to handle, how to handle, how to handle?

"No, I didn't," he said, still scowling. If she and Peter were happily married, what would she have done? She would have gone directly to Peter and told him what their son said so that he would feel like shit and would know his child saw what he was doing, that his lame attempt at being discreet didn't work when his kid was as observant as his wife was, and that he should feel ashamed—and he would either stop drinking so much or would get better at hiding it. But, since they were not happily married, what should she do? Ask her attorney? Put it in her back pocket and save it for later? Take Zach to counseling? What?

"Why did you tell me? Do you want me to talk to him?" she asked, hoping he would say no.

"No. I don't know why. I'll tell him myself," he said.

Five years old. Was he born a wise old soul or were his parents forcing him to become one?

On Monday, Zach cried when she tried to leave him at school, really cried, saying it was because he missed his dad. Great. After trying about thirty ways to comfort him, distract him, anything so that she didn't have to leave him crying, she said, "So you don't miss your mom, too?"

He said, "No, I don't worry about you, Mom."

"But you worry about your dad?" she asked, gently attempting to figure out the issue.

"No, I just miss him," he said, tears still overflowing.

After going through it three more times, she finally had to leave him, or she was going to be super late for a conference.

"I'm sorry, sweetie, but I really need to go," she apologized.

"It's OK, Mom. You can go. I'll be fine," he said, still crying, but trying to stop, wiping his eyes, trying to smile for her to make her feel better. Just who was the parent?

She cried all the way to the office.

15

than called her at her desk that Thursday, bailing on the Delta lunch they had planned for that noon. He said he'd been out of the office all week because of his stomach. He said it might be nerves. She asked him about why he thought that, but all he said was that "a long time ago" he'd had to drink Pepto or Maalox or whatever to calm his stomach. Peter had once told her about a time he used to do that. It was when he was cheating on his college girlfriend.

That Saturday night was the big One Metro holiday party at a rental hall, the usual decorations of a huge Christmas tree, poinsettias, candles. The band played cheesy holiday songs and pop music covers. Various food and drink stations were positioned around the perimeter of the carpeted hall, half of the hall filled with white-clothed round tables. A few hundred people milled about in their party dress, some of the men in nice suits, some in khakis and sports coats. Some of the ladies dressed to the hilt, some showing a bit too much leg or cleavage.

Tempe was bringing her new boyfriend and Monica, her husband. Jillian roamed around by herself in her little black velvet dress and silver heels, refilling her wine glass several times, chatting with various people. And then she ran into Lisa, an account manager. She was part of the drinking crowd that night. Jillian had no idea what Lisa might have seen but hoped maybe she'd had so much to drink that she didn't remember the details of the evening, either.

As soon as Jillian greeted her, Lisa said, "So, you're getting divorced, aren't you, Jillian?"

"Yes, I am. Word sure gets around, huh?" she smiled.

"So are you and Ethan still doing it?" Jillian about choked. What!?!

She tried to look puzzled. "Ethan…Chase? What are you talking about?"

"Oh, come on. I know what happened. I was there, remember?"

"Let's go outside and talk," Jillian said, already turning that way. Lisa followed in her blue satin dress and black heels, which clicked on the tile near the patio doors where the carpet ended.

As soon as the doors closed and the fresh air hit them, mixed in with the cigarette smoke wafting its way from the group on the next patio, despite the potted palms in between, Lisa dove in.

"I know what happened, Jillian. Ethan is such a handsome man. I wish you two were together."

"Oh my god, Lisa, what in the world are you talking about?" Jillian tried and took a big chug of red wine. That wouldn't help, but it was the only coping mechanism she had on her at the time.

"Jillian, you can't fool me. Why don't you just admit it? I was there that night, remember? I was the one who told you to have some fun. I was the one who sent you upstairs with Ethan after you two came back outside! The errand neither of you returned from? And the next morning when I asked you if you had some fun, you said you did! I know what happened," she said.

Monica came through the doors at the tail end of Lisa's missive. She looked gorgeous in a blood red dress and matching lipstick. Her hair was in a beautiful upsweep—Jillian had never seen her hair up before—and the red made her teeth look glowingly white, even more so than usual.

"For crying out loud, just forget about all that! I don't remember a lot of that night. I don't even remember you asking me about it the next day, I was still so drunk!" Jillian took another swig of wine.

Monica must have figured out what they were talking about. She also quickly assessed that Jillian had already had too much to drink and snagged her car keys right out of the front pocket of her purse before she could react. "Jilly, let's go back inside and get something to eat," she said, putting her hand on Jillian's elbow to guide her away.

"OK, let's go," Jillian said. She was anxious to get away from Lisa. She made her nervous.

Monica reached to take the wine glass out of Jillian's hand, but Jillian swung it out of her way and gave her a stern look. "No, you cannot have both my keys and my wine!"

Jillian sat at a table and nibbled on a few appetizers to pacify Monica, then stood up nearby with some other guests, chatting, waiting for Monica to abandon the keys so she could get the hell out of there. She didn't want to hang out with all these people anyway. Then she spotted Ethan. He was sitting with some other executives from his agency but was talking with the woman next to him, a petite blond with small features. Jillian didn't recognize her, so she assumed she must be Kelly, "the wife." She was turned half toward him, talking, and he was nodding his head.

Christ. Just what I want to deal with. Jillian stood there and talked to whomever wandered by, watching Ethan and Kelly, watching for her keys.

Ethan caught her eye and nodded for her to come over. Jillian held her index finger up—just a minute. She couldn't bear to go over there. She kept talking. About the time her most recent collocutors were moving away Ethan and Kelly were getting up. Kelly walked right by Jillian before she could even turn her head, but as Ethan reached her, he said, "We have to go relieve the babysitter."

"Whatever," Jillian spat, without looking at him. He kept walking. She was annoyed at everyone. Mostly herself.

Just a few moments later her keys were abandoned. She grabbed them and stormed out.

She bawled the whole way home—the effect of too much wine. She shouldn't have been driving but made it home safely. She was in bed—on the air mattress—when her phone buzzed; it was Monica, probably calling to make sure she was OK. At least someone called. She didn't answer it, though. She didn't want to talk.

She cried for more than an hour. She couldn't stop. The tears just poured out of her, like they had when she found out about Kate. If she let herself think about her situation and allowed herself to really feel sorry for herself, she cried so hard she couldn't breathe. It wasn't the first time, and not the last.

She started talking to Kate again. She needed her. She didn't pray to a god, to God, but she prayed to Kate, begging her to tell her what she should do, to give her something to hold onto, some hope, if there was any; that if she was depressed, to help her admit it so that she could get some help, though she didn't want to get counseling or take medication because Peter might be able to use that against her.

She chose to self-medicate with alcohol for a reason; Peter drank more than she did. He could hardly throw that in her face. But she did suspect she was depressed. How could she not be? The stress and anxiety of the situation were eating away at her; she was losing weight and didn't want to do a thing. But she was still stuck.

Maybe Kate could help in some way. She would be grateful if she could help in any way—any way at all.

The following Monday she emailed Ethan. "Sorry for the smart remark, but I was really annoyed at the time. I had an interesting talk with Lisa that you may or may not want to hear about." Send.

He emailed back "No problem." Sigh.

16

Jillian was alone on Christmas day. She was still in the house, not yet evicted nor released. After Zach opened about a hundred presents and played with the most interesting of them, Peter took him to the outlaws' house. Jillian started on some beers and, as evening set in, proceeded to light all the candles in the house, turning out all the other lights. It was kind of romantic, except that she was by herself.

She lit the candles knowing that she'd had too much to drink to supervise them properly, yet wanting to, anyway. She must have had fifteen on the fireplace mantle alone. More in the fireplace. More on the bookshelves and around the television, on the piano, and over the kitchen sink. She'd have put some in the bathrooms, too, except she'd run out. *Good. Let's use them all up.* Fewer to pack and move, and when she was ready for more, she could buy new ones, whatever kind she wanted, and they would be all hers.

The place looked beautiful. Sparkly and glowing, the shadows dancing, and none of the stains and cracks and dust visible during the day's light. The glow of the television didn't interfere with the orange and gold glow of the candles on the bookshelves and around the volumes of letters and words on bound paper, waiting for someone to disturb the dust and dive into the words and worlds within. If only the house could always look, feel, smell like it did then, with the shimmer of fire inside the white and red and green and orange wax, the smell of cinnamon and evergreen and cranberry and pomegranate. Cool rainy air came in from the open French doors to the porch, where the cat kept coming and going, in and out, in and out, looking for a comfortable yet interesting perch for the evening before she locked him in for the night.

She called her parents and talked to them for a record two hours. It was quite a relief to her conscience. She didn't have to feel any guilt about cutting them short like she usually did, nor about not calling them at all. Most of the call was their gossip about aunts and uncles and cousins, stuff that usually made Jillian mad because her parents were so unjustly judgmental, but she barely heard what they said. For the few minutes that they talked about her, she just gave them the basic facts about the situation. They didn't offer any sort of real advice or guidance, other than telling her they were certain she knew what she was doing, that they were there for her, that they supported her. Just words.

She called Monica, who didn't answer. If Monica called back, Jillian would be over her drama and embarrassed that she'd called her. Yet, she knew Monica would be able to offer some comfort, some insight, some hope that she would feel better tomorrow. But Monica was involved with her own family, her own holiday, her own relationships, and she couldn't help Jillian with hers on Christmas Day.

Tempe was at her family's place with Mark, her boyfriend, and the kids, in Indiana. Jillian started to call her but hung up. She put her phone in her pocket, though. She wanted nothing more than for it to ring.

Ethan was probably at home with Kelly and their kids, relaxing with his perfect family. Jillian was the furthest thing from his mind. Not only was he not thinking of her, but he didn't even want to be reminded of her. Did anything ever make him think of her, wonder what she was doing, where she was, if she was OK, if she was thinking of him, if there was anything he could do to help her, to help improve her condition? Ever?

She could see him with her, with their children, with their families. She wanted him to be a good father, the father he wanted to be.

What she envied the most was their intimate moments. Not necessarily their intimate moments (well, yes, those, too), but when they hugged, or touched each other in passing in the hallway on their way to taking care of their son or daughter. The touches on the cheek, or the quick peck of cool lips on the top of the head. Or even the quick, sometimes faked but not false, smile, in passing, while one went to one child and one went to the other, knowing that the child was most important and that they agreed on that, and were OK with that, and would make it up to each other later.

She was alone on Christmas, dreaming up her little fantasy life, envisioning not just the life she thought Ethan might have, but the life she wanted. All the candles were lit, and she drank, and walked around to make sure none of the flames ignited something they weren't supposed to. She knew firsthand how small, seemingly in-control sparks could quickly turn into a raging, unquenchable fire.

She had to pee frequently because of the amount of beer she was consuming. She thought about how much and how often she was drinking. Was she trying to mask what she was feeling? No. She was trying to feel it more strongly, to release everything that had been pent up all these years, to feel everything she had repressed, so strongly that maybe it would burn itself out and not have so much power over her, and she could be peaceful.

She relished the pain as much as the pleasure; at least she was feeling again. Whether it was positive or negative, it was reminding her, reassuring her that she was alive, which she hadn't felt in so long that she didn't care whether those feelings were elation or depression. Either one made her cry uncontrollably, from frustration, loneliness, anger, or release.

Expect a miracle. *God, am I losing my mind?*

She needed to change her expectations. She knew this! She didn't understand why she was having such a problem with it. She knew Ethan was not available, not interested. She knew he wished what happened hadn't; she knew he probably tried to forget all about it, or at least wished he could. She knew he didn't want to talk about it, not to her, anyway. And he probably wished she would just try to forget, too, and never remind him again. Were they happy? She wanted them to be because there needed to be happy marriages, or she knew she would never have one. But was theirs? Happy? How could she wish for it not to be? Why would she want them not to be happy? Because she wanted their life. Because she wanted to remove Kelly from their life and replace her.

Or did she? For god's sake, he used some of the same expressions Peter used! He was always late. He fake-laughed sometimes, and she could tell when he did. He wore dorky shoes. He didn't dress very well. He was obsessed with his hair. His shirts were always too big. His suit pants were, too. He even let her take the blame for what happened, after she apologized to him!

These were the red flags that were screaming at her, telling her what she already knew, what Kate had told her: that he was not the man for her. She didn't ignore them; she just couldn't change how she felt. She even knew that it was not really Ethan that she had feelings for, but for an imagined life that she so yearned for, and thought he had.

17

They sat at the bar in Carrabba's restaurant, which was packed to the hilt. Every table was filled, and every seat at the bar, too, with many patrons waiting for seats in the entry. Waiters in their starched white aprons flitted about, delivering drinks and pasta and steaks, tempting her.

Tempe sipped on her cosmo and Monica just watched Jillian calmly as she spoke, a little louder than she would have liked to, considering all the chatter around them. Jillian's eyes flitted from one place to another, never able to linger on any one spot for more than a moment.

"My New Year's oracle consult told me the past was at peace. I took this to mean Ethan has forgiven me and forgiven himself." She chuckled, trying to make light of it.

"What kind of scares me is that he'll disappear and I won't ever see him again, although that might be for the best. That's really the salt and the salve," Jillian said finally, looking down at her beer, then taking a big gulp.

"The what?" Tempe asked. "The salve? Yeah, that's what you think. I think you are just alive again and instead of crediting yourself for doing something courageous, you're giving the credit to this jerk!"

"I think so, too, Jilly," Monica added.

She sighed. "Yeah, well, The Future card indicated I would have to make a decision about what I really want, what my heart's true desire is," she said, not looking at them again.

"And? What is that?" Tempe asked. Man, she never pulled any punches. Jillian wished she could be so direct. Monica watched her, waiting.

"Just for all of this to be behind me. I want to fast-forward to when the divorce is final, I'm moved out, I know where I stand, I am over this infatuation with Ethan, Delta is a done deal…" she spoke, without even really thinking, tears welling.

"Hang in there, Jilly. I know it seems like a long road, but one day, that is exactly where you'll be, and you will be even stronger than you already are, and so proud of yourself for being so brave, and fighting for what you want, and for acknowledging that Ethan is not right and letting go of that," Monica said. Always so reasonable.

"And then," Tempe added, raising her glass, "will be time for you to live your life the way it's meant to be lived! Cheers!"

Monica and Jillian held up their glasses, too. Jillian forced a smile, and they told her how much they loved her and that she was going to be OK. She tried to believe them.

18

Ethan called that Wednesday and asked her to go to lunch—she was shocked—to talk about a prospective client. She cancelled with Monica and Tempe, who were none too happy considering who was replacing them. She was nervous as hell but expected that something was up. He hadn't invited her to lunch since the Monday after "The Incident."

They went to the same deli they had that Monday, and both ordered Cuban sandwiches and chips, and discussed the prospect—a financial services firm—and actually ate their lunch. They were having a normal business conversation, and then Jillian asked how his kids were.

"Great. We went to New York for New Year's and the kids and I had a great time."

"Do you have family up there?" she asked.

"Yes, some, but it wasn't quite what we expected. Kelly got a bad sinus infection right before and ended up staying home." He was looking down as he told her this.

"Really? Couldn't the doctor give her something for it?"

"He did. She was just afraid that she would be in too much pain if she flew. I looked for alternatives, but with just a week's vacation, we couldn't drive all that way, and trains were just too expensive." He sounded like he wasn't quite buying it.

"It's too bad she didn't get to go," she said, sensing an opening and trying to get more.

He mumbled something like "what's done is done" while doing a half eyeroll. He looked at her directly. "How's your situation?"

Well, well. He finally asked, if only to change the subject. But she managed to ramble on about lawyers and deadlines and agreements as they walked back to the car (yes, she drove again) in the crisp, cool air, with a sky as clear and blue as a Photoshopped image under keywords "perfect sky."

It really made her wonder, though. Would a happily married supermom not go on vacation with her family at New Year's because of a sinus infection? Was that really a good reason? Was it the real reason? She had her suspicions, but Ethan obviously did not want to talk about it any further, and she didn't want to make him uncomfortable. Of course.

"How are things with Delta on your end? Making any headway?" she asked, trying to keep the conversation going as they drove back.

"About the same. Same kind of resistance you're having, for likely the same reasons. They'll come around, though," he promised.

That night, knowing she would see Ethan at the official Delta meeting the next day, she asked the oracle cards how she should be interacting with him. Should she be all business, should she flirt, what?

They told her it was time to move on, to let go.

Letting go. She should have been an expert on that by now.

She'd had to let go of the babies. One year of trying to conceive with no success, then tests, and treatments, and finally three failed cycles of in vitro. Twice they had two healthy blastocysts and once four. Eight gone, flushed away with overwhelming grief, sadness, and a feeling of devastation. Peter never demonstrated such crushing feelings. Whether he had them or not, she didn't know.

Next was letting go of hope that she would ever be pregnant again, accepting that she would never hold another one of her babies in her arms. The happiest time of her life had been when Zach was growing inside of her. For the first time in her life, she wasn't alone. For the first time in her life, she had a blood relative, her own son.

Then, she had to let go of her marriage and her husband. Let go of the security—the image—of it, anyway. There was no reality to let go of, but she did have to accept that there really was a hole in her life, in her heart, that she had been ignoring and would have to face.

And the realization that she would also have to let at least partially go of her baby boy. Divorce meant custody, time-sharing, and there was no way Peter would ever give her full custody. She had been sure of that from the beginning. She had had to figure out how to let go of wanting, needing, daily interaction with her own son because she would not have that any longer. Unless Peter keeled over, which she was certain he would never do because it would be doing her too much of a favor.

Now Ethan and letting go of the man she never even had, but who had unknowingly—unwillingly—filled up some of those empty spaces in her with imaginings of what their life might be like together. Or the kind of life she wanted, anyway.

She wondered what she would have to let go of next: the life she could see so clearly? the love she yearned for? Was her life destined for heartbreak because her expectations were too high? As Wyatt Earp supposedly said, or at least Kurt Russell's version of him, when he'd finally met Catherine, the love of his life, while he was married: "For the first time in my life, I know exactly what I want, and who. And I can't have any of it. And that's just the damnable misery of it all."

She refused to believe it in her deepest, darkest, still-hopeful places that were getting harder and harder to reach. But the hopelessness had never had such a broad-reaching hold on her. For the first time in her life, she was damnably miserable. She wasn't curious about tomorrow; the thought of it just exhausted and depressed her. The most dreaded time of day became getting out of bed each morning to face god knew what, most of it maddening or saddening. Her favorite time of day became going to bed at night, to sleep, and escape.

Megan called to see how she was doing and get the update, so Jillian filled her in. Delta was limping along. They weren't making much progress, only waves that were annoying some of the strongest opponents, but Jack still wanted them to continue. The divorce was limping along, too. No progress there, either—just more deadlines or talk of scheduling a mediation, but no date yet. Jack was still visiting her almost daily, making her more and more uncomfortable. And she was becoming more fearful of being away from Zach unless she was at work, so happy hours with Tempe or Monica were few and far between. She was drinking at home almost every night, self-medicating in the only safe way she felt she could. Megan told her to be strong and be careful, and Jillian replied that she would do her best at both.

That evening she came home to a very clingy Zach. He wanted to sit right next to her, with his little hand in hers. He smiled up at her as they watched television. She supposed he sensed the tension, realized that his father and mother never spoke to each other.

And she also realized that every deadline extended and release from the house-prison postponed—torturous in so many respects— also meant that she still got to spend time every day with Zach, a luxury that would end when the ultimate deadline was reached.

19

That spring and summer, the longest of Jillian's life, were more of the same; the same routine; the same anxieties; the same back-and-forth with the Marital Settlement Agreement; the same frustrations and fantasies of Ethan; the same aggravation of seeming progress with Delta only to have to backtrack when a new objection was raised. The same the same the same. Alternating days with Zach and emailing with Peter when one or the other of them had an event to take him to or a school project that they needed to figure out how to handle while spending as little time with each other in the same room as possible. They were only even together for Zach's sixth birthday for less than thirty minutes, lighting the candles on his little cake and singing, then watching and helping him unwrap his zillion presents—presents Jillian had selected, then listed for Peter via email, purchased, and wrapped. But, of course, they were from them both.

Work dragged on with no real changes in anything. She would ease off Delta for a while, sometimes due to workload, and sometimes due to frustration and exhaustion. She used to be so happy at the agency, the perfect place for her combination left/right brain, allowing her to utilize her creativity in coming up with campaigns and tag lines and slogans, while also being able to efficiently plan out a project. Work used to be her refuge. But it had become just another prison, a place where she was watched and judged. A place away from Zach. She didn't even go to the annual conference that April because she didn't want to spend time with all "those people," pretending they gave a shit when they occasionally asked how she was, but either just being polite or hoping she would provide some fodder for the gossip mill. She didn't want to pretend to be having fun, to get along with all of those who were passively-aggressively opposing Delta, those who would smile at her and laugh and get her a drink, then stab her in the back first chance they got. She did her job the best she could, as always, but Delta really seemed to be at an impasse, and she wasn't known for giving up on things. She just had to wait until they changed their minds, or she did.

This anxiety-ridden, nearly silent routine was her life. She had no idea how she was surviving it and suspected that she might not be if not for Zach. But then, she wouldn't have been in that situation in the first place if not for him. He was the only reason she stayed.

The divorce mediation was finally scheduled for early September. Zach would be at school and Peter's mother—who still hadn't spoken a word to Jillian—would watch him after school if they weren't finished. It was a drizzly morning, gray skies as she drove downtown, just a couple of miles from the office. They met at a ritzy law firm complete with marble floors and huge flower arrangements, in separate rooms the mediator would bounce back and forth from, taking their offers or compromises for consideration.

Chrissie, his sister, who was an attorney, and who also hadn't spoken to Jillian since the onset of the situation, was there with Peter. Great.

It took eleven hours, but they got it done. Ninety percent of that time was spent on the timesharing schedule with Zach. Peter had objected to Jillian's original proposal all those months ago of Zach staying with him after school and her overnight, alternating weekends, because it was, in his words, too confusing. Yet, what they ended up with that day was far more convoluted—with Jillian getting Mondays and one Thursday a month—plus a holiday schedule that alternated years, who got him after school, who took him in the morning, what time he got picked up on Christmas, blah blah blah. Jillian was not happy with it, devastated over the number of days a week she would be away from Zach, but her attorney and the mediator both told her that if they went to court, she would likely get even less. How could that possibly be right? But she was so exhausted that she took it. She took it and ran.

At one point she had suggested leveraging the assets with the schedule, feeling that Peter was doing the same. The mediator told them that one had nothing to do with the other; that Peter felt—rightly or wrongly, not for him to judge—that he was the better parent. She felt like she'd been slapped across the face. But it was too late to argue about it unless she wanted to throw her hands up again, walk out, start over, and probably wind up in court. She took it and ran.

The last question the mediator brought was a request for a move-out date.

Jesus H. Christ. They had just signed the papers, the divorce wouldn't even be final for a few weeks, and he wanted to know when she was leaving! Fucker.

She arrived home that night before Peter did. His mother stood when she walked in. "Hello Jillian," she said, very formally.

"You can leave now," Jillian stated without looking at her, and kept walking.

"Thank you," she said, and left, not waiting for Peter.

The next day at the office, Jillian closed her door and researched hotels, ordered boxes and packing materials, picked a moving day, and arranged for a storage unit to store the few things she was taking from the house.

As she began sorting and packing over the next few days, she stacked boxes in the dining room. She wasn't taking too much with her, not even any furniture.

When the court date for the final judgment arrived about a week later, making the divorce official, she emailed it to Peter along with the date she was moving out and where she would be staying. He replied and told her how irresponsible it was to be packing in front of Zach. He was already mad at Jillian for telling Zach she was moving out, but she had asked Peter how he wanted to handle it, and he'd said he wanted them to talk to Zach separately. She had. She had sat down on the couch with him and tried not to make a big deal out of it. She gently told him that she and his dad were not going to be married anymore, that she was going to live somewhere else, that she and his dad both loved him very much and would still be his mom and dad, and sometimes he would be with his dad, and sometimes he would be with her in their new home, that both she and his dad would continue to love him and take care of him, and that it didn't have anything to do with him.

He asked her why, and it broke her heart. She wanted to be careful to not allow him to feel any blame, to not feel negatively about Peter or her, or about himself. To not be mad or feel guilty.

"Well, because being married is not making us happy anymore, and we want to be the best parents we can be to you. And I can be a better mom to you if your dad and I are not married or living in the same house together."

He looked up at her as she spoke, his little brows furrowed, trying to understand what she was saying.

"But you know how much we both love you, right?" she asked.

"Yes," he said.

"And you know we'll take care of you, right?"

"Yes."

"OK then. What other questions do you have?"

"None, I guess."

She was sure he did. He just didn't know what they were yet. But it was a start.

She emailed Peter to let him know. He totally lambasted her in his reply, saying how typical it was. Fuck him. It was done. He can like the way she handled things or not. He certainly never considered how she would want him to do things, so why should she offer him the same courtesy? It burned in her stomach. But the Final Judgment was finally only two weeks away, and the week after that, her Independence Day. Why didn't she feel any relief?

<h1 style="text-align:center">20</h1>

Jillian's friend Shelly, a public defender, who worked at the agency before she decided to go to law school, met her at the courthouse for the Final Judgment (that was really what it was called). It was only a couple miles from the office, so she went in to work that morning and slipped out for the hearing. She knew it wouldn't take long. Shelly volunteered to go with her since she worked at the courthouse, though Jillian wasn't nervous or upset. Just numb, she supposed.

Shelly met Jillian with Anthony, Peter's attorney represented him as he couldn't be bothered to even show up, and the judge asked the questions and they were done in ten minutes, officially divorced. Anthony hugged her, said congratulations, and left for another case. Shelly went with her to the filing clerk and waited while she had official copies made.

"Are you sure you're OK? How do you feel?" Shelly asked. Maybe she wondered why Jillian wasn't laughing or crying.

"Yes, I'm good. Relieved it's over. I guess it's kind of weird that it's official, it's taken so long," she said.

"So what's next? When are you moving out?" Shelly asked.

"The storage unit is being delivered on Friday, Monica's coming Saturday to help. I'm not taking much, mostly just my personal effects. He's keeping all the furniture, basically, and most of the housewares, so it should be easy," she said as they walked.

"I'm going to be at an extended stay hotel while I wait to close on my condo. Should be only a couple of weeks," she said.

"Well, congrats, and I'm so proud of you. I know this is a new beginning for you." Shelly gave her a hug. Jillian smiled and hugged her back, still dry-eyed.

Peter took Zach on moving day and Monica helped her move the boxes into a portable storage unit that had been delivered the day before, or into her car the ones that would go with her to the inn. It only took them a couple of hours, and they had a bit of fun, joking about starting a moving service called "Chicks with Trucks."

They also talked about Jack.

"He's weirding me out," Jillian said as they team-lifted a box of books onto the hand truck.

"What do you mean? What is he doing?" she said, standing up and putting her hands on her hips as they caught their breath.

"He's just visiting me almost every day, asking me how things are going, how I'm doing, what the progress is," she said, struggling to really define it. "It just makes me uncomfortable."

"I'm sure he's just concerned. Don't give it much thought; you have plenty else on your mind," she advised.

"You're right. I'm probably just over-thinking it," she said. But something, something was gnawing at her.

As they finished with the last boxes, Jillian smiled. *My Independence Day.* She was anxious to get out of the house, that prison, start relaxing, and start her new life, being the woman, the friend, the mother she wanted to be. It wouldn't be until years later, when she realized what a mess she really was during that time, that she would change the name of that day to "the Day I Left My Baby."

The next few weeks were spent on getting a mortgage and planning a closing and buying furniture and moving again—this time with Tempe and Mark's help—and getting utilities turned on and her address changed, her will redone, and all her investment and insurance beneficiaries changed. She called this group of tasks her wealth list, to complement her health and happiness lists, which consisted of the things she wanted to do, like cataloging all her books, learning to play guitar, taking golf lessons with Zach, doing yoga, and getting a new laptop, among many other wishes. She tried to do all this while being a normal and calm and good, loving, sane mother when Zach was with her. She missed him terribly when he was with "his dad," as she was training herself to say. She didn't want to use the term "my ex," as so many people did. She didn't want Peter to be her anything.

21

It was quite a job to set up house practically from scratch, and a great distraction from all the drama. Jillian got to make all the decisions herself, picking out a couch and rugs and dishes and beds.

It was fun, but it was also hard. She had prioritized what to get first and decided on a couch and beds. She finally forced herself to pick one store and not leave until she had ordered a couch. If she had unlimited choices—where to shop even?—she was overwhelmed. But if she forced herself to choose one or two places that would most likely have something she liked, she could handle it. Ultimately, it would take a full year to get everything she wanted, but everything she got was exactly the right thing.

Zach's room was the most fun; she knew he would change it little by little over time, as his taste in colors, styles, sports teams, or whatever changed, but she got a solid base to get him started.

She was finally getting her chance to live alone. She didn't really think about it as living alone, though, since Zach lived there, too. Just not all the time. The reality of how much time they were apart started to settle in.

As the months wore on and the chores required to set the place up dwindled, Jillian realized she did live alone for much of the time. It was very freeing in many ways; she could walk around naked, stay in bed all day, sing at the top of her lungs (even though she suspected some of her neighbors might occasionally be able to hear her), come and go as she pleased, eat and drink what she wanted, when she wanted, watch whatever she wanted to on TV, anything! No one to fight with, debate with, wait for approval from, watch for signals from, walk on eggs around. No tension, certainly.

No anxiety. No anger. No resentment. It was peaceful, calm, and quiet. And very, very lonely.

Every time she dropped Zach off at school on days he was going back to Peter's for several days, she cried all the way to the office, already missing him. They had a strict timesharing schedule, which Peter adhered to rigidly. When she picked Zach up, she knocked on the door of the home she used to live in, the house-prison, and waited outside, never invited in. In fact, if Zach had to get stuff together, Peter would close the door in her face, and she would stand on the front porch like some pizza deliverer waiting to get paid. Any schedule changes were requested via email. In fact, all communications between her and Peter were conducted that way. They were both better writers than talkers. Maybe that was how they should've conducted their marriage. Oh, no, wait. That wouldn't have worked, either, considering that if an email she sent to him was more than a sentence, he didn't bother to read the whole thing. Even when they were "in love."

They split holiday time with Zach, and she was thrilled that she could get him whatever she wanted without anyone's permission, so perhaps she overdid it a tad, but it elated her. Zach, being as grounded as he was, though, said that he got too many presents that Christmas. Who ever heard of a kid saying such a thing? She sure never had that problem. She remembered the year all she got was a new set of bed sheets with rainbows on them. And ten cans of tuna from her grandmother, because her mother had screamed at her for an hour when she'd eaten a whole can herself with some crackers as an after-school snack. Jillian paid her back the can.

And that February, they celebrated Zach's seventh birthday separately, Peter taking him to a party with "the family" on his actual birthday, and Jillian having a cake for him for breakfast the next day. Now, she wasn't the only one living two separate lives. Zach was, too, with no overlap.

They had agreed to sign him up for Little League that spring. At games, they would sit separately (Peter even got up and moved further away once), pretending they didn't even know each other, and Zach would look back and forth between them, waving to each in turn.

Occasionally Zach would seem sad, and Jillian would ask him what was bothering him, knowing all too well what it was. Sometimes he didn't know how to put it into words, or maybe he didn't want to say it out loud, fearing it would hurt her feelings. When he did talk, and sometimes cry, he would say that he didn't understand why they had to get divorced, that he didn't want to have to go back and forth, that he missed his dad when he was with her, and he missed her when he was with his dad. She explained the best she could that they both loved him very much, and that none of it was his fault or because of him, and that she knew it was confusing, and maybe one day he would understand it better, but for now what he needed to know was that he was the most important person in both his dad's life and hers, and that they loved him more than anything, and that their first priority was taking care of him. He knew they loved him, right? Yes, he would nod, his little face red, and his nose running. Nothing breaks a mother's heart like that. She felt like such a shit, so selfish, so broken. At her loneliest times, missing him so much, she wondered if she shouldn't have stayed.

22

I'm outta here," she said, laughing and turning to go, setting her empty beer bottle down on the nearest table.

"So am I," said Jack, right behind her.

They were at the same conference, at the same hotel on Clearwater Beach, where "The Incident" with Ethan had occurred two years before. The meetings were dull, the food unappetizing, and the drinks plenty afterward on the beach and in the new hospitality suite. She and Jack walked out of the suite together and both turned toward the elevator, still chuckling. Jillian pushed the Up button, and the doors immediately opened. They got in and she pressed 4. "What floor?" she asked, poised to push another.

"Same," he said.

"Oh, OK, well, that makes it easy," she said. The doors slid closed, and they stared at endless clones of themselves in the mirrored walls of the small space. When the doors opened, they exited into the teal and gold and white hallway. "K, night, Jack!" she said, and turned toward her room.

He turned the same way.

"Oh, you're this way, too?" she asked. The hotel wasn't that big. There were maybe eight or ten rooms down the hallway.

"No," he said and just looked at her.

"Oh, walking me to my room? How gentlemanly," she said, antennae suddenly on red alert.

She pulled her key card out on the brief walk so it was ready. No fumbling at the door. They stopped and she slid the key in. Green light.

"Thanks!" she said and pushed the door open, trying to slide inside and escape. He put his hand on the door and pushed it all the way open and strode right into the room after her. *Oh god. What to do, what to do, what to do?*

She set her things down next to the TV and headed straight for the other end of the room. She was drunk, or she would have realized she should have just said "What the hell are you doing?" and asked him to leave.

Instead, she opened the glass doors and went out onto the balcony, as far away from him as she could get.

He followed her out. He put his hand on her back and started sliding it up and down.

"Are you OK?" he asked. She was standing ramrod straight, hands on the railing, staring past the pool and the beach to the dark water in the Gulf, eyes bulging, heart pounding, breath shallow from trying not to move, trying to focus, think, what to do, what to do?

"Yes, I'm fine," she managed, still staring straight ahead at the dark Gulf waters, wondering how one of its sharks had made it into her room.

"Well, this is awkward, so I'm going to go," he said, and immediately turned and left. As soon as the door slammed, she ran to it and slid the security lock closed, the dead bolt closed, and then crumpled to the floor in a heap and started bawling her eyes out. Had her boss just hit on her??? Witness. She needed a witness! She called Monica's cell.

"What? What's the matter? Jilly, what's wrong?" She was at the conference but had brought her family, so skipped the drinking segment of the evening.

Jillian relayed the whole thing. "Oh my god, that pig."

"So you think he was coming on to me?" she asked, finally starting to get a hold of herself.

"Of course he was! Yes, he wanted something."

She jumped as the room's telephone rang, its red-light blinking. The last guest must have had the volume on high.

"Hold on, my room phone's ringing," she told Monica, puzzled.

"Hello?" she answered tentatively.

"Hey! It's Jack! I just wanted to let you know I'm in room 409 if you decide you need anything," he said.

"I'm fine," she said, and hung up. She picked her cell back up, starting to cry again.

"Monica! That was him! He gave me his room number in case I decide I, quote, 'need anything'." She was on the verge of hysteria.

"What?! I can't believe him! How much did he have to drink? Jilly!? What a pig! Calm down, calm down!" She'd never heard Monica really riled up before, taking note of her tone even in her drunken, wild-eyed state.

"What the fuck do I do? What do I do?"

"OK, first: calm down. Take a deep breath. He didn't try to kiss you or anything, did he?" she asked.

"No, just the back rubbing. Gross! I think I'm going to throw up!" She really was starting to feel nauseated.

"I'll be right there," she said.

She was, in two minutes, and Jillian flipped out, bawling, asking her if she thought he really was coming on to her, what she should do about it, if HR should be involved. Monica wisely advised that she should cool off first, wait a few days, see what happened, see how she felt when she was less emotional (and less drunk), and then decide.

Jillian couldn't face him the next day. She waited until she knew the morning meeting had begun and, with her sunglasses on in case she ran into someone she knew, headed to the front checkout desk.

"Can you tell me, please, if you keep a record of room-to-room calls?" she asked the clerk, trying to think ahead for once.

"What do you mean, a log?" she asked.

"Yes, meaning, if I wanted a printout of the calls to and from my room, including from inside the hotel, can you give me that?" *Please please please.*

"We have only a record of toll calls, so no, there's no record of internal calls, I'm sorry," she said, smiling.

"OK, thank you anyway," she said, disappointed.

As soon as she got in the car, her cell rang. It was a number she didn't recognize, so she let it go to voicemail and then listened to the message. It was Tom, the HR guy, saying that Jack asked him to call and make sure she was all right, noticing she wasn't in the closing meeting. Hmm. She'd have to think something up that wouldn't make it seem like she skipped out because of a hangover.

On her way home, she stopped at Best Buy and bought the smallest, most powerful voice-activated recorder they had, and practiced with it over the weekend.

She got into the office early Monday morning, trying to get there before Jack arrived. Candace then said he'd be out until Thursday. Good. She could close the door and get it positioned and tested.

If he was going to say something about what happened, or otherwise, she was going to get it on tape.

She went to Tom's office, which she usually avoided. She posed a question: "If someone told you about an executive coming on to them what would you do about it?"

"Well, I would have to conduct interviews and document everything, then determine if there had been inappropriate behavior," he said. We didn't get along well. He was anti-Delta.

"OK, thanks for the info," she said, turning to leave. She hadn't decided what she wanted to do, yet, if anything. And this was not the right person to help make that decision. Once it was out there, there would be no going back.

"Jillian, is there something I need to know?" he asked. She wondered if he would be reminded of Jack's request to check on her.

"Nope. All good," she said. *Caution, Grasshopper.*

23

S he arrived at the meeting room to discuss Delta again. Maybe the fact that it was a stark room—practically colorless, with no windows or pictures, only closed, solid wood doors—that kept them from progressing. After all this time, they were still taking one step forward, two steps back, and now the real meltdown was beginning. Everyone was tired of talking in circles and making absolutely no progress.

Those who opposed it had dug their heels in, and the harder the Delta team pushed, the harder those against were pushing back. A couple of people were even hostile, refusing to cooperate with any of them on any project, not just Delta. Jack still took no position.

After the meeting, Monica, Tempe, Ethan, and Jillian stayed for a few minutes.

"Well? What now?" Jillian asked, hoping for some new ideas.

"I still want to do this, but I think maybe we should back off again for a while," Ethan said.

He pushed his chair back from the wood table and leaned forward, his arms across his knees, looking up at us, the three non-blondes, as we had started calling ourselves.

"Why? How are things, really, on your side?" Jillian asked.

"Not good. I'm about the only person on board at this point, and I have so much else going on that I'm having a hard time devoting enough energy to it. I apologize, but that's about the long and short of it," he said, clasping his hands as if in prayer and leaning his chin on his fingertips.

"I can certainly understand your position, Ethan," said Tempe. "Maybe it's a good idea for all of us to take a breather and try to regroup once things settle down a bit."

Monica and Jillian looked at each other, sensing defeat. They nodded, then quietly left the meeting room, and went to their respective offices, too tired to even argue any more.

The next day Monica and Jillian met for lunch in the café. They had a brief Delta conversation, both deciding they didn't know what else to do except wait it out.

"Nothing's working anywhere. I'm tired. And I'm lonely," Jillian sighed.

"Why don't you sign up for an online dating service? Just see what happens? You don't have to do anything. Just check it out, see what it feels like?"

Jillian did think she might be ready to try, but she was nervous. Monica was right, though. She didn't have to do anything.

"All right. I will just go sign up or whatever and see what it's about," she finally agreed, mostly just to satisfy Monica.

"Good. Just take a small step. You don't have to commit to anything. It won't hurt." She smiled. Sure, it wouldn't. Wouldn't she be sending a message to the Universe that she was giving up on Ethan? Maybe she was just changing her mind.

That evening, she signed up, answering all the profile questions, and posting a few photos, and paying the fee. She even paged through a few of the matches to see if anyone piqued her interest. She half hoped she wouldn't find anyone. Good excuse to forget the whole thing. She shut down her laptop, went to bed, and fell asleep almost immediately.

That night she dreamed she was riding a go-kart through the streets of Tampa at a very high rate of speed, practically out of control, finally skidding onto a grassy lawn where a bunch of people from One Metro were wandering about in casual clothing. Must have been a picnic or something.

She hopped out of the kart and Ethan was beside her, grabbing her hand, and walking next to her. She looked sideways at him, wondering why he wasn't worried about someone noticing them together, their handholding. He noted her questioning glance and said not to worry. "Everything is going to be OK," he said.

Next thing she knew she was in a nursery of sorts, or playroom, mostly white. Ethan's daughter, Sophia, was in front of her, talking to her. Jillian handed her a book and smiled. Then she heard Kelly behind her.

"Why did you give her that?" she asked in a bitchy voice, accusingly.

"I lost something that was hers, so I'm trying to make up for it," Jillian replied, not really looking at Kelly, but smiling at Sophia, who took the book and smiled back.

Ethan was behind Kelly, sitting in one of his usual poses, leaning forward, elbows on his knees, hands in the prayer position under his chin to hold his head up. Kelly turned to him and snapped, "Get everything together and let's go."

He stood up and gathered various toys and things into a tote, loading himself down. Kelly snatched Sophia's hand and dragged her along as she stomped off ahead of him. He slouched under the weight of the bags, perhaps under the weight of more than that.

Then he did the most curious thing while Jillian sat there astonished at the entire display: He walked over to Jillian, bent down, put a hand over hers on her lap, and kissed her on the lips. "Don't worry," he whispered. "Everything's going to be OK. Just wait." He kissed her again, turned with his bags, and followed his family out the door.

She turned to see Monica sitting next to her, whose eyes were wide, and mouth hung open.

"What the hell was that about?" she managed.

Jillian started to laugh. "I have no idea." She chuckled. "But she is going to kill me. I don't know if she will run me over or push me off a cliff, but she is going to kill me for sure," she replied, laughing the whole time, as Monica looked on in amazement.

When she awoke from the dream, she felt a strong message: wait. Kate had heard her, and helped her, and told her what she should do. She wrote down the details of the dream and smiled all day that day, telling Monica about it on their way back to the fifth floor from an early meeting.

She was smiling the next day, too, even though it was Thursday and Jack was due back in the office.

Then, shock and awe.

She had the voice-activated recorder in place behind the reference books on her desk, ready to go. She was a bundle of nerves, practically quivering in anticipation, a feeling she had grown quite used to. She had no idea what to expect from Jack. Would he apologize? Or would he pretend nothing had happened?

Her guess was the latter. If he apologized, that would be admitting wrongdoing. He knew enough to avoid getting into that position—they did have HR law training once a year. That was if he even felt as if he had done something wrong.

She sat at her desk reviewing copy and creative for a new campaign—for a client she would have sent to Ethan's firm if the Delta deal were in place—when her desk phone rang. The caller ID said CHASE E and Ethan's cell number. She picked up.

"Good morning," he said.

"Hey! What's up?" she asked, trying to sound normal, casual.

"Well, there's something I need to tell you. I tried not to let it interfere with work, but it's unavoidable at this point, and I probably won't make our conference this morning," he stated mysteriously.

"What's going on? Are you OK?" she asked, sending concern she hoped he would note.

He sighed, then plunged in with the big news. "Kelly and I are going through a divorce."

All the blood in her body rushed to her feet, leaving her lightheaded and hot.

"I have tried to keep it separate from the office," he said, "but too much is happening and I just can't do it, not today, anyway."

"Oh my god, Ethan, I'm so sorry! Are you OK? What happened? Is there anything I can do?" she was freaking out. She couldn't think straight. She wanted to ask him a million questions—but didn't she just do that? She wanted to reach out to him, let him know she was there, would be there for him, however he needed her. But, as usual, she was tongue-tied.

"Please don't say you're sorry. I will be fine. I'll fill you in soon, but I wanted you to know I won't be able to make our meeting; we'll have to reschedule."

"OK, but please know that when you're ready, you know where to find me, and that a lot of people care about you and want what's best for you. Let us support you," she offered.

"Thank you. Yes, I know that, and I will. I'll catch up with you soon."

She practically ran to Monica's office, holding back tears and anxiety and hope, all ready to burst forth like so many tulip bulbs pushing through the last of the spring snow. She had quickly assumed the "wait" message of the dream meant "wait for Ethan." With news like that so soon after the dream, what else could it have possibly meant?

Monica was on the phone. She couldn't wait. She couldn't believe it. Monica looked at her suspiciously, trying to end her call. She wrote "Ethan is getting divorced!!!!!!" on a post-it from her desk and slid it toward her. Monica read it and nodded. She didn't seem surprised.

She already knew. She hung up and said, "I found out after we went to lunch, after you agreed to sign up online, after the dream. I couldn't believe it. And yet I couldn't bring myself to tell you because you were trying to move on, and I was so proud of you. I didn't know what to do!"

Jillian was stunned, her head spinning. She knew and she didn't tell her? How could she not tell her? Far less important. "It's OK. I get it. I just can't believe it."

"Are you OK? How did you find out?" she asked.

"He just called me."

"Well that's a good sign, that he called you and told you himself."

"How did you find out?" Jillian still wasn't sure what was going on.

"I heard one of his coworkers in the café. I didn't know it was for sure. That's another reason I didn't want to say anything to you, in case it was just a rumor," she went on.

"It's OK. He called to reschedule this morning's meeting on that prospect. It's OK. I'm OK," she stammered. She turned and left the office without another word.

She was back at her desk when she heard Jack's booming voice say good morning to Candace. Sure enough, he strode right in, purposefully, as always.

"How's my favorite vice president today?" he asked, a bit louder than usual, saying something for Jack. He stopped at the candy jar on the corner of her desk, always filled with Hershey kisses, his favorite, and reached in to grab one.

Hmph. It occurred to her she ought to fill it with something else. Like Harry Potter Every Flavor Beans. Maybe he'd get a vomit or dirt flavored one. She wondered what else he wouldn't like. This size of his belly told her not much.

"I'm good. The usual," she replied. "How about you? How was your trip?" She put her hands on some files on her desk instead of sitting back in her chair, hoping he would sense that she was busy.

"Good, good. Good to be home. So everything's OK?" he asked, chewing the chocolate, then wadding up the foil wrapper.

"Sure thing," she said.

"Glad to hear it," he said, tossing the foil ball into her trashcan and turning to leave. He paused at the doorway, putting his hand on the frame, and started to turn back, then thought better of it and continued on his way.

So, swept under the rug it would be. She was relieved and yet disappointed, and the tension, at least on her part, was undiminished. However, the news about Ethan outweighed it for the time being. It wasn't even 10:00 a.m. yet.

<h1 style="text-align:center">24</h1>

She wanted to comfort Ethan in some way, tell him everything was going to be OK, like he did for her in her dream, but she was afraid that if she told him that he would assume she thought he wasn't OK. She had to assume he was, and yet she knew he couldn't be. His world was falling apart.

What she did try to do was make sure she protected him when she had the opportunity. Plenty of gossip about his divorce started going around over the next few weeks. Had there been so much gossip about her own divorce that her friends had protected her from?

She wanted to yell and tell the gossips that they had no idea what he was going through and that they were fools who had things too good and didn't understand anything about adversity or courage or what it means to be dying inside and yet trying to do a job every day with a smile on your face, a job that meant nothing if the people you love don't love you or if you can't protect them. And yet you need to work because maybe that's all you have that keeps you going, keeps you sane, that makes you feel normal, and worthwhile, and like you should carry on, despite the feeling that you just want to crawl under a rock until someone tells you it's safe and worth it to come out again into the world of the living.

Holding back, always waiting for the right opportunity, for a door to open, for an invitation to arrive. Never able to say, do, what she wished.

They had their makeup meeting a few days later. Afterward, when they were going over the file, it seemed to her there was something else he wanted to say, that he wanted to talk to her about, but apparently, he wasn't ready. Sometimes he looked like he was thinking about whether to say something, and she would start rambling on and on to dispel the discomfort, talking instead of listening, again.

"How are you doing?" she asked finally, when they were wrapped up.

"I'll be fine," he answered. Typical male response. "My primary concern is my children."

She knew both of those things were true. She also knew, though, that he was hurting, not just because of the kids, but because of Kelly. According to the rumors, she had hurt him, had betrayed him.

"I've stopped asking why she did what she did," he said. She knew that he had to keep asking himself why she'd had a string of affairs and how she could have done that to him, to their family.

"You may never know. I don't know her at all, but I do know you don't deserve this. I can guess that she is a very unhappy, insecure person who had her priorities totally screwed up," she offered.

He looked at his watch. "Gotta go. I'm late again."

"You know where to find me if you want to talk. I've got some perspective, you know," she smiled. "You know I won't judge you."

"Thank you. I appreciate that, I do," he said, looking down, then gathered his things and walked out the door.

She didn't know if anything she ever said to him helped at all. He had once told her he was happily married. She didn't think he was. Otherwise, he wouldn't have done what he did with her. She thought he wanted to be happy, he tried to be. He may have fooled himself into thinking he was, or that he was at least content, like she had, so that he didn't have to face the consequences of the converse.

But he deserved—like everyone deserved—to be with someone who would love him, cherish him, be as committed to him as he was to her. She didn't know the reasons why, but Kelly obviously could not do that. He didn't realize he had to get out, either, until he was left with no other choice. It was a blessing. Jillian believed that. Now he could pursue his own happiness. She had no doubt he would find it if he let himself look. She wished she could be so sure about finding it herself.

25

A few weeks later, Monica, Tempe, and Jillian were off to a professional conference and trade show in Atlanta. The same people were there every year. They'd worked with many of them at some time or another, and there was a lot of socializing. That made it something to look forward to, in addition to being out of the office for a few days.

Zach was out of school for the summer, but the conference was during one of his two uninterrupted weeks with Peter, so Jillian's schedule was flexible.

Kayla, a project manager at the agency, was on Jillian's flight—Monica and Tempe had gone the evening before—and they decided to meet in the lobby bar after they checked into the hotel.

Kayla had been with Sagency for a couple of years, and they had worked together on a few projects, but Jillian didn't know her very well. At the bar, in the center of the marble lobby amid numerous small tables, intimate booths lining the floor-to-ceiling windows overlooking a garden around the pool area, they talked about work quite a bit, which clients they liked working with, which ones were kind of a pain, the projects they were working on. Jillian mentioned Black&Gray and even Ethan a couple of times. They slowly edged into their personal lives once they'd gotten to their third or fourth drinks. They ate dinner, still there at the bar, as it started to fill up.

Other coworkers, peers, business partners, and vendors stopped by, chatted, and took care of whatever expenses they had racked up. They sat there so long they started joking that the hotel was going to put their names on the bar stools.

The first time Cameron Taylor spoke to them, they totally blew him off. He just asked what company they were with, and they told him and didn't even reciprocate. He turned and walked away.

"Did you notice how nervous he seemed?" Kayla asked.

And Jillian said, "What man in his right mind wouldn't be intimidated by us?" They laughed. Jillian didn't feel like she'd ever intimidated anyone, but Kayla was a good ten years younger, blond, athletic, pretty. She could intimidate men. And probably a lot of women.

The bar got crowded and loud. More people they knew were hanging out, getting sloshed, and demanding their attention, so they finally abandoned their Jillian- and Kayla-seats, gabbing with whoever wandered into their little circle, preferably those who could entertain them or pay the tab.

Jillian was not sure when Cameron Taylor arrived back on the scene. They chatted for a while, and she noticed how tall he was, well over six feet. Well built, strong. Short dark hair, kind of wavy, pushed up a bit over the forehead. Beautiful green eyes. Smooth skin, well-shaven. Strong jawline, straight white teeth. *Hmm. Very nice. Wedding ring. Hmph. So much for that.*

Before she realized it, though, they were deep in conversation about their work, what they did, where they were from. Turned out he worked for Black&Gray, Atlanta office. Freaky.

"So what's your story? I see you're not wearing a ring," he posed in his soft Southern accent. A soft accent, but a strong voice, not loud. Sexy.

"Divorced," she explained.

"Dating?" he asked.

"Not really. Haven't gotten there yet," she answered, looking away.

"Why not? Seems to me like you would be in high demand." He smiled and kind of chuckled.

"Well, it's kind of scary out there, you know?" she joked. "I was with him for a long time, and a lot has changed. You never know who you're going to meet, right? Could be an axe murderer." Where the hell that came from, she had no idea.

"Yeah, I get it. Got to get back out there, though."

"I've had offers! None acceptable, though." She didn't want him to think she was pathetic.

"No acceptable offers, huh? What do you mean?"

"It just seems to me that all the men I would be interested in are either unavailable or uninterested, and the men who are interested are either unacceptable or unavailable," she tried to explain.

She and Tempe had started going to the Carrabba's bar almost every other Friday (when Zach was at his dad's), and there was always someone hanging about, lurking, looking. No one she had found interesting. She wasn't really lying, just spinning.

"What's your story?" she asked. "Married, I see."

"Yeah, I am. It's actually my second. First marriage was a shotgun wedding, which I finally bailed on. I needed to get my daughter out of that situation and that was the best way to do it. Most people ask me what took me so long, but I was trying to do the right thing. Then, I got remarried too quickly."

Wow. That was certainly more than she expected. Second marriage, huh?

"So what other family do you have? Brothers? Sisters?" she asked. After so many beers—she'd lost track of how many, even though she didn't think she was really feeling it—she was ready to see what else she could find out about Mr. Cameron Taylor.

"One brother," he replied.

"Is he tall like you? Where do you get your height from?" she asked, making conversation, and starting to lean toward flirting.

"Well, I don't really know; I'm adopted," he answered.

"Nuh uh. You are not," she stared, mouth agape.

"Yeah, I am," he smiled. "Why are you reacting that way?"

"Because I am, too," she answered. Wow again. She didn't know very many people who were adopted.

"Really?" he asked. "That's amazing! Was it as an infant?" he asked, looking right into her eyes.

"Yep. You too?" she asked, staring right back.

"Yep. It's kind of weird, isn't it? My brother is, too. Do you have any siblings?"

"Yeah, one sister, but we're estranged. She was adopted, too."

"Oh, yikes. What happened there?"

What the hell was with all the questions? It had taken Monica and Tempe weeks, months, years to find out all of this from her, and now this man she'd just met was getting all of it in an hour? He was asking questions, she guessed. Maybe she was no good at volunteering information but no good at dodging, either. Or maybe Monica and Tempe just hadn't been trying to get in her pants.

Tempe had finally made it to the bar, chatting with everyone like they were lifelong friends. Most recently Jillian had seen her talking with Jack, his hand on her back, leaning over in the commotion so he could hear her. She talked loudly enough that he didn't have to lean in, but he did, anyway. Perv. Made her skin crawl, seeing his hand on her back; made her feel it again on her own.

"Cam?" we heard. Tempe was calling him over. She knew this guy?

"Yes ma'am!" he replied, and dashed over to her.

She spoke to him quickly, and he came right back to my side. Jillian imagined, though Tempe claimed later not to recall what she said (that she'd confess to, anyway), that she said, "take her, she needs this," or some shit like that, like Jillian was some fucking charity case—charity fucking case? How humiliating. But she did note that he didn't talk with anyone else after that; he stayed focused entirely on her.

The crowd thinned as the hour got later, and Cam was sticking to her like glue. After most of the people she knew were out of sight (barring Tempe and Kayla), she started making sure she was touching him in some way. They were talking with Tempe and some people she knew, and she was standing in front of Cam, to the side a bit, and stepped back just enough so that her backside was brushing up against his thigh. She kept it there. Then, his fingertips were on her back. Down, then back up, then down again. She took a deep breath. It had been too long since "The Incident" with Ethan. (Had it really been two years?) She needed some intimacy, and she was ready to compromise.

It'd just be a one-night stand, anyway.

The bar closed and the servers started wiping down the tables. Kayla was in the corner with some man Jillian didn't recognize and Tempe was drunk and headed for her room. Jillian was pissed that she wasn't buzzing after all she'd had to drink. One vendor had even bought a couple of glasses of the $45-an-ounce Grand Marnier and shared it with Kayla and her. Oh ambrosia! Just the smell of it was freshly peeled oranges and it went down like maple syrup. She didn't notice it helping her buzz, though. She didn't know how drunk Cam was, considering she had just met him, but he wasn't swaying or slurring.

Cam asked, "Do you think they'd mind if we just sit here and talk?" as he took a step toward some chairs.

"Let's go outside instead," she said. It was far too bright inside.

"That's an even better idea."

They stepped out into the humidity, trees gently swaying, and headed for the pool, walking through the narrow path with high foliage on each side. But the pool was dark behind a locked gate, and as soon as she stopped and turned his arms were around her and his lips were on hers. Oh Jesus. She kissed him as enthusiastically as he kissed her.

"You are married, right?" she asked when they came up for air.

"Yeah, I am," he said quietly, almost apologetically.

She kissed him again. He smelled so good, like fresh laundry. His hands were on her back, her breasts, and her arms were around his neck. This was too easy, too comfortable. She pulled away.

"Are you OK? I'm sorry; I shouldn't have done that."

"I just wish you weren't married. You're not an axe murderer, are you?" she smiled.

He chuckled with his mouth closed, as he'd done several times earlier (which she found tremendously sexy and irresistible), and said, "Of course not."

She pulled him to her and kissed him again. Oh, so good.

"You really are a good kisser," he whispered, chuckling again.

Nervous laughter? Fuck it. "Thank you, but you know what? This isn't smart. Come on, let's go."

She grabbed his hand and took the lead, back down the path. She wasn't sure he knew what she meant. Was she going to ditch him because he was married? Or was she taking him to her room? She was so ready, and he did feel safe to her. His openness, their conversation, the fact that they were both adopted. It just felt right.

She kept his hand—he let her—and she led him back into the bright, chilly air-conditioned bar, straight through the lobby to the elevators, waited and got in, where it was just the two of them. She pushed the button for her floor, turned around, and covered his mouth with hers again. She wasn't nervous at all. Maybe she had had enough to drink after all. Enough to dull her usual nervous edge and her better judgment.

He ducked into the bathroom as soon as they got to her room, the two double beds with their thick down comforters and abundance of pillows calling to her. She really wanted to get naked but didn't want to appear too trampy, so she opened a bottle of water and checked out the view, coincidentally overlooking the dark pool.

He came out after a couple minutes, still wearing his suit and tie, but smelling of mouthwash, and they were on the bed making out before she knew what hit her. When he started to pull at her jeans and panties, she stopped him. "It's my turn to use the bathroom," she explained. She really did have to pee and didn't want to have to be holding it in.

She checked herself out in the bathroom mirror and thought she looked pretty darn good. She returned to the room, dimmed the lights, and they got right to business.

He kissed her, and they rubbed and groaned and kissed quite a bit more before he stopped and said, "I don't have anything."

She said she did and pointed to the nightstand drawer. What had possessed her to buy and bring condoms, she wasn't sure, but maybe it had sent the Universe a message, which It had taken note of!

Afterwards, he headed for the bathroom again and she lay completely naked on the bed awaiting his return.

He had never taken off his shirt, and as soon as he came out of the bathroom, he got dressed.

"Wow, you have a perfect body, you know that?" he said, as he eyed her up and down. He lay down on the bed next to her, put his arm around her.

"So why are you cheating on her?" she asked. Very bold of her. Very unusual for her to be so direct. Guess she was drunk after all. And not invested (yet).

"We're not having sex. I don't really know why. I'm a very passionate person, and sex is very important to me. For some reason, it seems she has cut me off."

"How long has it been?" she asked, curious.

"A couple months," he said. "How about you? When was the last time you had sex?"

"A couple years," she said, sighing.

"Wow. I guess you really needed this, then, huh?"

"I guess. Is this the first time you've cheated on her?" She wanted to get the real story. Was this a line, his way of easing the guilt? Hers or his own? Trying to make her feel sorry for him?

"Yeah. It's not really my style, but…I'm not happy about it. Like I said, I just got remarried too soon, I guess."

"Well, why do you think you're not having sex?" she asked again.

"I don't know. I've gained a few pounds, maybe she's not attracted to me anymore," he said, looking sad again.

His arm was still around her, right where it belonged. She turned and looked him directly in the eyes, just a few inches away from her own. "Cam, you are a very handsome, sexy man. That is not the reason," she stated.

He held her gaze in his and quietly replied, "Thank you."

She meant it. She kissed him on the lips.

Then there was a knock on the door. Cam flipped out. Jillian grabbed a robe and threw it on while he moved to the corner of the room, out of sight.

"Just chill out," she said. "I'm not expecting anyone. It's probably just the turn-down service."

She went to the door and had a quiet exchange with the housekeeper, telling her she didn't need anything. She did offer some chocolates, though, which would have been placed on the pillows, and Jillian accepted them.

She wasn't sure if Cam had heard. She shut the door and turned back into the room and found him standing in between the beds with his hands in his pockets, looking like he was about ready to jump out of his skin.

"Don't worry!" she said and, handing him a small foil-wrapped square, chuckled. "It was just the after-sex chocolate delivery service."

"Hilarious," he said, chuckling himself. "That's just frickin' hilarious."

Long into the future, thinking about that made her smile. When you smile when you're alone, it's real, right?

She didn't expect to ever see him again. They had a great time. He got laid; she got laid. Everybody was happy, right? Luckily, she hadn't fallen for him yet, so she didn't have any expectations of him.

The next day, even knowing where to find him, she didn't track him down. Really, she didn't do much because she was hung over after all, despite not feeling buzzed the night before (must've been that damn Grand Marnier).

Kayla was hung over, too, but neither one of them as much as Tempe. Kayla and Jillian laughed at her when she closed her eyes during one of the lectures. When she opened her eyes, they asked her if she'd had a nice nap. Weren't they funny? Jillian couldn't concentrate on the speaker, anyway, so she sent Kayla a text.

So what hpnd w/u last night?

Kayla turned and looked at her questioningly, then turned back to her phone.

What do you mean? What hpnd w/U???

I'll tell u if u tell me :-)

Jillian smiled, while staring straight ahead at the speaker.

Did u take him home?

Did U?

They were both smirking. They both had. Except Kayla was married. Well, Cam was, too, so she guessed these things happen, right?

As soon as the speaker finished, amid the chatter of relief that always comes after the forced silence of those things, Jillian put the pressure on.

"So? What happened? Who was that guy?" she asked.

"I've actually met him before," she replied.

"Oh, so you already knew him. Did you do him?" She laughed.

Kayla looked at her like she was misbehaving. "Jesus! You can't ask me that!"

"I just did! OK, I'll go first. Yes. I took Cam home with me last night. Well, to my room, I mean. It was amazing."

"Isn't he married?" Kayla asked.

"Aren't you?" Jillian asked.

"OK, yes, I did him. It was amazing, too." She didn't look happy about it, though. She wasn't glowing the way that Jillian imagined she was.

Tempe caught up with them after stopping in the ladies 'room.

"What are you two talking about?"

"Getting laid," Jillian said, and she and Kayla laughed.

"What?! Well, that's certainly a good topic! What about it?"

"About both of us getting laid last night!" Jillian laughed. Oh, maybe she was still drunk!

"Holy shit! What? Who? Jilly, did you take that guy Cam home? I knew you would! Kayla, what the heck? I didn't know you and your man were on the outs."

Kayla was frowning again. "Yeah, we are. Jay is married, too, but they're separated."

"That's not so bad. You're on a break, right?" Jillian said, and they all laughed. She was so high from doing it that she forgot she had morals. At least she used to.

They decided to skip cocktail hour that night to rest and recuperate from their hangovers. Jillian was in her room in bed watching the Discovery Channel when the phone rang. It was Cam. They exchanged a bit of small talk that ended with Cam on his way to her room.

She wasn't sure she could have sex again so soon. She was kind of sore, a good kind of sore, though. Hey, what the hell.

A few minutes later, he knocked. When she opened the door, he strode in, and she hugged him and kissed him right on the lips. Then she took him all in. He was wearing nice khaki drawstring shorts and a polo, flip-flops (thank god no dorky deck shoes), and a bead necklace. Holy crap! He looked so good!

They started talking, and he sat on the bed with her, putting his arm around her again, and they talked about the day. They chatted for quite a while and played footsie a bit, and she kissed him a couple of times. Once they started making out, though, it was all over. They got the condom on the first try and he nailed her. She forgot all about being sore.

He said he'd been in the bar before he called, talking with Jack. Oh sheesh. Cam said he told Jack that he'd met her the night before and Jack had said, "Oh, Jillian is such a sweetheart. I just love her." Cam said he called the bartender for another drink. She didn't say anything about "The Jack Incident."

They sat on the bed, leaning up against the pillows, usually with his arm around her, talking and talking and talking.

"I had some guilt today, for sure," he told her. He smiled when he said it, but he looked sad to her.

"Didn't stop you from coming for more," she answered. What was up with her? She was not usually this direct.

"I know. I just really like you and am really attracted to you."

She tried to quiz him some more about his marriage, and thought he answered her honestly.

Talking with him, being next to him, was so comfortable. It was like they had known each other for ages. It was so strange to be with a man who talked, talked to her about what he felt and what was going on in his head. A man, in her bed, talking to her, seemingly openly, and totally doing her! Astonishing. Even if she wasn't yet sure she believed everything that he was telling her.

After a while, he said he'd let her get some sleep and bailed. She slept, really, really well.

The next morning, she waited until seven-thirty to call his room. He answered the phone sounding like he was still asleep. She asked him where he was going to be so she could stop by and see him before leaving that afternoon.

She met Tempe and Kayla—Monica was still MIA—and they went to the auditorium, coming in late after having to get coffee and Diet Coke, and found seats together about ten rows up on the far side. The beige room was cavernous; there must have been folded chairs set up for a thousand, plus the stage at the front with three video screens. They couldn't find Monica anywhere and she wasn't picking up her cell, bad reception inside the hotel.

She didn't want to admit it, but she looked for Cam; he said he'd be there. About twenty minutes into the speaker's presentation, she realized he was sitting in the same section, about thirty rows up. It was the least populated seating area so there weren't as many people in between, just one who had kept her from spotting him earlier. He was wearing a suit, sitting kind of sideways in his chair, with his arm around the vacant seat next to him, legs crossed.

She pointed him out to Tempe. "Oh, yes!" she said.

Finally, he looked around and spotted her. They smiled at each other, easily crossing the distance over the sea of chairs. His eyes, his whole face, softened when he smiled, like it was coming from the inside out.

During the session, he used his left hand a few times to smooth the back of his hair—maybe he could feel Jillian's eyes boring into the back of his head—and the light in the hall reflected off his wedding ring. Sexy, even if that ring meant his commitment to some other nameless woman.

There was a break between the speaker and the next segment, during which some of the crowd took the opportunity to leave the session. Cam came back and sat in the row behind them, saying hi to Tempe and Kayla and that he was going to the exhibit hall. Jillian told him she could meet him there after but that she wouldn't be able to stay long; she had a lunch meeting. He looked so handsome in his suit.

Tempe commented as he left the room. "Damn, he is a good looking man!"

After the session, Jillian booked it to the exhibit hall, practically mowing over Monica in the hallway. "There you are!"

she said as she kept walking, practically backward so that she could keep moving.

"Sorry!" she said, and held out her hands, palms up, and looked at her like she was nuts (she knew she was, anyway). Jillian just smiled and kept going.

She figured he would be in the common area of the hall, and she was right. He was facing away, by himself, but he happened to turn around as she was approaching. He saw her right away and gave her that face-softening-but-brightening smile again. He had plenty of time to eye her as she walked up, and he certainly looked appreciative. Not in a leering way, but in an I'm-so-glad-to-see-you way.

They found a couple seats together and sat down. She crossed her legs and her foot slid up his leg.

He turned to her, and she looked right in his eyes and said, "Do you have any idea how hard it is for me to not be touching you right now?" to which he replied, never taking his eyes off hers, "I'm feeling the same way."

She reached for her purse and pulled out a business card. He chuckled, "Aren't you supposed to give me your number before we have sex?"

She squinted her eyes at him suspiciously and said, "Well, you didn't ask me for my phone number. You asked me for my room number." They laughed.

She had to go; they knew it would be the last time they would see each other. They stood and she reached out just to touch his arm, and before she knew it, they were embracing. She wanted to kiss him so badly she could barely stand it, but they were in public. And that was that. She hoped he was watching her as she rushed away.

26

On the plane back, Jillian wondered how she would feel when she saw Ethan, having finally been with another man. Would the infatuation have dimmed, lost some intensity now that she'd had a distraction? They say the best way to get over someone is to get under someone else. She had. Would it make a difference?

She didn't get a chance to find out. The following week, Zach was out of school for a few days, and it happened to be "her turn," so she took time off work to spend with him. They had a great time playing Wii, going out to breakfast, watching movies. She was getting better at switching back and forth between her two lives—one as Zach's mom, the other as a single woman. She usually needed about twenty-four hours to make the complete shift, but once she was past it, she was good to go. It was hardest to switch from Mom to single, missing Zach so much.

The next day back in the office, Monica nearly repaid her for blowing by her in the hall by about mowing Jillian over as soon as she stepped out of the elevator.

"Did you hear?" she was antsy, very unlike Monica, usually cool as a cucumber.

"Uh, hear what?" Jillian asked.

"Ethan's gone! I hoped you hadn't heard; I almost called you, but I didn't want to disrupt your time with Zach," she said.

"What do you mean he's gone?" she asked, her chest tightening.

"He quit, supposedly. You know he's been out a lot, and I guess with everything that's going on, he and his boss had it out and he walked out," she said.

"Holy shit! He doesn't need this right now. How can he quit in the middle of a divorce?! Kelly will have his head!" Jillian was almost panicked. Could she call him? Should she call him?

"I didn't even think of that! All I could think of was you and how you would feel. Of course, I feel terrible for him," she said.

"Thanks for telling me. I think I need to call him and find out how he's doing," Jillian said.

"I know. Let me know if he needs anything. Are you OK?" she asked.

"Yep. I'll call you. I have lots to fill you in on," she answered, though she wasn't sure she was OK. She wasn't quite hyperventilating, but close. She hadn't even finished her first Diet Coke.

Jillian was shaking as she dialed his cell. It felt like the entirety of her insides had crawled up into her throat. No answer. She didn't leave a message. She called Monica to keep her in the loop and said she would give him a couple days. Maybe he'd see a missed call from her and take the initiative for once and call back. She and Monica decided to meet for lunch. It was going to be a long morning.

Monica arrived in Jillian's office a few minutes before noon, and they decided to go to a restaurant a few miles away; they could talk more openly without worrying someone they worked with was sitting nearby. Monica offered to drive, so they got in her silver Acura and took off.

"Are you sure you're OK?" Monica asked again. She had to know Jillian wasn't. She didn't even know about Cam yet! Good grief.

"Have you ever experienced an event that made you feel like the hands of the Universe were grabbing you by the shoulders and standing you up at the crossroads, telling you it was time to change direction—and it's going to help you, or has already done so, and you just weren't aware of it yet?" Jillian felt a bit manic.

"Um, I'm not really sure I have, but fill me in," she said.

"My head is spinning! I am not trying to be overly dramatic, but even you will wonder. No matter what you think, what you believe, or how you feel today: in a week, or a day, or an hour, or an instant, it can all change, in ways you never expected. Or maybe in ways you hoped it would but never dared dream would be possible." Frantic.

"Okaaay," she was still waiting. She was probably happy at that point with her decision to drive. Jillian probably would have run them off the road.

"I haven't even told you what happened in Atlanta, yet! Just wait, although I'm not sure you're going to want to hear it. Where do you want me to start? Do my eyes look buggy?" Jillian asked. They felt like they were about to pop out of her skull.

Monica laughed. "They look fine. Start wherever you want to," she said. Typical Monica.

"I met someone. He's amazing. We had such a connection, like I've never felt before. Like I've been trying to forge—force—with Ethan, but we had it practically instantaneously!"

"OK. Who is he? What happened?"

"For one thing, he's adopted, like me. We found that out like in the first hour we were talking. He's very sweet, handsome, very sexy. And he talked to me, asked questions, like Peter never did, like no man ever has, like he was really interested in me as a person," Jillian gushed.

"Wow. Sounds great! Where's he from, why was he there?"

"Believe it or not, he's with Black&Gray, the Atlanta office. Isn't that bizarre?"

Monica parked and they walked into the small, dark, Thai restaurant and were seated at a two-top by the wall. The natively dressed server handed them menus and asked what they'd like to drink. Water with lemon and Diet Coke.

"Seriously? But he's not married, right?"

Jillian's jaw dropped. God! She went right for the throat. Why would she even ask that? Jillian sighed and her shoulders drooped. She didn't need to answer her after that.

"Jillian! What the hell are you doing?"

"I know. I know! It was supposed to be a one-night stand. I am so lonely! I want to be with someone, and we really connected, and it was just supposed to be one night. But it turned into two nights. I was going to say good-bye to him when I ran past you in the hall."

Monica sighed this time. "So what's his story? Are they separated or something?"

"No, but he said he got remarried quickly after his divorce. His first marriage was a shotgun wedding. And now there's no sex in the marriage." It sounded totally lame even to her own ears as Jillian said it out loud.

Like a story. A cheater's story.

"Maybe it will at least help you move on."

"That's just the thing! That's the rest of it, what I'm talking about! That Ethan's gone! Can you believe these things happened like this?" Jillian asked, the frenzy renewed.

"It is pretty freaky when you think about it," Monica said, still ever so calm.

"Which is what I've done nothing but since this morning. It's just too much. It's like I've been transported from one reality to another, practically overnight," Jillian said. She still hadn't processed everything.

"It's a good thing. It's what you need. And you know what? This guy's marriage is not your problem and not your responsibility. I wish he wasn't, for your sake, but if he makes you happy, well, then, do what you need to do. I just hope you're not in for even more heartbreak," she said.

Always the even-keeled, realistic one. That was why Jillian needed her.

"I know. I can't help it. He's so different from any man I have ever met. And it's not like we're having an affair. How could we when he lives so far away? I don't want to break up his marriage. We'll be friends, maybe. That's all," Jillian said.

"Sure," she said.

They ordered, ate, and Monica filled Jillian in on what she knew about Ethan. The whole time Jillian felt abashed for sleeping with a married man (again) because of the way Monica looked at her when she'd told her. She'd contemplated leaving out the part about him being married, but Monica had asked her so directly, how could she have avoided it without a direct lie? She couldn't have. She knew. And now they would see what happened, on many fronts.

27

Cam emailed Jillian several times and called her twice over the next week. The second time he called, she was on her way home from work.

"Hey, it's me," he said. She could hear the smile in his voice.

"Hey, me. What cha doin'?" Jillian asked, smiling, too.

"I'm on my way home from the office. It's about the only time I can call you. How was your day today?"

"Good! Same old shit. How about you?" she asked. Weird to have this kind of conversation. It had been so long since anyone acted like they gave a crap about how her day was. Had anyone ever?

"Good! You know, this is weird. I'm not sure what I should be doing here, you know what I mean?" he asked.

"I know. Me, too. I am very happy when you call, Cam, but I certainly don't expect you to. I hope you do, though, and I'm trying to keep my hopes and expectations separate. Call me when you can, when you want to. No expectations."

"That's good to know. I wish I could call more. It's just difficult. I do want to talk to you; I want to see you. In fact, I need to come down there for a meeting, should be in a few weeks," he said.

"Really? That would be great! Do you think we'll be able to spend any time together? Or should we?"

"I want to! Things aren't really any different at home. I'm still totally shut out. I don't know what's going to happen."

"You need to talk to her, Cam," Jillian advised.

"I know. I just avoid confrontation," he said. Boy, she knew how that went.

"Don't look at it that way. Look at it as talking to her. You're great at talking to me. What are you going to do, just let things slide? Coast every day until there's no hope for recovery? Hope

148

she'll change, that something will change? Cam, you're strong. You are passionate. You know what you want. Talk to her and try to figure things out. Don't you both deserve that?" she offered. Funny advice coming from her. She knew it seemed so easy from the outside but was so difficult to act on. If only people could tell us not just what to do, but how to do it.

"I know you're right. I will. I just have to find the right time. Hey, I'm about home. I'll call you again soon, OK?"

"Sure thing. Take care of yourself, big guy," she said. She refused to tell him she missed him, but she did. How could that be?

"You, too. Have a good night."

And so it went.

The men who had come and gone in Jillian's life had all gone with good riddance. They either dumped her and she got over them because she sooner or later figured out they weren't for her, anyway, or she left them, usually after getting over them, in some kind of adore-to-abhor process.

Even with Ethan, no matter how much she cried over him, the signs were there, she just kept ignoring them. The way he treated her; the way he let her take the blame. The way he ignored her most of the time. She knew he wasn't interested in her. She knew he was a fantasy, that she was living in an alternate reality as a way of coping with the stress of the divorce. She removed herself from that situation and became infatuated with the "perfect life" she thought he had and that she could have with him. He had none of it, either.

Just when she needed him most, without even realizing it, Cam appeared right in front of her, inserting himself into every fiber of her being. She didn't even know it was coming. All she wanted was a one-night stand to relieve some of the pressure. She got one. The second night, it was for fun.

He was incredible, and she was so turned on by him that she went for more. The connection was firmly established in the first few hours, but she still had no expectations. Not after the second night, either.

But he continued calling once or twice a week, and they would chat for a few minutes. He always asked her how she was, what she was doing, how her day was, what her plans were. Not in a demanding way, but in a very conversational way, like he was truly interested. His voice was so sexy. She told him about Delta, and he said he thought he'd heard something about it the last time he was in Tampa but didn't know much. And she told him about Jack's little visit at the hotel. He laughed and called him an old pervert. Jillian laughed, too.

They emailed several times a week, too, joking around, flirting, him filling her in on his plans for his trip. Closer and closer they got. It turned into a long-distance affair. They talked to each other like they were dating. And he told her more and more about his situation with his wife, Mary Beth, and Jillian counseled him— in the beginning, anyway. Each time he called, they talked less about Mary Beth and more about his day, Jillian's day, his trip to Tampa.

As the communication pattern emerged, Jillian did start to have expectations, despite willing herself to deny them. When she didn't hear from him when expected, she was disappointed. But she tried to distract herself with work, with Zach, or with one of the zillion projects from her health, wealth, and happiness lists that she was working on at home to keep from feeling lonely when she was alone.

She started relying on his emails and calls. It almost felt like he was her boyfriend, like they were a couple, though far away from each other. A call or email from him warmed her, comforted her, for hours, days even, depending on what he said. Only a handful of times did she email him first, though she always replied quickly to him. And she never called him; too risky.

She started caring about him, damn it. He got to her. She let him. She was so looking forward to seeing him again. Would it be the same?

She had jumped out of the frying pan and into the fire, from a one-night stand with a married man, to a full-blown affair. Did she have no morals? She always thought she did. Maybe she didn't. But she really and truly just didn't care that he was married. Well, she did, but only in the sense that he couldn't be hers if he was committed (legally) to someone else.

If Mary Beth was taking care of him, or if they had the kind of relationship in which he could tell her how he felt about their lack of passion, he wouldn't be spending time with Jillian. Would he? Was that the kind of excuse cheater-enablers always made?

Some may think it was because of the risk, the daring, the rebelliousness of sneaking around, of doing something you're not supposed to be doing that keeps that kind of thing exciting. Not to Jillian. She hated that she couldn't call him whenever she wanted to. She hated that she couldn't send him a good morning text or email without worrying about how it might be interpreted.

She had just never had that kind of rapport with anyone she had ever dated. Ever. She didn't have it with Peter, not even in the beginning. With every man she had been with, she'd felt guarded with her feelings, with her sexuality, like she wasn't quite safe with them. The best sex she ever had was with men she barely knew. She was self-conscious, reserved. Maybe she'd been too young, too inexperienced.

With Cam, she felt comfortable and safe in every way. She knew he was looking for sex that first night; so was she. Even the second night, sex was on their minds. And it surely continued to be. But she thought they made a connection neither one of them had counted on. She felt one, anyway. She didn't think the opportunity would ever come to find out what might have happened with Ethan if he'd given them a chance. She did know that she could not try any longer. He already felt so far away, and it had only been a few weeks since he'd "left the building." How would she feel if she saw him? What would happen? Would it be even more awkward than usual?

She knew what would happen when she saw Cam. She would run up to him, wrap her arms around his neck, and start making out with him! With Cam, she felt she could do it and not just fantasize or dream about it, like she had with Ethan. Cam told her one of the things that bothered him about Mary Beth was that she didn't act happy to see him when he got home, that she told him it took a while to get used to having him around again. Jillian knew what that rejection felt like, for sure. She promised Cam that it certainly wouldn't take her a couple days.

What was Mary Beth's problem? What was his? Why couldn't he tell her, and why couldn't she sense it? Jillian certainly knew when she and Peter stopped having sex regularly and knew that he wasn't happy. She knew she just didn't want to. And she got to a point where she would no longer force herself to try.

If Peter had made her feel like he gave a shit that she was around instead of like she was the nanny or the maid, maybe things would have been different. But he didn't. And she didn't know how to ask him in any way other than the ways she did. When she stopped feeling that he really loved her, she stopped wanting to have sex with him. Was that where Mary Beth was?

Jillian wanted to ask Cam if he'd planned that night, if he had been planning on hooking up with someone, if he had already made a conscious decision to cheat and was just looking for the right woman to cooperate, or if it was just circumstance, and he was an opportunist, and she was just irresistible.

When Jillian was with him, when she talked to him, even if he was working her, she felt happy, confident. Those two nights, he told her that she was a great kisser, that her lips were soft, that she was a gorgeous woman. Sure, they were all probably lines, but she gave the man props for delivering them with genuineness. When he said them, she felt like he meant them. When he told her he enjoyed talking to her, that he felt comfortable with her, that he valued her opinion, that he didn't want to hurt her, and that if she wanted things to be platonic between them, he would still want to be friends, she believed him. A part of her wondered if it was all just to get her back in the sack, but, of course, she ignored that part.

She was curious to see what would happen after his trip. Would he still call? Would they plan the next time they would be together? Would she cry when he left?

Thinking about him and their interactions made her feel less lonely, like maybe she wasn't alone after all. Every time she talked to him, she wanted to tell him she missed him, that she missed talking to him. But she didn't. She promised herself that she wouldn't say that unless he said it first. The problem was that she was no good with promises to herself. There was only herself to hold her accountable.

Cam had also said he was unsure of how he should be handling things. Did she believe him? She hoped he didn't expect to show up and just fall into bed together again, hang out watching TV for an hour, and then leave! No way that was going to happen. He did allude to spending the night; she hoped they would spend the night, many nights, together.

It had been more than two years since she had a man in her bed all night. When was the last time she had had one there that she enjoyed having there? Years. And years. And years. Peter liked for them to stay on their own sides of the bed. He rejected snuggling early in their relationship. With Cam, she planned to sleep naked and snuggling all night. She wanted to give Cam everything. What the hell did she have to lose? He was already married to someone else. He lived in another state. He shared custody of his daughter there. So what? He would eventually break up with her? She'd be no worse off than she was before, and neither would he.

Except for what could have been. Maybe it is sometimes for the best to never know what the potential is, what you might have had. But she decided to go for it. Her foot was in the door, and she was going to barrel through it and see what was on the other side. If it was disappointment, so what? She would move on. It certainly wouldn't be the first time.

He said he'd call when he got his rental car, and they would meet up and have dinner and hang out. Her plan instead was to pick him up, make out, go have dinner and some cocktails, maybe even watch the sunset on the beach. She was about to have the time of her life.

She had dinner with Megan that week, who was in town visiting relatives. Jillian told her all about Cam. Megan stared at Jillian, wondering who she was, she supposed, as Jillian rambled on and on about Cam and how she felt. She told her everything he'd said about his marriage and why he was cheating. Megan looked down at her plate.

"Makes one think about their own situation," she said.

"Everything OK?" Jillian asked, suddenly concerned.

"Oh, yes, definitely. But it can't hurt to check in once in a while, right?" she smiled.

Tempe told Jillian she was playing with fire—again!

"Why? Because I could get hurt? That's bullshit. That doesn't scare me. I have been through worse and made it, right?" Jillian scoffed.

"Jillian, just please be careful," she said, then let it be.

28

Cam called when he was at the airport waiting to board. He called again when he was walking through the terminal to the tram after he arrived in Tampa. He gave Jillian the name of the hotel he'd booked, just ten minutes from her condo, and asked if she would come get him there.

She called when she was pulling in, and he gave her his room number, saying he'd just walked in.

The door was blocked open, so Jillian knocked softly and pushed it open, hearing him say, "Come on in!"

Oh, that first sight of him! She caught her breath. He was even more handsome than she remembered. Had he lost a few pounds? He said he'd been working out a lot. He looked great!

He walked right over to her, their arms encircled each other, and they kissed. He groaned, his hands moved to her ass, and it was hot, and she loved it. She didn't want to stop there, but she also wanted to save it for later, back at her place, so it would have to wait. It was going to be an amazing night.

They finally tore loose from each other and, as he was unpacking, he started talking about his flight and his bags and how he had to pack a certain way. Jillian flung herself across the double bed in the small but nicely decorated room, waiting for him to finish. She asked about dinner, what he wanted, and he said maybe something on the beach. Perfect! They would go to a great place in St. Pete Beach, a three-story restaurant and rooftop bar, The Hurricane, perfect for the sunset.

Jillian drove, since she knew where they were going, and they enjoyed the thirty-minute drive over Tampa Bay. They talked the whole way about work, what had been going on, what his trip agenda was. He was wearing shorts, a T-shirt, and flip-flops. Perfect. So handsome. So sexy.

She managed to find a parking space, checked her makeup in the mirror and got out her lip gloss, then turned to him and said, "Kiss me again, you, before I put more of this stuff on." And he did.

But there was a little nagging voice in her head already. He had been unpacking in the hotel room. He didn't touch her on the drive over. Maybe they were in a readjustment period after all. Maybe he had to get used to having her around again.

They made their way up to the second-floor restaurant, climbing the winding concrete stairway after waiting too long for the elevator, him climbing up behind her as she wondered if he was looking at her ass. He rushed to open the door for her on the landing.

They were seated, ordered, and had dinner. They made a lot of eye contact, but there was not a lot of touching. Jillian reasoned it was because they were in public and he had his wedding ring on, and she was obviously not wearing one.

Then, he dropped the bomb.

"There's danger, you know, in what we're doing," he said.

"What do you mean? What kind of danger?" she asked.

"Danger to my daughter," he answered.

Jillian wanted to make sure she understood him perfectly, so she asked him how.

"There's a danger that we could fall in love."

He smiled and chuckled as he said it. Danger that they could fall in love.

What was that, something to make her feel better? Like he could fall in love with her? What was he trying to say?

"I am concerned about how it will affect my daughter. I need to do what's right for her."

"Of course you do. It's all your decision, Cam. I don't have anything to lose here, and you have everything, so it really is up to you."

He nodded, looking down at his plate instead of at her.

They changed the subject, finished eating, tried to laugh. The rapport was still there, like they had known each other for years. Maybe they knew each other in a former life. It was enjoyable, but what she really wanted was to be touching him, for that intimacy.

He paid the check. "Let's go up to the rooftop and watch the sun set over the beach," she suggested.

"Sounds great, let's go." He smiled. They climbed up another concrete staircase to the deck and found a couple of front-row seats for the sunset. The humidity was at its peak and it was still super hot, but she hoped that being on the beach in the evening would at least provide a breeze, and it did. She kept having to brush her hair out of her face while Cam was at the bar getting a couple of beers.

"You know," he said softly, handing her a cold beer in a flimsy plastic cup, "you have got it all going on over here. The way you look, your hair blowing in the breeze. You certainly have got it all going on."

"Thank you," she replied quietly, smiling, pulling another lock of hair away from her eyes. Maybe things would go well that night, after all.

They drank their beer.

"So what's up with Jack? Has he come on to you again?" he asked, chuckling, leaning one elbow on the wall.

"No. Things are definitely uncomfortable between us, or at least on my part. I used to have so much respect for him, but the past couple years—between that incident and his failure to push Delta—has diminished that quite a bit. I mean, he is my boss. What am I supposed to do? Have a 'talk' with him?" she chuckled.

"I guess not," he replied quietly. "But, speaking of talks, I finally tried to have a talk with Mary Beth. I don't know how successful it was, but it was a start."

Her chest gave a squeeze. "What did you say to her? How did she respond?" she asked, putting her good-friend hat on.

He sighed. "I told her that I really need passion in our relationship, and she pretty much admitted that she'd cut me off.

She said some things that sounded more like excuses, but at least it was a start. We did end up having sex that night, so, that's progress, I guess."

An elephant sat on Jillian's chest. The voices in her head were getting louder, and her mood started changing, hope diminishing, her dreams for the evening—for them—beginning to sink with the setting sun. "What were her excuses?" she managed.

"I'd been thinking that maybe she had stepped out on me, and I happened to mention it to one of our friends one night when I'd had too much to drink. She told Mary Beth, who then felt like I didn't trust her. But I'm not sure I buy it. The timing of it just doesn't make any sense to me. And why wouldn't she say anything to me about it? Anyway, I don't expect this is the last of it, but it's at least out there now."

He sounded sad and rejected. Dejected. His eyes had dimmed a bit as he spoke. Rejection, even if only perceived, was hurtful to everyone, but to adoptees it was especially painful, considering the people who conceived them, those who were supposed to love them the most, rejected them the first chance they got. Not knowing what their reasons were for doing so only added to any feelings of inadequacy they had, because they made up their own reasons.

She smiled at him, trying to encourage him. "Good for you. I'm proud of you for taking that step and trying to do something to improve the situation." But her heart was breaking for him, and for herself. How could she have not expected this?

"I really am just concerned about my daughter and about how this would affect her. She has a stable environment with us that she doesn't have with her mother, and I want to be able to give her that. She and Mary Beth are really bonded."

"Well, like I said, Cam, it's your decision. We both have to live with whatever we do, whatever we've done. Of course, I want to be with you. But I will respect your decision."

Why did she say these things when she didn't really mean them? And when she didn't know if she would really be able to follow through? Because it was the right thing to say, she guessed. What she really wanted to do was stand up, stomp her feet, cry, and yell, "Pick me! Pick me!" But, of course, she did no such thing. The voices, however, were screaming.

He got up to get a couple more beers, and she pulled him back. "The sun's about to set; I don't want you to miss it." He stood there with her. He didn't put his arm around her, didn't hold her hand. But they did talk about the sunset and the clouds, and how he couldn't see such a wide stretch of the horizon in Atlanta. It was beautiful. But no touching, no romantic kiss, at sunset.

Not good. They were in public, and he was nervous. Or maybe it was much, much more.

When they finally decided to leave, with Jillian saying they needed to drive home while they were still able, she asked if he wanted to walk out onto the beach. They took the staircases in reverse, and he did finally take her hand as they walked down the sidewalk under the streetlights. As they passed by the patio section of the restaurant, they heard a server ask, "So, have you made up your mind yet?"

They looked at each other in disbelief and cracked up laughing.

They crossed over to the beach side and took their shoes off on the boardwalk, walking out onto the sand barefooted. They tried the water, and he was surprised by the warmth of it. They talked about the sand and the ocean, what was in the dark waters. Jillian pointed out some spots on the horizon where she could see that it was raining. He was worried that they would get caught in it, but she knew it was too far away.

They walked back up the sand to a bench and sat down. She put her legs up over his and they kissed. It was so nice, so romantic.

She felt at that moment that she could fall in love with him, that maybe she already had.

But it didn't last. They got up, and he drove her car back, with her directing him to her place without asking him until they were almost there if he wanted to come over. But he said of course he did, he wanted to see her place, hang out, so they went.

She gave him the nickel tour, and he commented on how nice everything was, with its rich burgundy and brown and orange decor, so comfortable and homey.

He asked to use the bathroom, and Jillian ran to hers while he was in the hall bath, checking her hair and blotting the glow from the humidity off her face. Then she went to the kitchen and grabbed a beer from the fridge and decided not to get a second. He came out, sat down on her camel-colored leather couch with her, and asked where his beer was. "I didn't want to assume you would be staying long enough to drink one, but I will be happy to get you one if you'd like."

"Well, if they're just in the fridge, I can help myself."

Jillian got up. "You're my guest. I'll get it."

They sat on the couch and talked some more. Again, they rehashed "the decision." She kept telling him it was up to him, but she was willing him to go for it, even though she knew it was not the right thing for him to do. She had her feet up on the ottoman, and he threw his legs over hers. She traced the outline of his kneecap as they talked, and he told her about a client he had from California. Cam and his boss went out with her one night, and she and Cam were dancing a lot, but even though it got "pretty flirty" (in Cam's words), she said she wouldn't have sex with him because he was married. Over the next few months, she made some overtures, and he became uncomfortable. "Kind of like I am now," he said.

Jillian quickly removed my hand from his knee, as if it had burned her. "Sorry." She was immediately unsure of herself, confused.

"Do you have any music?" he asked. Did she? She had a playlist she'd made just for this very night.

He used the bathroom again, and she jacked it up in her bedroom, where her speakers were. He hesitantly came in and sat next to her on the end of her queen bed, with his feet on the floor.

"Jilly, I don't know what's going to happen. I don't know if things will take two months or ten years to figure out, but I have to feel like I have done everything I can to make my marriage work, and I don't feel like I've done that, yet."

She just nodded, looking down.

"I really expected Mary Beth to say she wanted out, but she didn't. Maybe you and I will have a chance someday, but I know people who have been in our situation and have had affairs. Their marriages have broken up, and they've tried to have a relationship, but they don't trust each other."

Jillian smiled. "Are you asking me to wait for you?"

He laughed and said no, that if she told him she had found Mr. Right, he would be totally happy for her. "I just feel it will be easier and better for us to end this now."

"So, you want me to take you back to your hotel?"

"Yeah, I think that's what I'm saying."

"OK. Let's go right now." *Before I make an even bigger fool of myself.*

She found her shoes. She was destroyed. Tears started leaking down her cheeks. She tried to hide them from Cam, but he saw them on their way to the front door.

"Wait wait wait," he said gently, as he pulled her back, sitting down on the entryway chair and pulling her onto his lap.

"Why are you crying?" he asked softly, pleadingly. She couldn't talk, fearing that all that would come out would be a sob. "Please, tell me. This is what I did not want to happen. I so did not want you to be hurt."

"I am hurt. I am rejected. I feel like I'm losing something." She was quivering, trying to hold it in.

"Please, please don't feel rejected. I want you so badly. Ninety-nine-point-nine percent of me wants to be with you right now, but my head is warning me off." He was stroking her knee with his thumb.

"I do feel proud of you," she said. "But, I feel terrible for myself."

He sighed. "Thank you so much for saying that. You've been coaching me, encouraging me to work on my marriage. That means so much to me." His arms were finally around her, where she wanted them to be all night, for the last few weeks, for her entire life.

"I just felt like I could say anything to you, do anything with you, and now that's lost."

"You can say anything…" he trailed off, knowing what she meant.

"Can you tell me what happened? When you decided?"

"Well, just when I was in the bathroom, my head took control. When we were together, it was really an in-the-moment time for me, and so much is going on in my head now. I am so messed up right now."

She got up. He held her hand as they went to the car. She let him drive again, giving him directions as they went. He asked her if she still wanted to go to dinner the next night, and she said she did.

"I still want to be friends, you know."

Tears started running down her face again. He held her hand. He asked her a question she couldn't answer because she was again afraid a sob would betray her. He didn't ask again, he just drove.

When he pulled up to the hotel, he asked if she wanted to come up so they could talk some more, and she said no, it would be best if they didn't. They got out of the car, and he held the door for her as she got into the driver's seat, then kissed her gently on the lips.

"Call me after your meeting tomorrow, and we'll make plans."

"Sure thing. You OK?"

She nodded and tried to smile. He walked backward a few steps after shutting the door, looking in at her, smiled, then turned and walked away.

She cried all the way home. She slept about two hours the whole night. But he was coming in to One Metro for a meeting in the morning, and she had a conference to attend—one where Jack would be present—so she had to go in. Great. She was tired, depressed, and hung over, but she got up, showered, dressed, and made it in almost on time.

She stopped at security and asked them to call her when Cam Taylor arrived, and to ask him to wait in the lobby for her. When they called, she went down to meet him. He smiled when he saw her. He looked so handsome in his suit and tie.

"Hey there," he said, as she led him through the security doors and into the elevator. "God, you look amazing," he said, smiling as the doors closed.

"Thank you. You clean up pretty well yourself." She wanted to touch him, kiss him, hold him so badly she ached.

"What a night, huh? Pretty intense." He was still smiling, but talking softly, and she thought she could see the sadness in his eyes again, despite the smile.

"Yeah. I hardly slept at all. Too much beer. But I wanted to see you this morning, make sure you were OK." She smiled and winked at him.

"I didn't sleep well, either, but I'm OK. You?" He stopped smiling and cocked his head a bit to one side.

"Yeah," she managed, just as the elevator stopped and the doors opened on her floor. "I have to go get ready for a meeting," she said, pushing the button for his floor. He stuttered something, obviously tense, distracted, and she gave him a little wave as the doors closed.

She headed straight for the restroom, worried that she was going to either throw up or start bawling, but she did neither. She went back to her desk and cleaned up emails until meeting time. She couldn't think, couldn't concentrate. She kept spacing out. She went to the conference and tried not to meet Jack's eyes. She couldn't even hear what the others were saying. She barely contributed.

Afterward, she told Candace she wasn't feeling well and was going home.

"Yes ma'am!" she said, staring at Jillian, knowing better than to ask.

She cried the whole way home again. When she got there, she really let herself go for a while, then tried to calm herself down. She cleaned up and changed her clothes, then texted Cam (assuming that his meeting was over), asking how it went.

"Really well!" he texted back.

She crawled into bed and slept for a couple of hours, got up, ate a Pop-Tart, drank some water, took some Tums and Tylenol, and lay down on the couch. She contemplated tossing some pennies to ask the I Ching what she should do, but she was afraid of what it would tell her.

At about four o'clock, she started freshening up for dinner. She wasn't sure what time he would call, but she was just dozing off on the couch again when he texted and asked if she could pick him up.

Instead of rushing right out again, she made him wait for a little while. When she did finally walk into the lobby, he was reading the paper.

She drove, and they decided to go to Outback, which she knew would be packed.

He finally said, "Oh, I could have driven! Sorry!"

But she told him she didn't mind. "Take a load off, bug guy!" She gently gave him a punch on the bicep. Any excuse to touch him. But she did note to herself that she had pulled back, either in trying to respect his decision or to protect herself, or both, but that the walls were up.

He told her about his meetings and repeated that he hadn't slept well. "There's no reason you shouldn't have," she offered.

"That was pretty heavy, intense, last night."

"I know, but you should have a clear conscience. You did the right thing."

"Thank you for saying that, for being so understanding."

"That's what friends are for, right? Don't worry about me. I'm a big girl. I'll be over it in no time." She smiled.

"You just have to get under someone else, right?" He smiled.

Hm. Maybe he wasn't so happy about that prospect.

Luckily, they found a close parking spot and made their way in, him rushing to open the door for her again. They sat in a booth in the bar. She ordered water, and he ordered an iced tea. No beers that night! They had a nice time talking about work and their aspirations. They joked about starting a business together; he said they should do it. They talked some more about Delta, and how Ethan had essentially bailed before he left. Maybe Cam could help. Or maybe, again, she was just inventing a reason to connect, throwing out another sticky thread in one more relationship web she was trying to spin.

After dinner, he asked if there was an ice cream shop nearby, and she knew of two, so they went on their way.

"Thank you again for dinner. I'd give you a big kiss, but I don't want to make you uncomfortable," she said, teasing. He smacked her thigh and gave her a look. Ha! The sarcasm was back; her defense when she was hurting.

They had ice cream, and it was fun, and he told her again that she looked great, and that she looked amazing that morning, just as she did then, and that was why he wanted to go out instead of stay in, that he didn't know if he could resist, be as strong, again. She just smiled.

In his hotel lot, she pulled into a spot so they could say their goodbyes. "Thank you again for being so generous with me, so understanding," he said.

"Cam, I knew this would end. You have a wife, a daughter, your whole life, your family, your job, everything, there, and I am just a woman hundreds of miles away. I can't compete with that. I knew I would lose. I just didn't expect it to happen so soon."

He was looking down, nodding his head. He didn't respond right away. When he did, it was very softly, almost a whisper. "I know. I didn't either. I just really think it will be easier this way."

"I know. The whole 'let's be friends' thing is so cliché, but I hope you were being genuine about that," she said, still steady.

"I was. I hope you were, too." He was staring at her.

She was still shockingly dry-eyed, which told her that she truly had shut down. "I am. Hey, enjoy the rest of your trip, OK? Good luck getting all your paperwork done tonight," she said.

He hugged her. A long, strong hug. He thanked her again. He hugged her again. He kissed her on the lips. He got out of the car, looked in at her once, and walked away.

As soon as she pulled away, the dam broke again. She cried all the way home.

She slept poorly, waking often from confusing and unsettling dreams. She turned to Kate again for guidance. She had told her that Ethan was not for her. She hoped she would help with Cam.

Maybe she would if Jillian promised to listen to her this time.

She called in sick the next day. She hadn't called in sick once during the whole divorce because she would have just been living in her car, driving around, unable to hide from her life, either at the office or at home. Now, she had the luxury of locking herself in the condo, her kingdom, her cave, where the only thing she had to fear was herself.

She alternated between the couch and bed that day—thinking thinking thinking. Replaying everything in her head. It was overcast and rainy out, the perfect weather for pajamas and her mood.

She hadn't asked Cam if he was still in love with Mary Beth; if he thought she was in love with him; if he was trying to make his marriage work solely for the benefit of his daughter; or if his marriage was what he truly wanted. Jillian wanted to know if he got over her because he got back under his wife, and if they hadn't had that conversation, and they hadn't had sex that night, would he have been with her. She wanted to know if there was something that changed from that first passionate kiss when she walked into his hotel room, to when he could have followed through on it, if there was something she did, or said, that changed his mind, or had he arrived knowing they wouldn't be intimate? Did the guilt get to him? Did she turn him off? Did he really reconsider? Did he really think that if he was with her, he would be getting in deeper—too deep? She tried to convince herself it didn't matter. She had tortured herself with questions when she was obsessed with Ethan and never got any answers, and now they didn't matter to her at all. One day these questions wouldn't matter, either.

Monica and Tempe both called her, and Tempe texted, too. She didn't answer. They were both going to be ticked, but she really didn't want to talk to anyone, let alone someone who could say they told her so. Of course, she sent Cam a text to make sure he'd gotten home OK, and he replied that his flight was perfect, but he'd kept waking up the night before worrying that he would be late. He asked her if she was OK, which she assured him she was.

She didn't know what to expect. She wanted to ask him, but she was withdrawing from him and didn't want to dwell and seem needy, so she didn't. She decided the best thing would be to expect nothing. She would try to expect to never see nor hear from him again.

29

I want a do-over," she confessed to Tempe at lunch in the cafe the next day, finally together long enough to talk about it. "I am trying to learn not to assume anything, but not making assumptions means you have to have the courage to ask, and sometimes that's hard," she explained.

"It also means thinking on my feet, with clarity, perspective, which is also difficult when I'm so emotional," she said. She kept playing the whole thing out in her head, trying to figure out what she should have done differently.

She thought she owed Cam an apology. *Like when I owed Ethan an apology?* Cam had told her that if she ever decided she wanted their relationship to be platonic, that was OK with him, he would respect that, and he would still want to be friends. And she told him that worked both ways. Yet, when he did try to tell her that was what he wanted, she didn't clue in early enough, or respect what he was telling her.

"I was just so confused. All the messages I had been getting were telling me that he didn't want to end our physical relationship. However, I could have been reading things the way I wanted to. I should have asked," she continued. "I'm confused about when things changed, and why. I totally understood and respected the reasons he gave me at the time. I was just not sure I completely believed them. Did he know before he got there that he wanted to be just friends? Was it because he had sex with his wife and felt like they were back on track? If he didn't want me to touch him, why did he kiss me, or let me kiss him? Why did he hold my hand? Why did he even come over? Was he just playing me? Has he been playing me this whole time?"

God, so many questions, all of them tugging on her, chattering in her head, standing on her shoulder squawking in her ear. *Leave me alone!* She stopped; she was out of breath and getting too worked up. She looked around the café to see if anyone had noticed her agitation. Everyone seemed to be involved in their own conversations.

Tempe stared at her, shaking her head, looking kind of disgusted.

"Well, don't make it out like you did something wrong, like it was your fault," she accused. "It was not! He said it wasn't you, and it wasn't. Everything you've told me points to the fact that he was confused. He wanted you; he wanted to have sex. Of course, he did, he's a man! He's back in his wife's bed, so he thinks they still have a chance. I've been there. You have no idea what I went through with Mark. So many times, I thought, 'What the hell am I doing?'"

And now Tempe and Mark were getting married! They'd lived two thousand miles apart, she was married when they met, and Mark told her over and over he couldn't leave his kids, they needed him. Yet, there he was. He left his job, the only home he'd ever known, his family, all his friends, and his children to move to Tampa, to be with Tempe. Jillian knew this. Why wouldn't she think that the same could happen to her? She shouldn't have, though. She had never been the princess in the fairy tale. Her wishes didn't come true.

"I just feel like the balance of power shifted. In Atlanta, I felt I was in control. He wanted me. As soon as I walked into his hotel room in Tampa, I knew it had changed. I knew that because I had started to have feelings for him, he had the advantage. It terrified me. I wasn't confident. Then I felt rejected and dejected because he didn't have sex with me. But he still talked to me. He was open with me. He told me what he was thinking, what he was afraid of; he asked me questions, he asked me how I felt, as if he gave a shit."

"Yeah," Tempe replied. "I don't get the no sex thing."

"The damn thing is that I just keep trying to find the signs, the ones that should warn me off, tell me that he is not who I think he is. Like the signs I saw, but ignored, with Ethan, even with Peter, the signs that would make it easier for me to let go, to move on, to realize that he isn't who I think he is or want him to be—and I just can't find them."

Tempe looked at Jillian with her eyebrows raised. "Really? You mean besides the fact that he cheated on his wife?"

Jillian's heart skipped a beat. "I can hardly judge him for that," she replied. "Does a small part of me feel like he was working me? That the whole thing was just an ego trip for him? Or that maybe it had been revenge sex because he thought his wife had cheated on him, and since he'd evened the score, he felt better? Or that maybe once he saw me again, he didn't want me anymore? That was the possibility that would devastate me the most, that he saw something in me that turned him away. That I turned him away, and he said all those things just to make me feel better, like it wasn't me, that he hadn't used me, maybe to ease his own conscience."

"All of those things could be true. They are not necessarily in conflict. Except for the part that you did something. You definitely did not do anything wrong. He still loves his wife."

Tempe was firm in having Jillian's back, that was for sure, but that she did not want to hear.

"He never said it was because he loves her, or is in love with her, and wants to be with her. And I didn't ask him."

"You should have," she said.

"I know."

Jillian ate a few bites of her sandwich in silence. She did expect that Cam would drift away from her. But she felt it would happen after his trip here. He would come and they would have an amazing couple of nights together, and she would cry after he left, and then they would slowly drift apart, him calling her less and less often, and her refusing to call him, and eventually she would stop crying because he'd abandoned her, like everyone else.

She had told him that she was proud of him for not having sex with her. No matter how rejected she felt, he was right. He did the right thing. And even if it was a line that it would be easier if they ended that part of their relationship because it was too dangerous, that was the truth, too. It was hard enough. If they had been lovers when he was there, if he had spent the night with her, with his arms wrapped around her, naked in her bed, she would have completely fallen in love with him.

She was not sure that she hadn't already. She felt so safe with him. He was so smart, and well spoken, and he could talk to her about things, about work, about being adopted, and he got it.

She knew, though, there had to be something else going on, just like there had been with Ethan.

There always was. She decided to keep her eyes and ears open for the signs and pay attention to them for once. That was, if they even kept in touch.

"What I do know is that I can't wait for him," she finally said. "I won't cry over him for months. I'm lonely. I'm alone. I'm so tired of being afraid to do anything about it. For months now, I've felt as if I'm drifting, not really making any decisions. If Zach is home, I ask him what he wants to do, and that's what we do. At work, I'm driven by meeting schedules, deadlines, emails, and my own conscience to do the best job I can, no matter what. You've been driving my personal life. If you ask me to do something, I usually do it. Otherwise, I just don't feel like doing anything, I don't want to do anything, and I don't. I just come home from work, force myself to eat, and watch TV. It gives me a lot of time to think and obsess."

"You are right about that. If all you do when you're by yourself is think, you shouldn't spend so much time alone. You think way too much. You need to start doing more. I know it's hard, but you just have to." Tempe scraped the last bits of her yogurt out of its plastic cup.

"If Cam isn't the one for me, I need to find someone a lot like him, if I ever get around to it. Someone who will draw me out, and ask me how I feel, and listen, and tell me I'm gorgeous, and how much he wants me. I thought our connection was real—maybe it is, was—but maybe I don't trust him after all." Jillian looked down at what was left of her sandwich. She wasn't hungry. "I think, though, I just don't trust myself anymore."

"Why the hell not? You can't see inside other people's minds or lives and know what's going on, where they're coming from! It's impossible!" Tempe was mad now, disappointed in Jillian for her lack of confidence.

"Well, I think either my instincts are failing or I'm terrified that the part of me that is suspicious is right. I don't want to believe in the part that gnaws at me, saying that Cam is just the kind of person who is open and makes a lot of friends, and that the bond we formed so quickly, the kind that I make so rarely, is an everyday occurrence and therefore meaningless to him. I just felt so safe with him in every way, and I haven't felt that in a long, long time. In fact, I'm not sure I have ever felt so safe and at home with another human being. That's what makes me question myself."

"I understand that. Just like with Ethan, though, you don't have any perspective right now. Trust yourself and give yourself some time and distance. What has really happened here will become much clearer."

30

Forrest stood in the doorway of Jillian's office with a glass vase overflowing with gorgeous yellow roses. He was in his usual khakis, short-sleeved oxford, and penny loafers. He smiled at her but had a slight blush on his pale, puffy cheeks. They hadn't spoken much since he offered his counseling services so long ago. She spoke to him when she needed to for business purposes, and he must have been doing the same.

"Oh, for me? Where did they come from?" she asked, sitting up straighter. *Please don't say from you, please please please.*

"Happy birthday! They're from me! Enjoy!" he said, setting the vase on her conference table, looking as proud as a kindergartner giving his first teacher an apple.

"Well thank you!" she said. "They're beautiful!" They were. He smiled smugly and walked away. Thankfully.

Jillian was admiring the flowers, enjoying their scent, when Candace appeared in the doorway. "Oh my gosh, they are gorgeous, Jillian! Who from, am I allowed to ask?" she said, as she bent over them and took a deep breath.

"Forrest," Jillian deadpanned; the smile gone from her face. *Let's see what reaction that gets!*

Candace stood straight up, and her head spun toward Jillian. "Forrest? Our Forrest?" she said, tilting her chin down to look at Jillian over the top of her reading glasses, eyebrows raised.

"Yup, that one," Jillian said, now frowning. "You want them?" she asked.

"Nope." Candace turned and walked out without another word.

After Jillian told the third visitor that the roses were from Forrest, she had to get rid of them. She didn't need any rumors flying around. Really, though, it was probably already too late. She felt like a hypocrite, keeping them from someone she had so little respect for—someone she did not want to be seen as aligned with in any way whatsoever. She had enough issues.

So, she picked up the whole vase full, a little regretfully considering how gorgeous they were, and decided to just set the whole thing in the kitchen garbage can. But on her way, she ran into Jack's lovely wife. Julie was much younger than he was, apparently had been his secretary at his last firm. She was cute, and blond and apparently a handful. She couldn't imagine Jack settling for a woman who wasn't.

"Oh, Jillian, those are beautiful! What's the occasion? Where are you going with them?"

"Oh, thank you! My birthday. They are beautiful, but they're making my allergies act up. Would you like to take them? I hate to just throw them away," she lied smoothly.

"Really? Oh, I'd love to! You can't just throw them out! Really?" She was all gaga. And Jillian would score some points.

"They're all yours, then. Enjoy!" Pay it forward, right? She set them down on the end table next to the chair Julie was parked in, turned, and strode back to her office with a smile on her face.

Forrest was still kissing Jack's ass.

She didn't want flowers anyway. Yeah, it was her birthday, and just about the one-year anniversary of the divorce, and what would have been her and Peter's ten-year wedding anniversary. Whoop-de-fucking-do.

She did get a birthday card from Cam, but she hadn't talked to him in days. She got back from lunch and had a happy birthday email from him. She emailed him back, telling him she was just going to dinner with Zach, and mentioned that she had some things to dialog with him about when he had the time, no rush. He emailed back that he would call her on his way to pick up Lauren, his daughter. Wow. She wasn't expecting him to say he would call that day. Of course, he could have picked up the phone and called right then, and she only suspected he didn't because he suspected that she wanted a serious talk.

For the rest of the afternoon, she practiced what she was going to say to him. She even typed it out so she could get things in the right order, say each measured word at the right time, not have to backtrack, like writing a letter, or a speech. She shook with nerves, so rare in anticipation of an interaction with him. She didn't know if he would be OK with her having that conversation with him. He said she could say anything, right? If he meant that, he'd be fine.

She was still pondering whether or not she believed in god or the Universe, but she wondered: if they did exist, why were they punishing her so? She didn't understand what she'd done to deserve such misery and pain, why she would be given such a small taste of the kind of man she had yearned for her whole life, only to have him snatched away from her without him ever really being hers.

Being shown the kind of love that she dreamed about—the man who would make her feel whole, like her true self, safe and alive, and like she really mattered—only to have him leave her because he was afraid of falling in love with her.

She mourned what could have been, the life they could have had together. Gone, before it was.

She wanted to believe that the Universe supported her and wanted her to be happy. She almost believed that when she was anticipating Cam's visit. She almost believed that she had finally been offered up what she had been looking for, without knowing it, when she least expected it.

And then it was crash and burn time. It terrified her to think that Mary Beth would want a baby and that he would give her one, and Jillian would lose him forever. She still hoped he would want to be hers, that he would choose her. She didn't expect him to, but she didn't understand why she was given him, and then was asked to give him up so completely.

She couldn't be just his friend. She debated whether to wait for the opportunity to tell him how she really felt, or to step out on a limb and go for it, realizing there was nothing left to lose. Should she wait for him to come to her, realizing that might never happen? Or should she approach him, tell him, and let the chips fall where they may? What was the right decision? Did he deserve to know? Or did she deserve to keep her feelings to herself? Again, she was weighing the odds of what could happen if she did, or what could happen if she didn't.

She was going to take a risk. She was going to throw out that four-letter word. Not in the context that she felt it for him, or he felt it for her, but in that she didn't think he felt it for Mary Beth. That was truly what she wanted to say to him for his own good, to make him think about it; but of course, she also wanted to find out whether he did love Mary Beth, and that was a safe way to get it out there.

She would let him off the hook, not make him answer her, for sure. She wasn't ready to push things that far. But it would be a start.

She also planned to find out a little more about what happened when he was here and what had happened at home since. She was trying to go back in time to those first two nights and the first couple of phone calls, when their conversations were more about where he was and her offering guidance to him without emotion. They were just friends, after all, and that was what friends did for each other, without getting their own emotions all tied up and invested in the situation, right?

He called ten minutes before five, and she was ready. He asked if he was calling too early. Of course not. Could he ever really call at a bad time?

"No, it's perfect. Thank you for calling, Cam. I know you don't have a lot of time."

"No, it's OK."

"Good. Well, I certainly don't want a total rehash of what happened when you were here, but there are a few things that I really want to say to you if that's OK."

"Sure, go ahead." He sounded cautious.

"First, I want to apologize for putting so much pressure on you."

"Oh, stop…"

"Please, let me finish. It wasn't right. We had an agreement, and you tried to tell me several times, and I just wasn't getting it. However, I do think that it was maybe because I was as confused as you were. I mean, the implication had been that we were going to be together, based on things that you had said. And the kiss we had when I came to pick you up? And that you let me kiss you again, and you held my hand, and you told me how great I looked and everything? That really made me feel something different from what you were saying to me. I was really getting mixed signals. I hope you will forgive me for pressuring you and then being such a brat about it when you wanted to go."

"My head was really so messed up…"

She interrupted him. "There's more, if you can stand it."

"Sure, go on."

"There is something I want to thank you for. I feel I'm finally getting the courage up to stop living in fear of asking for what I want, because of how I might be perceived or what I might be giving up by going out on a limb. The past couple of years have been extremely difficult on me, and I've done somewhat of a retreat. You may not understand how you have helped change that, but what has happened between us has started me on that path, and because you've told me I can say anything to you, I'd like to practice, if that's OK."

"Yes, please, go ahead."

She imagined he was terrified at that point, that he thought she was going to say she was in love with him. He would be much relieved when she was finished.

"OK. I totally understand and respect where you are and the decisions you've made. It tells me a lot about the kind of person you are. Whatever happens, know that I will always respect you for that. I know I don't know the whole story of Cam, or Cam and Mary Beth, but regardless, I respect you for not going for it with me, whatever your reasons. I know saying some of these things may turn you away from me. I know this may make things less comfortable between us, as friends, and that maybe you won't even want to be friends with me anymore, but, in my newfound courage, I want to tell you that, as your friend, I want to make sure that you've thought about what you're doing and why you're doing it. If you feel that staying with Mary Beth for Lauren's sake is what you need to do, I respect that. But make sure you are not sacrificing too much of yourself. One thing you have never said to me is that you are still in love with her and want to spend the rest of your life with her, or that you want to make it right because you know you're supposed to be with her. Maybe you do feel that way, and maybe that is what you want, I don't know. But I do feel that if that were true, you wouldn't have been with me, even if it was just a momentary lapse, or revenge, or I was just too irresistible to you—ha ha—or whatever it really was. It seems to me that you two are good friends; and a husband and wife should be. But what you said is critical, that you are lacking passion, and if you can't get that back, you are making a huge sacrifice. As your friend, I'm telling you that you deserve passion, Cam. I don't just mean sex. You deserve the kind of relationship that makes you feel happy, and good, and positive. Not one that makes you doubt and feel bad about yourself. I also worry that if you're staying because of Lauren, that you will eventually grow to resent one or the other of them, or both, and you will give up the strength you demonstrated when you were here and start living a double life. Which, sooner or later, will take you down."

Silence.

"I'm not asking you to respond to any of this. I know you didn't ask my opinion, but I did promise to be your friend and, over the past couple of weeks, these are the thoughts that keep bubbling up, that I have hoped to share with you. OK?" She felt relieved that she had delivered her speech, but anxious about how he would react.

"What you've said is pretty much dead on," he finally replied. "You've nailed it. I know, and we're still working through it. She has tried to turn the tables on me saying that I don't listen to her, but I don't know. I think maybe it's improving, but I don't really know for sure."

"Well, what else has happened lately? Will you tell me?"

"Well, she's initiated sex a couple of times, but now I really feel like I'm just being serviced, you know? Like she's doing it out of duty or something and there's not really any desire there. I don't know if it's just a lose-lose situation. She still is just not acting thrilled to see me when I get home and that really bothers me. But I do want you to know something else, Jillian. Please don't ever think that I wasn't with you because I didn't want to be. I am so attracted to you. Please don't think it was that. After I left there, I realized I did really want to be with you and truly wondered why I didn't just go for it again." He chuckled.

"I would have gone for it, too, you know. But you still made the right decision. And thank you for telling me that. You didn't have to say that." She was dying inside.

"I still don't know what's going to happen. But I do really appreciate you pouring that out to me."

"Well, I practiced it. I had a lot to say. Did I sound rehearsed?" She laughed.

"No, not at all. You sounded strong, really strong."

Funny how many people told her how strong she was, yet she never felt that way.

She could hear noises in the background, like he had arrived at wherever he picked his daughter up. Time was short.

"Well, please know I care about you, Cam, that's why I wanted to say these things to you. And I hope you know you can say anything to me, too, and if you want to talk about anything or try to work anything out or, whatever, you know how to reach me."

"Yeah, I do. Expect a call."

They said their good-byes.

Well, he didn't retreat. Did she feel any better? Yes. Did she feel relieved and proud of herself for telling him all of that? Yes. Did she want to tell him that she was in love with him and that she wanted them to be together? More than ever.

Jesus, why do I have to be so fricking life-or-death dramatic about everything? I have the patience of a gnat. She wanted to get back to looking at the bright side of things, like she used to. If the Universe truly did support her and want her to be happy, then she needed to believe that and look for the ways It was doing that. Instead of feeling like she was looking at her potential happiness through a glass window, not being allowed to touch it, she should find the happiness in what she had, right?

Cam was a gift to her. He appeared at just the right time to save her from herself. He saved her from the fantasy of Ethan, helping her to move on from that unhealthy infatuation. He improved her self-confidence. And, most importantly, he gave her hope that there was a Mr. Right out there for her.

The new question was, what were the odds? What were the odds that she would meet a man like him at all? Were the odds against that type of thing happening, or in favor of it? She'd lived on the planet for forty years and had never met a man like him. Not as an acquaintance, not as a friend, and certainly not as a lover. She had wondered if men like him existed. She did find one, finally— were there more? There had to be, right?

She didn't hear anything from him for a couple weeks. She finally emailed him after struggling with it for quite a while because she kept promising herself she wouldn't. And she had told Monica that she wasn't contacting him first.

She emailed him a book review she'd been saving. Nice, safe topic.

He emailed back ten minutes later, opening with "Hi stranger!" He gave her the lowdown on his schedule, who he'd been meeting with, how many trips he'd taken. And his last sentence was, "I'm going to call you later this week, if that's cool."

She emailed him right back and worked in that his nice long drive home seemed like an opportune time to call if he had something to talk about but, of course, call any time. No response. No call that night.

Or the next.

Or the next.

At first, she thought, OK, he wants to talk about what's going on at home, with Mary Beth. Great. No big deal. That's what friends were for, and that's what she had been encouraging him to do, so what else could she expect?

Then she thought (hoped), well, maybe something had happened. Maybe she hadn't heard from him because not only had work been crazy, but home had been, too, because he'd been moving out! Too much to hope for, she supposed. If he was, why would he wait to call her, anyway?

Then it hit her: he was calling to ditch her. Again. He was calling to say, "Look, it would be best if we didn't have any contact with each other for a while." Maybe Mary Beth suspected something.

Maybe she ran across one of their emails or found Jillian's number in his call log. Maybe they were working things out and he felt guilty. Maybe they were going to try to have a baby. Maybe she was already pregnant. Maybe his boss suspected something.

She waited and wondered why he didn't call when he was traveling.

She wondered why he was waiting. God, her Tasmanian devil brain was driving her insane!

She tried to assume (stop assuming!) the simplest reason for the call, if it ever came, that he wanted to just catch up and fill her in.

She also kept expecting the worst: that they couldn't even be friends anymore. Would she have the chance to convince him they weren't doing anything wrong?

If he did ditch her, would he ever be back? She couldn't help but be hopeful that he would one day. How could he not if he felt the same way about her that she felt about him? Did he?

She talked to Tempe, who said there was no way he was going to ditch her. He had no reason to.

The first thing Monica said when she told her she had emailed him was "Why?" And not the kind of "why" that's like, oh, what did you have to tell him? More of the "why in the world did you do that?" kind of why.

Sheesh. Jillian finally told Monica she just wasn't going to talk to her about him anymore, to which Monica responded that that was only because Jillian didn't like what she had to say. Hmph. Same reason Jillian wasn't talking to Kate or the oracles.

Monica and Tempe were the two extremes of Jillian's own subconscious: Tempe on one side telling her to be confident, of course he would call, of course he wanted to be with her, and Monica on the other telling her to be totally suspicious of his motives, don't trust him, and don't make a fool of herself. Maybe they were both right.

Not like Jillian hadn't thought of all that. Not like she didn't know. Maybe she would put all that out there when or if he called, depending on how the conversation went. She toyed with ways to deliver it.

Unless you have been lying to me this whole time, you're not in love with your wife and your marriage is eventually going to fail. If you're lucky, it will be sooner rather than later, and not when I'm remarried and have ten more kids. Ha. Or...

You asshole. You have just been keeping me on the line this whole time. Has this been like some big ego trip for you or something, some game? Fuck off. Or...

I love you. I'm in love with you...

Choose me! Please choose me! For god's sake, for once, can't somebody choose me?

He didn't call. She went to a concert with Tempe and Mark that weekend. She tried to act normal, meaning she drank too much, acted wild, and hoped no one would think anything was wrong. But all she wanted to do was sit down and cry her eyes out. It was the first time he ever said he was going to do something and then didn't. The beginning, or continuation, she supposed, of "the end." She supposed they were moving toward the same thing that he and his little California friend had, talking once every few months. Was that why he told her that story? Had he been setting the expectation?

Why did she even care? Why did she care? Why did she want him so much? Why couldn't she just accept the fact that he was married, and he used her, and now he was cutting her loose? Why couldn't she just be dignified about it and say fuck off and move on?

Why didn't he call? Why didn't he? Why why why? It would have been so easy, even if he was calling to tell her he wasn't going to call anymore. Why didn't he just do it? Just cut her to the quick and get it over with?

Maybe she had to do it herself. Maybe she just had to say that he didn't have the courage to do it, so she had to assume that was why he was going to call, anyway, and let him off the hook, and just fucking move on. That was all she could do anyway until he told her otherwise.

31

Jack asked Jillian, Tom the HR guy, and a couple other senior associates to join him at a meeting with some potential new clients. After schmoozing most of the day, he announced that they were going to go on a bus tour of the city, ending at the hotel where the clients were staying, with drinks and dinner at the ritzy steakhouse inside. He sat with Jillian on the bus tour, and she did her best to keep it strictly business. Why wasn't he sitting with one of the prospects? Sheesh.

They arrived at the hotel, and she almost enjoyed the preamble of drinking and appetizers, flitting from one group to another and doing her best to avoid Jack.

At dinner, Jack was more concerned with them than with Jillian, so she chimed in occasionally and had a couple more glasses of wine, and he kept drinking his scotch, and the food was good.

Afterward, they were to retire to the bar. She'd had enough to drink at that point that she was ready to keep it going, Jack or no Jack. The bar lounge was huge, with five or six groupings of couches and overstuffed chairs, a piano, the main bar area, and some high-top tables. The seven or eight of them imbibing after-dinner drinks made their way to one of the living room setups. Even in her half-drunk state, she paused to see where Jack would sit so that she could avoid sitting next to him. However, her delay worked to a disadvantage. Although he sat in a chair, by the time she made her way in, the only spot available was the end seat on a couch right next to him.

They all continued talking about the meeting, and business, and the tour, and then started making comments about the others in the bar area around them. They were certain that the woman in the white shift and spike heels with a Middle Eastern-looking man was a high-class call girl. They peered over their drinks trying not to be obvious, but also attempting to garner evidence in support of their suspicion. None was forthcoming.

"What are you staring at?" Jack sneered at Jillian, leaning forward in his chair, his scotch in one hand. Then, to her shock, he slid his thumb up her calf. Wearing a skirt had been a major error on her part.

She moved her leg and looked across at Tom to see if he'd noticed. Tom looked Jillian right in the eye, but she couldn't discern any indication that he had.

The tux-clad server came up and asked how they were doing, and Jack ordered another scotch and "another of whatever she's drinking" before Jillian had the chance to object. A few others declined, bade their goodnights, and excused themselves. Then a couple more. Then it was just Tom, Jack, and Jillian. Jack asked her about an element of the meeting, and she started to offer her opinion when Tom stood up and said, "Sorry, I need to go. I'm just beat. Goodnight."

Jillian stopped mid-sentence, caught off guard and realizing she would be alone with Jack. She should have jumped up and said, "Me, too," but she didn't.

"Good night, old man!" Jack boomed, and, as soon as Tom neared the exit, popped off his chair and bounced onto the couch next to Jillian. She immediately moved to the front edge of the couch, prepared to spring, and continued with her answer. It was not to be, however.

Jack's hand reached out to her back and started the up-and-down thing.

"You know, I need to go, too," she stated, without looking at him, her skin crawling. And still without meeting his eyes, she stood, grabbed her purse, and walked off.

She wasn't freaking out, though. She was pissed. Un-fucking-believable. What the hell? Anyone could have seen him. He must have been wasted. What an idiot. And did Tom leave so suddenly because Jack had given him some silent signal to leave them alone? What a joke. Some HR guy, protecting her like that.

She got a cab home, leaving her car, having had too much to drink. She shook her head the whole way. She texted Cam when she got into bed. "The perv strikes again! Can't keep his hands off me! You're my witness!" It was the first time she'd ever texted him during nonbusiness hours. She hardly ever texted him at all. Too dangerous. She was wasted. She was pissed. Who gave a shit?

Cam didn't reply then, of course, but he did call first thing the next day and asked to hear the story. He laughed at how brazen Jack was. Then she asked him about why he hadn't called.

And she asked about Delta, as a diversion.

"I'm sorry, Jilly, I've been sick. And I can't really get involved with Delta right now. You know I want to support you. You know I want to help, but I just can't handle it right now," he said. "As far as Jack goes, I think you should report him," he said.

"You were sick? What's wrong? Are you OK?"

"Yes, I'm fine, just a bug. Seriously. Report him," he said.

She thought he was probably right, but she was nervous. Jack was such a prominent figure in the industry and in the community, and she was worried about how it would reflect on her.

She visited Monica and told her the story, too, and that Cam said she should report him. Monica said she'd support Jillian in whatever she decided to do, but that she should be careful, agreeing that it could boomerang and hurt Jillian more than it hurt Jack. Jillian told her that Cam said he couldn't help with Delta, either.

"Well, since we've let go of it for a little while, the tension seems to be easing, but things are reverting to the way they were before. No referrals."

"I know. I'm exhausted. I'm sick of banging my head against the wall and sick of feeling like everyone is dissing me behind my back. Maybe something else big has to change in order to tip the scales in our favor," Jillian said. She was disgusted, but she also knew that to continue to push their agenda would make life more difficult at every turn. Asking for any further support from Jack was out of the question. In fact, she was getting closer to thinking she really should report everything. What the hell. Maybe she needed another liberation. Maybe she should just quit altogether and start over somewhere else.

She sat next to Tom at a late morning meeting. When she was sure no one could overhear, she asked, "Did you see Jack slide his thumb up my leg at the bar?"

"Yes, I did. I'm so sorry. I noticed he ordered you another drink, too. I intended to stay, to not leave you alone, because I thought maybe something was going on, but I was just too beat. And I had to go take my medicine," he practically whispered.

"Well, it didn't end there. Thanks for sticking around," she said sarcastically. "Let's discuss it later."

"Of course."

That afternoon she went to Tom's office.

"What do you want me to do?" he asked.

"Well, I think I would like you to just fire a warning shot. Let him know that I said something to you," she hedged. Maybe that would be enough.

"Are you sure? Because I have to do whatever you tell me to," he said.

"I don't want to file a complaint or anything, I just want him to stop," she said. Reporting it to him was one thing. But file a complaint? Was she suicidal? Not only was he her boss, but he was also the CEO. Everyone in their industry knew him. She certainly was not well known. She'd just be a whiner who was asking for it, right? Forget it. It could be a lot worse. He could be chasing her down the hallway trying to kiss her like one of Tempe's former bosses did to her. She did file a suit against him. She lost her job. Her boss didn't.

A couple of days later, Tom walked into her office and shut the door behind him. Her throat tightened.

"Jillian, I talked with Jack. He was mortified. I think he almost started to cry. He said he never intended anything, that you are a very important part of this company, and he doesn't want you to feel uncomfortable. I don't suspect you will have any further issues," he stated.

She didn't necessarily believe those were Jack's genuine feelings or opinions, but at least it was out there, and he knew, and Tom knew. Hopefully that would be the end of it.

Her nights of crying were returning, though. The dilemmas with Cam, Jack, and Delta were piling up on missing Zach so much and feeling lonely. She wasn't talking with Monica or Tempe about Cam, either. She was feeling shut down at every turn, once again.

She tried to soothe herself, but it wasn't working. Her eyes stung the next morning and her face burned; her stomach hurt from keeping her sobs inside so the neighbors wouldn't hear. She cried at night until she was physically exhausted. Then she would close her eyes and try to soothe herself in her self-mothering way. She would imagine Cam there with her, behind her, holding her in his arms, telling her it would all be OK. She would finally start to calm down. At times she could almost physically feel him there. Nothing had ever felt so right to her before. Then she would sleep for a while.

Sometimes when she awoke, she would start crying all over again. She felt so alone. One night she had a talk with Kate. She asked her to please help if she could. She told her that if she had anything to do with bringing Cam to her, she was so grateful to her for doing that, that she felt he was a gift to her, even if it was just temporary, to help her move on to whatever was next. She was trying to convince herself because, when she allowed it to hurt, it hurt worse than the divorce did. It hurt far more than her unrequited desire for Ethan ever did, though she'd cried so many tears for him she lost count. Or maybe she just lost time.

Pulling the bandage off in one quick stroke had always seemed the wrong method to her, highly over-rated. It may get it over with faster, but it still hurt like hell. A much better option was a good soaking in warm, soapy water, contemplating the hurt beneath the healing, what it was, and what it may have become in the time it had been hidden away. As the water did its work and slowly cooled, so that you didn't even really notice the cooling, some gentle picking at the edges of the stickiness could begin, allowing the water to seep further in and loosen the next millimeter or two. Then more picking, until eventually the bandage was completely detached from the skin and the hairs on the skin and even from the wound (or former wound), and you hardly felt a thing.

In fact, you're feeling gleeful that the leech had been removed without the quick rip, the ouch, and the stinging and rubbing required of that sadistic—or masochistic, depending upon the ripper—ritual.

Cam was a gift to her. And she reasoned that if he must be taken away, she wished him to gradually fade away so that she might notice his going less. Maybe that way she would be able to fill the inevitable void in her heart and soul left by his absence with something or someone else.

Much easier to slowly, steadily, almost scientifically and calculatingly pull away, one little notch at a time, until one day she would wake up and realize he was part of her past, than cut it to the quick and risk bleeding to death.

As she drove home from the office the next day, for once willing herself not to cry instead of indulging, she talked aloud, telling herself it was worth it, there was no reason to cry, that everything would be OK, that she needed to stop being such a wuss. It was raining a bit, not enough for the wipers to come on. When she came around a bend in the road, there they were: two huge, gorgeous, full-spectrum, horizon-to-horizon rainbows. She shouted out loud, "You have got to be fucking kidding me!" And then burst into tears, anyway.

32

When Jillian was a kid, she loved rainbows. She had posters and pictures and a bunch of tchotchkes, interspersed with all her unicorns in her lavender bedroom. Well, her bedspread was lavender.

Nothing else matched, she just pretended it did. Redecorating was not in their vocabulary because it was not in their budget.

She had a black velvet poster that she'd colored, too, that she had gotten for her birthday or Christmas. She even had her lone-Christmas-present rainbow sheets (that she eventually took to college with her) and pajamas. Most adults said "Wow!" when they came in her room, making her prouder of her collection, though she knew as an adult they were probably chuckling at her.

She still loved rainbows, the promise they gave, the fact that they appeared when you least expected them, in the most unexpected places. Sometimes you really had to focus to see the range of colors and even then, some eluded our weak human eyesight. Sometimes they are so bright and bold that you wondered who had a big enough brush to paint watercolors across the sky.

A few times, rainbows had appeared when she had really needed them. The first was when her premarital relationship with Peter was reaching a breaking point. Was he ever going to ask her to marry him, or should she move on? They had a long discussion (well, long for them, meaning at least ten minutes), at the end of which he said they would be getting married. It was on a weeknight, and she was starved for dinner. She wanted to go get some fast food, and as soon as she walked out the front door, she saw it. It told her everything was going to be OK. He proposed officially, ring and all, three months later.

Another time was the morning of the final divorce mediation. She was taking Zach to school, and it was a drizzly morning, but the sun was still peeking through, so typical in Florida. She was a jangle of nerves; terrified, yet hopeful of what the day might bring. And they did reach an accord that day; she wasn't happy with it, and she supposed Peter wasn't either, but they had a signed agreement.

Tempe was helping Jillian a lot, or not, depending on how things turned out. She was encouraging Jillian to have courage, to be brave and ask for what she wanted, which is what she wanted to do, who she wanted to be—not the nervous, self-conscious, and sometimes self-defeating drama queen she so easily sunk into.

They had baseball tickets, one extra, and Tempe suggested that Jillian call Ethan and ask him to go with them. "All he can do is say no," she said. Well, duh, she knew that. She wondered if she agreed just because it was what she wanted to do anyway and she needed someone to validate her desire, or just to prove to Tempe that she wasn't chicken.

"You think too much," Tempe told Jillian in her usual direct manner. "You have got to get out of your head and out of your own way."

So, instead of hugging the trunk this time, at least she was venturing out onto the limb, even if she wasn't jumping up and down on it or hanging and swinging. She sent Ethan a text. She didn't expect a response, and if she did get one, she expected that he wouldn't want to go. And even if he did say he would go, she would expect him to cancel at the last minute with some family emergency crap, like he used to. He did reply but said that he couldn't go. "Ask again sometime." Phpht. Doubtful.

That week, she also asked Cam if he could be her date for the wedding of a co-worker she'd been invited to. She expected him to deny her, but you never know. Of course, he said there was no way. How could he possibly explain it?

She also decided that she would email Cam whenever she wanted to. She wouldn't be so bold as to call him or text him, never knowing where he was or who was with him, but she could at least email him. It was her life. She was, for once, going to try to live it on her terms.

33

It was time for one of the big annual national conventions that Jillian usually attended as a representative of the firm. She hadn't gone in two years because of the divorce. That year it was in Las Vegas, and Cam was going to be there. What happens in Vegas stays in Vegas, right? She would find out if anything would happen worth leaving there.

Kayla stopped Jillian after a meeting to ask if she was going. Kayla said she knew a couple people who would be there. Kayla wanted to go, and Jack said she could (of course), but her workload was too heavy, and she decided she had to pass after all. She gave Jillian the names of her friends in case she ran into them.

"Is that guy from Atlanta going to be there?" Kayla asked, which struck Jillian as kind of odd. They hadn't discussed any of that since they got back to the office.

"Yeah, I think he probably is," Jillian said, wondering if she should hedge or just be honest.

"What's going on with him?" she asked as they walked down the hallway.

"Not much. What's going on with you and Jay?" Jillian asked. Two can play that game.

"Oh! I'm surprised you remember his name! Just drama, as always. I'm sick of it," she said.

"Yeah, me, too," Jillian said, smiling. She felt kind of surprised at herself for keeping her trap shut for once.

She called Cam—yes, called him!—as soon as she arrived at the baggage carousel at the Vegas airport. He had arrived the night before and was already at the bar. He asked her to meet him there.

It took her longer than she expected to get to the Luxor, check in, and freshen up. She was so excited to see him. Not nervous (well maybe a little) but happy they were going to get to spend some time together.

She walked what seemed like two miles to the sports book where he was waiting, calling him when she was on her way. He said he'd meet her outside the book in the casino. She wove through the slot machines and tables, the chink of change, bells of the machines, music, and general controlled chaos that all reflected her amped-up mood. She turned a corner and there he was in jeans, sneakers, and a polo, hands in his pockets, bouncing up and down on his heels. He broke into his soft smile as soon as he saw her.

"Hey!" She smiled as she approached.

"Hey back at cha!" he said, pulling his hands out of his pockets and stepping toward her. As soon as she reached him, she wrapped her arms around his neck and pulled him to her. He felt so great. She didn't want to let him go.

"Oh my gosh," he whispered.

She knew he was probably self-conscious, aware of the eyes of their associates on them, perhaps sparking some eye-narrowing suspicion among them if they embraced a moment too long. She regretfully let him go.

She filled him in on her trip as they strolled back to the bar of the sports book. He introduced her to some others and went to get her a beer.

They all hung out there, drinking, eating, generally cavorting for a couple of hours, and she made some new acquaintances. Cam made fun of her for eating French fries for dinner, but he watched her as she ate, once winking at her when she turned to him laughing, catching him staring at her. She threw her best smile at him and winked back. He took a big swig of beer, as did she.

Then they were ready for some true partying. Cam led the way, and the group followed, drinking, laughing, joking, occasionally dancing down the aisles as they moved from bar to club to bar, Cam practically skipping at times as he waved to them to come, come on! He was like the Pied Piper, taking the town's trusting children toward the cliff, but he had no such evil intentions. She didn't think.

They arrived at the top floor bar in wherever, who cared, selecting a wide booth they could all fit into, and she slipped in right next to him. However, as soon as everyone was settled, he excused himself to the restroom, and when he returned, sat in the booth next to them with the overflow.

Frustrating. After a little while, everyone started moving around anyway, and soon they were close to each other again, sitting just across the table, talking in the same group. Once again, she turned to him to catch him staring at her, and he winked again. No smile this time, though. Was that just his way of sending a secret hello? She winked back, wondering what was going on, where he was, where they were.

The night ran on, and they were all drunk, but eventually decided to call it a night. They made it back to the Luxor somehow, where Cam and a couple of his associates were also staying, conveniently, but he headed toward a different set of elevators. She thought about calling him, at least texting him, but decided that if he wanted to see her, he needed to make that move. And so, it wasn't until her contacts were safely in their case and she was in her pajamas, crawling into bed, that her phone rang. Her heart leaped when she saw that it was Cam.

"Hey you," she said.

"Hey. Make it back OK?" he asked quietly.

"Sure did. I had a great time tonight, a lot of fun. I wish we had more time to catch up, though," she baited. Even drunk, she was keeping her dignity and not asking him to come.

"Well, why don't I come over and we can do just that," he said.

"Of course. I'm in 444, but I may have to come get you. I don't know if your key will work in my elevator," she said. Something in her made her stop. She had a sense of déjà vu. She couldn't place it, though, so she dismissed it.

"Sure it will. I'll call you if I have a problem," he said. Sure enough, a couple minutes later her phone rang again. She put her bra on under her pajamas, left her glasses on and headed to the elevator. As soon as it opened to the lobby, there he was. With glasses on, too! She imagined he had been getting ready for bed, too, and couldn't stop thinking about her and finally could not resist any longer. It made her smile.

They rode up in the elevator, talking about the night, the people, how crazy Vegas was. All she really wanted to do was put her arms around him and plant her lips on his.

As they walked back to her room, he asked if she'd gotten his email about his mom.

"No, is she OK?" she asked, suddenly concerned.

"She had a small stroke. My parents are traveling in Europe, so not much I can do, but I'm worried. My dad said everything's fine, they don't want us to worry." He seemed worried anyway.

They entered her dark room, with the drapes drawn and only a single table lamp on. He sat down on one bed, and she sat across from him on the other.

"Do you need to go to them?" she asked.

"No, they're OK. My brother's going to make sure they get everything they need. Apparently, it was pretty small, but since they're out of the country, it kind of freaked them out. And us, I guess."

"I can see why, of course. What can I do? Are you OK?"

"Yeah, I guess. There isn't anything I can do, really," he said, and lay back on the bed, putting his hands to his forehead and closing his eyes.

She moved over to sit next to him on the bed.

"I'm sorry you've had that on your mind all night. You seemed like you were having fun, though," she said.

"I did. How can you not, here? I am worried about her, though," he said, staring at the ceiling.

"Well, lie here with me for a while and get your mind off of that," she said, laying down next to him and putting her head on his chest.

"That will help, I think," he said. They lay there for a few moments, each taking a few breaths, then he moved his arm around her, she put her hand on his chest and started stroking it with her thumb. His hand reached for her knee. It was all over at that point. She turned her head and reached for him, their mouths on each other in a flash.

Afterwards, he excused himself to go to the bathroom. He returned, completely naked, and got a bottle of water. She wanted him in bed with her. She wanted him to stay the night with her. She wanted him to stay forever.

She walked up behind him, wrapped her arms around his chest, his stomach, closed her eyes and pressed her cheek against his back, between his shoulder blades, her hips against his buttocks, pressing together every inch so that he could feel her enveloping him, soothing him, warming him, lightening his heart, she hoped, easing his fears, sending love and acceptance and strength to him for whatever he needed, to ease his guilt, to reassure him that his mom would be OK.

"Let me hold onto you, Cam. OK? Take what you need from me, find strength in me, know that I'm here for you, valuing the good, kind, wise, talented, beautiful man that you are." She would go back to that night many times later, conjuring up the feeling of his body against hers, remembering how he took her hands in his, turned around, hugged her close. They didn't speak for a long time.

"Lie down with me," she said quietly.

She got in bed, pulled the covers back and motioned for him to join her. He paused for a second, then crawled in, lying on his back. She curled herself into him, her head on his shoulder, his arm wrapped around her, her hand on his chest, his other hand on her forearm.

"Just hold on to me. Everything's OK." She tried to soothe him, and tears started leaking from her eyes.

"Why are you crying?" he asked, surprised, as he felt them drop to his chest.

"Good reasons. I'm so glad you're here. I'm so happy you called and came. I've realized what a gift you are to me, Cam. I feel so safe with you, like I'm home, when we're together," she said.

"You never felt that way with Peter?" he asked quietly.

"No, never. I've never felt that way with anyone," she whispered.

"I didn't with Lauren's mom, either. Mary Beth and I were great at first, but it's changed…" He trailed off.

She could hear the hurt in his voice but didn't pursue it. She didn't want to know. She didn't want to talk about her. She wanted the time to be about them. "Friends can love each other, right?" she asked.

He stopped stroking her arm briefly, then, "Of course, they can," he said hesitantly, surely wondering what was coming next.

"We're friends, right?" she asked.

"Yes, we definitely are. You are a gift to me, too, and we will hold on to each other," he said.

They dozed for a little while, and then awoke, and he said he had to go. She fell into a deep sleep as soon as he left.

Her phone ringing woke her up just a few hours later—already lightening outside—and it was Cam. Shit was she hung over. But happy. So happy. He had grabbed her glasses instead of his own when he left. Hilarious. He was coming to swap them out.

She could tell as soon as she opened the door that he was not feeling the elation she was. He looked concerned. He looked guilty. He handed her the glasses and said, "Here's your room key, too." His way of saying he wouldn't be needing it?

"How are you feeling? What do you hear about your mom?"

"They're OK. I'm OK." But he didn't sound it. He was still standing. She walked up to him and wrapped her arms around him.

"Cam," she started. "Don't worry. She'll be OK. You will be OK. Everything will be OK. Just do what you need to do today and know that."

He closed his eyes and nodded his head. "Mm hmmm," he agreed.

She pulled away. He was so tense.

"You needed me, Cam. I'm glad I could be there for you. I am happy to be here for you now. You just tell me what you need, what you need from me, and it's yours. You know that?" she smiled.

"Yep. Nice to know. Thank you," he said quietly. He was withdrawing again. He felt guilty. He was nervous to be around her, feeling regretful.

"So what's on your agenda today?" she asked, trying to lighten things up, and he filled her in, and she filled him in, and he said he'd see her later and left. She almost cried but restrained herself. She knew he was gone again. He did send a text later, asking if she was coming to dinner with them. "Of course. Time and place?" she sent back.

She walked into the restaurant and was the last one there. He'd ordered a beer for her. They were right across the table from each other but, again, a few minutes later, he moved to another table. So irritating.

The night was fun again, though. She socialized, danced with different men who were in the group, but not with Cam. They all got drunk again. Then they were making their way into a super crowded dance club, the lights flashing and music pounding, and she had no idea where they were.

Cam happened to be right behind her, so she asked him not to leave her. He said OK.

Ten minutes later, again, he excused himself to the restroom and never came back. One of his associates escorted her back to the Luxor, and she was sure he was awaiting an invitation, but none was forthcoming.

She ran into Cam in the conference center the next morning. He looked amazing in a crisp white dress shirt, his white undershirt peeking out over the top button, and sharply pressed navy slacks. Yummy. She so wanted to wrap him up in her arms and make out with him right there. She didn't think he felt the same way, although when she walked up, his first quiet words were, "Wow, you look great."

"You, too. Very nice," she said, smiling. "What happened to you last night?" she asked.

"Yea, let's talk about that later, OK?" he said, and chuckled a bit. Great. Just fucking great.

"I'll call you later about dinner."

"Promise?" she asked, still smiling.

"Yep, promise," and off they went, their separate ways. She was terrified that this was how they would end.

She made it through the day and back to her room and took a nap. He finally called and gave the scoop for dinner. "Do you want me to go? Because if you would have more fun if I weren't there, I'll skip it. I don't want you to feel pressure, or be uncomfortable, feeling like you have to run away," she offered. Always the martyr. Sickening. That is so not what she wanted. Coward. She was a coward.

"No, I want you to go," he said, but he didn't sound convincing.

"OK, I'll meet you all down there then," she said.

As soon as she hung up, she had a voicemail from Tempe. "Hey, Jilly, it's me," she was crying, upset. "I'm so sorry to call you out there, but my stepdad died early this morning. I can't pick you up from the airport, the funeral is at the same time. I'm sorry," and she'd hung up.

Oh no. Bob was a great guy, a friendly, helpful man, but he'd been in ill health lately. She decided right then to fly back early so she could attend the funeral. She called Cam back.

"Change of plans. I just got a message from Tempe; her stepfather passed away, and I need to pack and make plans to fly back tomorrow," she said.

"I'm sorry to hear that. Is she OK?" he asked.

"I think so. I haven't talked to her, yet, but I'll call her next. I'm going to skip tonight so I can get things together," she said. Good excuse to not have her heart broken.

"OK," he said. No argument.

"Let's try to have breakfast or something tomorrow before I leave, OK?" she asked. They still hadn't talked about why he'd left without her.

"Definitely. Call me in the morning and we'll decide," he said.

"OK. Have fun tonight. Not too much! Ha ha. Tell everyone I'm sorry?"

"Sure thing. Night."

Her heart gave a squeeze. Whether it was from missing him already or from another piece of it being crushed, she couldn't tell.

She called Tempe, talked with her for a while, made sure she was OK, told her she was coming back early. She texted Candace, asked her to call, which she did right away, and then asked her to change her flight. She packed, leaving out only what she'd need in the morning. Then she sat and stared at the television until she fell asleep.

Cam messaged early in the morning that he was on his way to get coffee; could she meet him? She was already up and dressed, ready to leave for the airport in about an hour. "Of course. Be right down." Time for damage control. Don't be a drama queen, she kept telling herself. *Be calm. Don't freak out. Don't freak him out. Be normal, for crying out loud. Don't cry.*

She spotted him right away as she neared the food court, pulling her suitcase behind her. He broke into his face-brightening smile as soon as he saw her, and she watched him look her up and down.

He reached out to give her a big hug as soon as she was close enough. He'd already gotten a Danish and coffee, so she waited in line for a Diet Coke while he found seats.

They chatted for a few minutes about the conference, and he asked if she was able to get her flight changed, how Tempe was doing. They talked about everything they could, avoiding the elephant in the room.

"So why did you run out on me the other night?" she asked.

"We shouldn't have had sex again. I don't want you to be hurt, and I'm afraid that I've set expectations again, and I can't do that, I don't want to do that," he said.

"I don't have expectations of you. You don't owe me anything," she said.

"I had to go. I was drunk. You looked so great. I wanted to be with you again. I couldn't! I felt it coming, so I ran. I really did just intend to go to the restroom, but some of the guys were out at the bar, so I sat down with them for a minute, and then they were ready to go, so I decided it would be best if I went, too. I knew you were in good hands. I wouldn't have left you alone," he said.

"So you bailed because you were tempted again," she said.

"Yeah, that's right," he said, chuckling.

"Cam, please don't run from me. Please don't ever run from me," she said.

"I'll try. I just am trying to do the right thing, and I just am not sure I know what that is any more. I am wondering if maybe we just shouldn't minimize our contact for a while, kind of turn down the intensity. Cool off."

She was holding her breath. There it was. Again. A lump was rising in her throat, hollowing out her insides. *Control, control, control.*

He continued. "Maybe eventually we can truly be just friends with each other. That's what I really want. I want us to be friends. I just don't know how to get from here to there any other way," he said.

She nodded. "If that's what you really want, Cam, of course. I will have to respect that. I didn't come out here expecting to be with you. You already made it clear that we would be just friends, so I didn't think that would happen. I'm glad it did; I don't regret it. I love being with you. But I don't want our being together to be hurtful to you. I don't want to be your mistake, your regret," she said.

"It shouldn't have happened, I should not have let it. But I do love being with you, too. In another time…" he trailed off. "That's just why I think if we distance ourselves from each other for a while, maybe it will help," he said.

"Fine. I'll follow your lead. Now that we have all of that on the table, can you stand one last minute of intensity? Then I promise to dial it down?" She smiled, trying to indicate it wouldn't hurt too much.

"Sure," he replied.

"Everything I've said to you here, including that you're a gift to me, I've meant. I meant every word of it. I hope you won't forget that," she said.

"I won't. I meant it all, too. We'll keep in touch, I promise," he said, and smiled.

"OK. I need to go. You need to go. I could stay here forever with you, but I have a plane to catch," she said. She really didn't want to go. Ever. She couldn't stand the thought of walking away from him again, of not knowing when she would hear from him, when she might see him again. But it wasn't up to her. It wasn't her choice.

They got up, hugged, long and strong, and she kissed his cheek, smiled up at him. He grinned widely and said jokingly, "Get going! Seriously, have a safe trip back, OK?"

"Yeah, you, too," she said, and rushed off with tears in her eyes that she hoped he didn't see.

A few hours later, in her window seat on the plane, staring out into the light, her tears finally fell, and the distance between them expanded once again.

34

Tempe wanted to know everything. They got through the funeral, then went to the bar for cocktails. And Jillian told her the whole sordid Vegas tale. Tempe shook her head almost the whole time.

"Oh my god. That man does not know what he wants!" she said.

"Well, I know what I want. Him! But it's not just up to me, is it?" Jillian said. Was she destined to live like the Cimmerians, enduring constant clouds, and fog, never seeing the sun? Maybe it was the closest she would ever get to the life, the love, she longed for. Maybe it was the most she deserved.

Her mantra had become that Cam was a gift to her. Every time she started sinking, feeling sorry for herself, convinced that they would never be more than they had already been, she tried to pull the gratitude card, that he was a gift from the Universe, from Kate, from whatever was out there, giving her hope. She tried not to want, ask, for more.

She did want Cam to be happy, but the thought of him with Mary Beth made Jillian sick to her stomach. Imagining him telling her that Mary Beth was pregnant made her head spin and her insides feel like they were trying to escape her body in any way they could.

35

She sent Cam an email from her desk the following Monday. He replied within ten minutes, but it was ice cold. She didn't know what else she expected, but it cut her to the quick.

Jack and Kayla both stopped by that morning, asking how the conference was. Kayla asked if she had run into any of her friends.

"No, sorry. There were so many people there and so much going on, I didn't even really have a chance to seek them out," she apologized.

"Did you see your friend?" she asked, smiling.

"Yeah, I did. I went to dinner a couple times with him and some others from Atlanta," she said, hedging again.

"Oh good. Did you have some fun?" she asked.

"Yeah, it was fun," she said, smiling, but on alert. Something about the way she asked made her hesitate to provide more details.

"Good! Maybe next year I can go," she said.

"Yeah, maybe," she said, and Kayla walked away.

When Jack came by, Jillian told him it was interesting, rejuvenated her, was just what she needed, and that she would write up some notes for him. He said it wasn't necessary.

"I know it's just a jaunt. I thought you needed some time out, so I'm glad you went and that it helped," he said. "Did you have any fun?" he asked, smiling.

What? She stared at him, alarms going off in her head. What was with all these "fun" questions?

"Well, it was Las Vegas, how can you not have fun?" she said. *What the hell?*

"No, I mean, did you have any fun?" he asked.

"What do you mean? It was a conference." She looked at him, puzzled.

He laughed and said he would see her later, throwing his Hershey's Kiss wrapper at her instead of the trash can as he usually did. Strange. Very strange indeed.

A couple days later she got an email from Cam, asking her how she was, what was going on, totally casual. She emailed him back with a casual response, and they exchanged a few more messages, bantering back and forth like old friends, not lovers. Jillian was relieved. It did make her smile and give her hope that he had not abandoned her. He was thinking of her and had resisted the urge for as long as he could. Lord knows she had wanted to reach out to him every day, every hour, every minute, and the struggle to restrain herself was physical, palpable.

How do you really know when you love someone?

She knew she loved Zachary. She felt it in her stomach, her chest, her throat, her eyes, when she listened to him sing, when he yelled "Mom!" when she came in from work, when he told her she was the best mom in the world and he loved her one hundred percent, and when he drew his brows together and pursed his lips, like she did, when he disagreed with something.

She also felt it to the depths of her soul, if she had one, when he said he loved his dad one hundred percent, but her only fifty percent; when he cried and said he made a mistake when he said he wanted her to put him to bed instead of his dad; when he corrected her, saying "No, Mom, Dad doesn't do it that way;" when he asked her to leave him be.

She was in high school, sixteen years old, when she fell in love for the first time. She and Richard had only been "going out" for a month when he broke up with her out of the blue. She didn't understand why, only that his note said he needed to do it "before our love made us crazy" or some crap like that. She was devastated. They'd never even said they loved each other. She yelled at him, bawling, the hormonal vampire raging, in their second-period music classroom before the bell rang. She wanted him back. She wrote him notes endlessly. She lay in bed every night asking herself why she was acting the way she was. Did she love him? Was that why she couldn't let go, why it hurt so badly? She so wanted the answer to those questions. Finally, she had decided that she did love him—she was in love!—and she was so happy that she was in love, that she had finally realized, or decided, that she was, that she forgot he wasn't even her boyfriend anymore.

It wasn't the first time she had said she loved someone, though before then she wasn't being honest when she said it, and knew she wasn't—just like she wouldn't be later when she would say those words to Mike.

When she was in ninth grade, still in junior high school, James, the Adonis of the neighborhood, who was wildly popular and already in high school, looked her way. All the kids they hung out with and played kickball in the street with, then spin the bottle with, whatever with, wanted to be near him, to be him, because he was "cool." At sixteen, he was six feet tall, slender, olive complected. Brown hair, light green eyes framed by long dark lashes, making his eyes seem to glow against his darker hair and skin. Strikingly handsome, almost pretty, athletic, and a huge partier. His nickname was Mad Dog.

"I want you to be my girlfriend," he'd posed one afternoon right after school started in August, as they sat on the neighbor's unpainted cinderblock wall, as their friends skated up and down the crappy blacktopped street—finally paved!—trying not to trip on the stray gravel thrown from the few driveways that weren't just packed earth. Jillian didn't skate much anymore. It made her sweat and messed up her hair. She usually just sat or stood around, chatting, watching, or drawing pictures in colored chalk on the street. What else was there to do?

"Why?" she'd asked, looking at him out of the corner of her eye, in what she hoped was a flirtatious peek, the best she could do at fourteen.

"Because you're the prettiest," he'd said. Good a reason as any, she supposed.

"What about Dawn?"

"What about her?"

"Well, she's my best friend, and I know when you took her out on your motorcycle, you kissed her," Jillian had replied. "Doesn't that mean something?" Maybe she wasn't a good kisser.

"No, not necessarily. That was just for fun. With you, I'm serious," he said.

"OK, but if you're with me, you're with me, right?"

"Absolutely," he said. And kissed her. Not a quick peck, but no tongue, either. Wet lips. Not hard or soft. Just very wet.

Besides, Jillian wanted to be "cool," too. What better way than to be James's girlfriend?

She did eventually fall in love with him, years later, but he said he loved her relatively early in their drama.

They were sitting on a homemade stage in the lower level of the church they went to because their parents made them, and all their friends went there anyway. He had mouthed "I love you" to her and she had mouthed "I love you too," knowing she was lying, that she didn't even know what that kind of love was, let alone know that she felt it for him. She smiled, but she didn't feel it, didn't believe. It was just easier to say it and not cause any upset.

She and James dated on and off all through high school. They broke up the first time after she found out he was kissing someone else after all, setting a pattern for the rest of their relationship.

"Jilly, I've told you, it's just for fun. It doesn't mean anything. I am serious with you!" he would argue. And she would forgive him.

They had been going out again for a few months when she was a sophomore and he a senior. She stopped by his house on her way home from school. He got out early for work release but hardly ever went to work. His house was never locked, so she leaned her bike up against the fence, let herself in and, after failing to find him there, sat down and turned on the TV. Dawn showed up shortly after, saying she saw Jillian's bike outside. Then Greg, another friend of theirs and James's best friend. Greg practically lived there. They chatted for a few minutes, and then the phone rang. Greg answered it.

"OK," he said, glancing over at Jillian and Dawn. "Are you sure? OK," he said. He hung up and walked back over to the girls, sitting down, looking none too happy.

"That was James. He said he wants you out of his house," he said, looking directly at Jillian.

"What? What are you talking about?" Jillian asked, surprised. "Are you kidding?"

"Ha, Greg. You're so funny!" Dawn said.

"No, I'm not kidding," he said, staring at the ground, no longer meeting their eyes.

"Greg, what's going on? Why would he say that?" Jillian asked, confused, still thinking it was some joke.

"Jillian, I'm not supposed to tell you this, but when he asked you out again the last time? When he said he and Terry were broken up?" he said, still staring at the ground. "They weren't. He's still seeing her. He just called from her house."

Jillian heard Dawn say something to Greg, arguing with him, but Jillian just got up and left, pedaling her bike home calmly and slowly. No one followed her. She wasn't surprised. But when she made it home to her own empty house, she bawled her eyes out. About a half hour after she got home, the phone starting ringing. She answered it the first time, and as soon as James said "Jilly," she hung up. It rang again and again that afternoon until dinner time. She didn't pick it up again. The next afternoon, again and again. She didn't answer. And the same again the next day.

They rarely saw each other at school, and Jillian purposely avoided any place where there was even a remote chance that they could run into each other. She shut him out. He left her alone for a couple months.

Then he tracked her down, and she took him back. Again and again and again.

It was more of the same all through high school and college, lies, cheating, heartache and heartbreak, jealous classmates, his "real" girlfriends—the ones he had sex with, because Jillian wouldn't give it to him—who said Jillian was just a little girl, a phase. Each time, she would try to convince her own friends that it would be different, while her male friends warned her off him because he drank and smoked and drove his motorcycle and Corvette way too fast. Finally, they went their separate ways, never suspecting that the last time they saw each other would really be the last time. She did love him, and she thought he thought he loved her. But she didn't think either of them really knew what that meant.

Would you rather believe you are in love and one day realize you're not, or know that you are and realize it will never be returned? Always these choices, these made-up ultimatums about deciding which misery was worse. Always these options that were not really options at all.

Just ways in which to torture ourselves.

Why did she never imagine what the rest of her life would be like with Peter before she married him? That she would always be wanting more, would always want to feel more important to him, more valued by him, truly loved by him, but would always be shoving her aggravation, her disappointment even, down and away into the bottomless pit? Perhaps not bottomless; it had filled up and overflowed.

Was it karma, for not being totally honest with Peter, not telling him how she felt, what she wanted, and not giving him the chance to do anything about it?

Was it fate, inevitable, a cruel hand dealt by the Moirai at her birth, something she could not have prevented?

Was it preparation for whatever was next, whether that was a life with Cam or someone else?

Assuming any of that was defined or predetermined. If you didn't believe in God, or a god, or karma, or fate, it just was what it was. It was just her own imagination, her own wish and desire, manifesting a world that was safe for her, that brought her hope, that allowed her to see a life beyond what she had, that helped her know she was alive and wanted to live. She did feel. She could be happy. She wanted to be happy. She could love and she wanted to love. She so wanted to love. She wanted to be loved. She wanted more. She deserved more, didn't she?

But she was also terrified. Not of leaving what she had; not of living alone or of being a divorced mother to her son; not of being judged, gossiped about, stereotyped, categorized, criticized; not of failing or succeeding or explaining; not of leaving the past behind and making no excuses for blazing a hot trail to the future she wanted. But afraid, terrified, that the love she yearned for—cried for, wanted more than anything, a love that consumed her—would never be.

She spent Thanksgiving with Tempe and Mark again; it was Peter's year to have Zach. The next night they all met for happy hour at Carrabba's. It was finally colder, maybe staying that way for Christmas for once. They took their jackets off and put them on the backs of the bar chairs and ordered drinks.

Ryan, the weekend bartender, was chatting it up with them, as usual.

A few drinks in, Tempe leaned into Jillian and whispered, "Um, he is being very attentive tonight."

"What do you mean?"

"Well, usually, he's buzzing around talking with everyone, but he's been over here a lot tonight," she said, raising her eyebrows at Jillian.

"Oh, please. I haven't noticed anything. He is pretty cute, though, if you look," she said, peering at him out of the corner of her eye.

Too quickly, Mark was already ready to go. He didn't really like it there and wanted to go to the dive bar next door and play pool.

"All right, all right already!" Tempe said.

Ryan brought the tab and, when Jillian signed it, she also wrote him a note on a napkin: "Ry, give me a call sometime. Jilly." And wrote her number.

"What are you doing?" Tempe demanded, spying the napkin. She slid it out from under the receipt and showed her. "Good for you!" Tempe said and laughed.

They walked next door with their hands in their pockets, even though their drinks had warmed them up a bit and armed their thinned-out blood with a bit of heat. The place was dark except for the neon beer-brand signs and single lightbulbs over the pool tables. It was pretty busy, but they managed to get the last three seats together at the bar.

As soon as they sat down, Tempe elbowed Jillian hard.

"Ow! What the!?" But as soon as Jillian looked at her, she nodded across the bar. Ryan was standing at the other end. His shift must have ended, and he was ready to have a few drinks of his own.

Just then, he saw them, too, smiled, then suddenly looked down and grabbed his phone. He picked it up, answered, and smiled.

"Oh, fuck," Jillian said, guessing what had happened. Ryan had probably left without seeing her note, and this call was someone from Carrabba's telling him about it. How embarrassing.

"What?" asked Tempe. Jillian explained her suspicion.

"So what? So maybe he'll come over here and talk to you! What's wrong with that?!"

What was wrong was that it put her on the spot. If he'd gotten it later, he could ignore it, and she could pretend she'd never left it if he never called. No big deal.

Ryan didn't come over right away, but he did look their way several times. Jillian, Tempe, and Mark drank and talked with others at the bar near them and had a good time, but Jillian was nervous the whole time, self-conscious that Ryan was staring at her. Finally, she excused herself to the restroom, which happened to be behind where Ryan was sitting. He smiled at her as she walked past. When she came back out, he had apparently stolen a bar chair from somewhere and motioned for her to sit, and she did. They immediately launched into flirtatious conversation. "Sooo, what's up? Why'd you leave tonight without saying goodbye?" she asked.

"Sorry. As soon as I'm done, I'm done, I'm out. What's up with you? Did you follow me here?" he asked, winking.

"No, I certainly did not. I think it's just a lucky coincidence. Lucky for you, that is," she said, teasing.

"I think you're right. I think it is definitely my lucky night," he said, looking her in the eye.

He put his arm around her chair. A server handed her a beer, and she took a swig. She looked across the bar to find Tempe and Mark, and they were in deep conversation, arguing even.

"Yikes, look at that! Wonder what's going on?" she asked.

"Don't know, doesn't look good. Do you think they'll miss you if we go play pool?"

"Doubtful. Let's go." And they grabbed their drinks and went to find a table.

They played a couple games. Jillian wasn't very good, but Ryan was, so he beat her quickly. She made sure she bent over the table well when she made long shots, so he could get a good look.

"Hey Jilly, what are you gonna do? We're ready to go," Tempe announced as she and Mark walked up. Jillian looked at Ryan questioningly, should I stay?

"I'll drive you home, if that's OK," he said.

Jillian dug her keys out and gave them to Tempe. "You OK to drive?" she asked.

"Yep, it's only a few blocks. We're good. Are you sure you want to do this?" she asked.

"Yep. I'm fine. I'll call you if I need you," she said, and winked.

As soon as they left, Ryan walked over to her, grabbed her face in his hands and kissed her. Mmmmm, he was a good kisser. She kissed him back. "Wanna get outta here?" he asked, still close.

"Yeah, I do," she said. Couldn't wait. He grabbed her hand and led her outside, into his Mustang, where they made out for a little while. Then he started it up and they took off.

His apartment was nearby, but certainly nothing to be impressed by. In fact, it was a serious bachelor pad. Hardly any personal items or decoration. They went straight to his room, and he closed the door, lit two candles, put music on, and asked her if she wanted a drink.

"Some water would be great," she said. He pulled a fresh bottle out from under the bed (a great idea she later adopted), and she sat down and took it, cracked open the top, took a slug, and recapped it.

They didn't sleep much that night. Jillian certainly wouldn't classify the sex as earth-shattering, but the kissing was great, and she liked the intimacy. They didn't talk much, either. She would awake from a short doze and turn to him and wrap herself around him, enjoying having a warm body in bed next to her, and kiss his neck or his ear. He would seem to ignore her advances until she gave up and turned over. Then he would turn to her, brush her hair back, kiss the nape of her neck or behind her ear, or the top of her shoulder.

They chatted for a few minutes in the morning, and he drove her over to Tempe's without offering coffee or breakfast or anything. Hmph. A one-night stand it would be. Fine with her. No connection here, just sex, and not even great sex. Guess it was better than no sex. Maybe.

<h1 style="text-align:center">37</h1>

Jillian was nervous the next time they went to Carrabba's a few weeks later, the week of Christmas, wondering what an exchange with Ryan might be like. Maybe he wouldn't be working. It was his regular night, though, so, of course, as soon as they walked in, there he was.

"Hey there! Great to see you guys!" he said, putting napkins on the bar for drinks. "The usual?" he asked, winking at Jillian.

"Yes, please!" Tempe replied, while Jillian just smiled at him. She sure didn't want him to think she had any kind of issue seeing him or that she was embarrassed or anything.

He brought Tempe's cosmo and Jillian's beer and, as he set them down, leaned forward over the bar to her. "Hey, Jilly, I'm sorry I haven't called. My mom fell and had to have surgery again, and I've been over there helping her and my stepdad out. Between that, here, and my day job, I've been kind of consumed," he said.

"Yea, whatever, no problem. Your mom doing OK?" she asked.

"We'll see. This is like the fourth time, and I think I may end up moving in with them to help. Not thrilled about it, but you do what you have to, right?"

"Sure," she said, smiling again.

They drank, and he smiled and served their drinks, and it was no big deal.

He called the next day and asked to meet him for a drink that night. She did. She knew there wouldn't really be anything meaningful between them, but he didn't seem to be an axe murderer, either, and she was sick of feeling lonely. She could waste a few weeks spending time with Ryan while Cam was off trying to make good with Mary Beth, right? No harm in that.

They went out a few times, had average sex, and made no real connection, but it was nice to be close to someone.

38

So what cha been up to?" Cam's email posed on the first day back in the office after New Year's.

"Hey! The usual. Zach and I had a great Christmas but, of course, I missed him when he went to Peter's. How about you? How are you and Mary Beth getting along these days?"

"Things are OK. What about you? Any dates lately?"

Strange. Almost like he knew, like he sensed some other man's presence around her even from hundreds of miles away.

"I'm not sure that's any of your business," she hedged. "But, I will tell you I've taken up with a bartender just to kill some time," she replied.

No response. Was he laughing? Shocked? Jealous?

Twenty minutes later her phone rang. It was Cam. She smirked to herself. It had worked like a charm.

"This is Jillian."

And he just continued their email conversation without another word: "So have you had some fun on the bar?" He chuckled, in what she recognized as his closed-mouth laugh, her favorite.

"I don't think I'm going to give you that much detail, mister. I'm not going to let you live vicariously through my adventures," she said.

He laughed again. "Oh, you are bad," he said. She could see him: his eyes were probably closed, he was shaking his head, trying to shut out the images of her in intimate positions, feeling guilty. She wondered if Mary Beth was around. She guessed he wouldn't have called if she were.

"Is it serious?" he asked.

"God no. I'm just having some fun," she said.

"What's he like?" he asked.

"It doesn't matter. There's no real connection. He can be kind of negative, not my thing. I think he's just passing the time with me like I'm passing the time with him," she said. She shouldn't tell Cam that if she wanted him to be jealous, but it was the truth.

"Passing time? What do you mean?"

"I mean, neither one of us has anything better to do, so we do each other. Better than nothing, better than being alone all the time," she said. OK, Jilly! Enough!

"We do what we need to do, I guess," he said, but the laughter, the smile, was gone from his voice. Was he disappointed in her? Thinking she was tramping around?

"Look, Cam, I get lonely, you know? He's not a bad guy. He's just not 'the one' either, OK? Please don't judge me. You don't want me, and I just don't have the energy to take on much more right now. I know it's not the right thing, but it's easy for now, OK?"

"Jilly, I do want you! You know where I am! I have to try! I'm sorry! I am not judging you. I hope you have some fun; you deserve it. Look, I need to go, OK? I'll talk with you soon," he said.

"Yeah, OK. Figures. I miss you," she said.

"I'll talk to you soon," he said and hung up. So much for no pressure, no drama. She felt like shit. She wanted to cry. Total backfire. Why did she feel so cheap, so manipulative? Had she been with Ryan just to try to punish Cam or to make him jealous, knowing he would eventually ask, and she would tell him? Now they both were hurting for no good reason.

Ryan called a couple of days later and asked if she wanted to meet for drinks. She said she couldn't, she had other plans. They never went out again.

39

Cam was back in town and at One Metro. He'd flown in that morning, and they hadn't had a chance to talk yet. They were all standing in the hallway waiting for the conference room when her cell rang. She picked it up; it was her doctor's office.

"Hi, Jillian. We have your labs back, and we have some news for you. Are you the excitable type?"

"Um, I'm not sure what you mean by that. What's going on?" That was weird.

"Well, your labs came back as positive that you're pregnant."

"Excuse me?" She quickly walked to the nearest exit and stepped outside into the cold February air. "That can't be. It must be a mistake," she said. Her heart was pounding, and she was sure the blood had drained from her face, from her entire body.

"Are you sure? Because the labs say…"

"The blood work says that or the urinalysis?" she managed. *Can't be. Can't be. Can't be.*

"The urinalysis. If you're pretty sure, we need to send you back in, and we'll do bloodwork to confirm," he said.

"It's got to be wrong. Believe me, I would know. When can I pick up an order for the rework?"

"I'll have it ready right away. You can pick it up any time."

"Thank you. I will take care of it right away."

Holy shit, couldn't be. She'd had two periods since she and Ryan were together last, hadn't she? They were light, but that was because of the new pill she was on. She had decided to go back on it for a couple of reasons: one, because the thought of getting pregnant terrified her, and two, because she didn't really want to have a period. What was the point. Right? Good god.

Was there any chance she could be pregnant though? Was there any chance it was Cam's? Oh god, could it be Cam's?

What the hell? She was not pregnant. She would have known.

She walked back into the hallway and scanned it for Monica. She finally found her, and she happened to look over at Jillian. "Can I talk to you?" Jillian mouthed across the crowd. Monica immediately headed her way.

"Can we step outside a sec?" Jillian asked. She didn't want anyone to overhear, for sure. Especially since Cam was about fifteen feet away.

They crossed their arms against the cold. "My doctor's office just called. My labs came back with a positive pregnancy result," she said.

"Holy shit! You're kidding!"

"I can't be, right? I mean, I'm on birth control. I've had two periods since I had sex last. I can't be, right? I mean, Peter and I tried everything! I thought I couldn't get pregnant again. It can't happen like this, right? Right?" She was starting to panic.

"No, you are not pregnant. You're right. You would know by now. You know your own body. You've been pregnant before. You are not. What did they say?"

"Well, he said it was the urinalysis, not the blood work, so the urinalysis could be wrong, easily. They just let it sit too long or something. If it was the blood work, I'd be fucked for sure. I'm going in for blood work to confirm or refute, as the case may be," she said.

"Good. Good, get it done ASAP. Leave now and do it," she said.

"I can't go now! We've got this meeting, and Cam is here for god's sake! Oh fuck! What am I going to tell him?"

"Nothing. You're not going to tell him anything. It's just a mistake. Blow it off, get the confirmation, and we'll laugh about it later," she said. She was a rock. Oh, to have an ounce of her composure.

"OK. OK. I'm OK. I'm not pregnant. Take care of business, go to the lab tomorrow morning, everything's fine," Jillian said. They both took a deep breath and walked back inside.

The next two hours were a blur. She couldn't concentrate. She was caught off guard a couple of times, her mind wandering.

What if she was pregnant? What if it was Ryan's? God, she didn't want to be tied to that man for the rest of her life. Maybe she wouldn't tell him. She didn't need money. She would have her own child. It would be all hers and she wouldn't have to share him or her with anyone else, like she had to share Zach. Was that fair? Maybe not, but that was life.

Could it be Cam's? No way, too long ago, almost four months. What if it was? What if she did get pregnant by Cam? What would he do? Would he walk away? He hadn't with Lauren. Would he leave Mary Beth to be with her and their child? Would he think she'd done it on purpose to try to trap him? *Shit. Shit. Shit. What the fuck?*

A couple of times she and Cam caught each other's eye. Both times she had looked up to find him staring at her. Both times he'd given her a subtle questioning glance, sensing that something was wrong.

Finally, the meeting ended, and she rushed into the restroom across the hall to get a grip before anyone could catch her. Deep breaths. Couldn't be, couldn't be. When she came out, Cam was standing there waiting.

"What is wrong with you? Are you OK?" he asked quietly.

"You are never going to believe the phone call I got right before we went in," she said. She couldn't believe she was going to tell him. He stared at her, waiting.

"My doctor's office called. They said I'm pregnant," she whispered. His jaw dropped, and his eyes about popped out.

"You're kidding," he finally managed.

"I know that I'm not; it's a mistake. I'm not. I would know if I was. I am definitely not. I should be laughing, it's so ridiculous, but it's kind of freaking me out," she said.

He took a deep breath, held it with his cheeks puffed out, then slowly let it go.

"The bartender's?" he asked.

"Cam, I am not pregnant!" She stared at him, then looked around to see if anyone might've heard.

"OK, OK! You're sure?"

"Yes, I am sure!"

"OK, then. Let's go. We're expected for drinks," he said.

She called Tempe from her car. Tempe cracked up laughing. Seriously cracked up.

"Are you serious? You're kidding right?" she said, still laughing.

"No, I'm not kidding," Jillian said. What was so god-damned funny?

"Oh my god. Wouldn't that just be your luck, wouldn't that just…"

"What the hell is that supposed to mean? I don't have bad luck!" Jillian yelled. She was insulted. How rude.

"I just mean your whole situation, and everything with Peter, and then you get knocked up? That'd just be fucking hilarious!"

"Maybe hilarious to you! Not hilarious to me!" she said. Tempe was seriously ticking her off. "I'm not, anyway. I've had two periods since Ryan. I am definitely not; it's a mistake," she said. Convincing Tempe or still convincing herself?

"Stranger things have happened, girlfriend. Haven't you heard about those women who give birth having never even realized they were pregnant?"

"Yes. But those women are ignorant, or stupid, or in denial. I am not any of those, and I am not pregnant," she said. "I'm at the bar. I've got to go. I'm going in for bloodwork tomorrow. I'll call you," she said, and hung up on her.

She partied that night like she wasn't pregnant because she wasn't, and Cam whispered sly jokes into her ear about "drinking for two" whenever he had the opportunity, and they were their usual jovial, joking, flirty, public selves.

On the way home she stopped at an all-night drug store and bought a pregnancy test. A two-pack. She took one right there in the public restroom. Negative.

First thing in the morning she took the second one. Negative. After showering and dressing for work, she went and picked up the order from the doctor's office, went to the lab, and had blood drawn.

After work, she stopped at the drugstore again and bought another two-pack. She waited until she was home to take the third test. Negative. She took the last one the next morning. Negative. The doctor's office called at 8:15 the following morning to say no, she wasn't pregnant after all, and that she should write a complaint letter to the lab for their carelessness.

She cried. Out of disappointment or relief, she wasn't sure.

40

At the end of a business email, Jillian asked Kayla if she'd talked to Jay lately. She used only his initial, though, being careful.

"Ack. I need counseling," Kayla replied.

"What's going on?" Jillian asked, not sure if Kayla would share.

"I'll fill you in later," she replied. Jillian assumed she didn't want to send the scoop via company email.

She showed up in Jillian's office a few hours later.

"Do you have a few minutes?" she asked.

"Of course! What's up?"

"I have talked to him. But I'm trying to work things out with my husband, for my son's sake," she said. Jillian could see the sadness in her eyes. She recognized it easily after seeing it in her own for so long.

"I just feel like, though, maybe I'm missing out on something better. I know it's terrible to think, but I can't help it," she said.

"You seem to be going about it the right way, though. Don't give up until you're absolutely sure there's nothing left, so you don't wonder, don't have regrets," Jillian said.

"I know. That's what I'm trying to do. He's still way over there, still with his wife, anyway, so I guess it doesn't really matter," she said. Painful place to be, Jillian knew.

"Has he said anything—that he wants to be with you, or anything?" Jillian asked.

"No, he certainly hasn't made me any promises. I think the whole thing has just made me realize how unhappy, how unsatisfied, I am in my marriage. We've been separated twice already, and I filed for divorce once before, but that was all before Chance came along. Everything's different now. I have to consider his needs, too," she said.

"Sure you do. But part of what he needs is for you to be the best mom to him you can be. I left Peter because I knew I would be a better mom, a better person period, away from him. And it was the right decision in that regard. But that was my life, my choice. You have to make your own choices," Jillian said.

"I know. It sure isn't easy. What finally did it for you?" she asked.

"My situation was certainly not yours, but when I started thinking about the person I was with Peter, and how different I was from how I am everywhere else, with everyone else, I realized that 'his wife 'was not who I wanted to be. She was not me. I didn't like her, and she was killing me. I had to get out before she won," Jillian said.

"I am just so confused about everything. I feel so out of control," she said.

"I know what you mean. It's very frustrating. It seems so simple now, but it was gut wrenching, heart-breaking, mind-boggling, the choices I had to make, the parts of me that I had buried over the course of our relationship. Over time, the compromises that I had made to keep peace between us just became festering open sores in my soul. And the more I tried to ignore them, the more they hurt," Jillian said. She wasn't sure where all of that was coming from, except that she was trying to help Kayla in some way, trying to help her not feel alone, like she wasn't the only person who felt what she was feeling.

"But, I made the choice," Jillian continued. "I am living by it. It's not all relief and freedom. Sharing custody of Zach is physically painful to me. He loves spending time with his dad, so he doesn't miss me so much when we're apart, but it's difficult for me. But all that being said, I sure am being the kind of mom I want to be now, and that thrills me," Jillian finished, smiling.

"So it's going to get harder before it gets easier but, if it's the right decision, it will all be worth it, right?" Kayla said but didn't seem convinced.

"Something like that. Just don't make it about Jay. Make it about Kayla, and Chance," Jillian suggested.

"Good advice. Thank you for the chat. You look really great, by the way. Even if it's not all 'relief and freedom,' as you said, something's working," she said, and finally smiled.

"Well thanks a lot! That is sweet of you to say! I'm here any time. Good luck," Jillian said. She smiled to herself. Maybe she had finally made it through to the other side.

"Hey, by the way," Kayla asked, turning back. "Whatever happened with that guy, Cam, or whatever his name was?"

"Oh, nothing. No big deal," Jillian said, hedging.

"Didn't he work for the place upstairs, with Ethan? I thought I saw him in the building a few weeks ago," she continued.

"Yeah, he does, out of their Atlanta office," Jillian admitted, unable to figure any other way out.

"Has he been helping you with the Delta project?" she asked, biting her lip.

Jillian froze. "Not that I am aware of. I don't know that he knows anything about it."

"Just curious. See you later. Thanks again for the talk."

"Any time." Yes, it was curious. Very, very curious.

But what was the right thing for her to do now? The right thing for whom? Respect Cam's marriage? Why? He didn't. He was the one who cheated. Yes, she enabled him. She kept trying to tell herself to want the right thing, which was to be friends and nothing more; that of course she didn't want their marriage to end. She didn't want Cam or Mary Beth or Lauren to be hurt by a divorce.

No, she didn't want them to be hurt. But who was getting hurt now? She was. She was, that was who.

Why was she the one who had to make the sacrifice, giving up on him, letting go, doing one of the hardest things she'd ever had to do in her life, for a woman she'd never even met? When she wasn't even sure that she loved Cam, or that Cam loved her?

She had told Monica that she didn't want to be the cause of their breakup if they were to break up. But that she did intend to stay in his line of sight in case they did. Always trying to do the right thing, say the right thing, think the right thing. Exhausting.

One of the therapists Jillian had visited during the divorce process told her that "to thine own self be true" is the path to freedom. Don't deny what you really want. That didn't mean you necessarily acted on it, but you at least admitted it.

She finally admitted it. Yes, she wanted them to break up. She didn't care how it happened. She wanted Cam to be free so that he could be with her. And you know what? She did want them to break up because of Jillian. She wanted Cam to decide that he was in love with Jillian and that she was his soul mate and he wanted to be with her. He would tell Mary Beth all of this, and she would move out, and he would come and get Jillian. She didn't want him to call her and say they had broken up for whatever their own reasons were and now he could be with her. She didn't want to be his consolation prize, his second choice. She wanted him to choose Jillian. She wanted him to decide she was more important to him. She wanted to be first. For once, just fucking once, she wanted to be first.

Some days she was completely confident that they would be together one day. Something would happen, and he and Mary Beth would be done. He would come for her, and they would be together. He would lie in bed next to her, they would go to dinner together and hold hands, and even kiss in public. They would go to Zach's baseball games together, and to movies, and love, love, love each other all day, every day.

Some days she was still terrified about Mary Beth getting pregnant, and she would know she and Cam would never have their chance. She would push it out of her mind as hard as she could. She tried to phrase all her thoughts positively—*we are going to be together, we will love each other, he is coming for me*—instead of no and not, because the Universe doesn't hear those words anyway. She could not impregnate Mary Beth with her thoughts, but she was certainly not going to give any energy to that possibility. Push those thoughts away, shut them down.

Jillian finally screwed up the courage to make an appointment with her psychic. The psychic told Jillian that Cam was coming to a major ending of some kind, that he was getting away from something soon. Of course, Jillian's first thought was "Thank god! They will soon be over, and we will be together." It didn't occur to her until much later, when she hadn't heard from him in a few weeks, that the ending might be them. Nope, wouldn't accept that. That wasn't it, couldn't be. The psychic told Jillian she was thinking too much, looking for too many answers. She should turn it over to the Universe.

It became a game of push and pull. When she didn't hear from him for a while, she could almost sense the email coming. She could almost time it. Most of the time, she still resisted contacting him first. He was a married man, after all. And Jillian wasn't desperate. She wanted him, but she needed him to come to her. If only for her own conscience. And he did.

If she didn't get an email when she expected one, she would start to panic. Occasionally, she would find an article or news story that she thought might interest him, or some little tidbit from a client, and she would send him an email with no other message. He would always email back with questions on how she was doing, what she had been up to.

As soon as his name would pop up in her Inbox, she would smile, and her whole body would relax. She would reply, and answer his questions, and ask a bunch of her own, trying to find out what was going on. Sometimes he was more forthcoming than other times. He usually didn't answer any of her questions about Mary Beth. Jillian didn't appreciate being ignored. She thought it was rude of him, but she knew why he didn't. That salted the wound even more.

He would always tell her how work was going, sometimes how Lauren was, sometimes how his softball team was doing, once that he had been in a minor car accident, but that he was OK.

Sometimes he would text when he was traveling, once even when he and Mary Beth and Lauren were on vacation. He said he'd call when he got back into town. He did.

When he called, Jillian bravely decided to make a play. "I just want to tell you, Cam, how happy I am that we met, how much joy knowing you has brought into my life. I don't know how it happened, how you did it, but you've managed to become one of my dearest friends, Cam. Please don't ever go away," she told him.

"Not going anywhere. I'm really glad we met, too. I've decided to go to the conference, hoping you'll be there. I'd love to see you," he replied.

"Yes, I'm going. We'll spend some time together?" she asked, trying not to sound too excited.

"Of course. We'll talk more then, OK? I need to go."

"Sure thing. Thanks for calling," she said politely, and hung up, happier than she was before he'd called.

<h1 style="text-align:center">41</h1>

The conference was only a couple of weeks away. She had been afraid to ask Cam if he was coming, afraid he would avoid it, avoid her, or be too busy, or would be coming but would be bringing Mary Beth with him. Ack.

God, the conference. Why the hell was so much of her life revolving around what happened at the conference? Damn thing. Was it the center of her Universe, or what? Maybe if she quit she could work in a different line of business and not have to go to those damn things.

She told Tempe that Cam was coming.

"Good! Maybe you two can finally get some things straightened out!" she said.

"What do you mean?" Jillian asked.

"Jilly, I know you're in love with him. And I haven't heard you tell me anything about him implying that anything else is going to happen between you two. Has he?"

"No. We're just friends," she said, looking away. Why couldn't Tempe just be happy that Jillian was happy?

"No, you're not. He might be, but you are not. Don't wait for him," she said.

"God! I am not waiting for him! I have told him, and I have told Monica, and now I am telling you, again, that I am not waiting for him! Just because I'm not out tramping around or signed up for online dating or whatever does not mean I'm waiting for him!"

Jillian was pissed. How dare she! How dare any of them tell her what to do! It was her life. If she wanted to fucking wait for him for the rest of her life, she could, and she would. She couldn't stand dating. She was terrible at meeting new people. That was why she drank when she went out, because it eased her tension, her anxiety. That was why she dated (or slept with) men she worked with—she already knew them; they already knew her. They didn't have to go through that awkward stage of meeting, deciding whether they were worth getting to know a little better. What if she didn't like him? How did she get out of it? That's how she and Peter had met, for crying out loud. She really wasn't a snob, or cold, like some people thought. She was introverted, extremely self-conscious, and aware of everything that was going on around her. Dating sucked. She was a serial monogamist, even when it was only a one-sided emotional relationship. But maybe that's an oxymoron. One-sided does not a relationship make. Better one-sided than no sided. She told Tempe so.

"So just lay off, OK? Why can't you just be happy for me?"

"I'm worried about you! You're spending too much time alone. You are in love with a married man. You aren't meeting any new people. Is this how you want to live your life? I don't think it is. If it is, tell me you're happy with the way things are and I'll leave you alone. Tell me. Is this what you really want?"

"God, no. But Cam means more to me than any man I've ever met in my entire life. He is the kind of man that I have always wanted, that I thought I would never find. I can't give up on him. I can't."

"OK, Jilly. OK," and she gave Jillian a hug.

42

Cam confirmed he was coming, but just for one day and night. Jillian was so excited and looking forward to it. She wanted to tell him that she loved him. She didn't want it to be a big drama, a big show.

She just wanted to say it like she would say it to Zach, or to Monica, or as if they had been saying it to each other since the beginning of time. No big deal.

He'd emailed that his annual blood workup indicated that some things were off. His doctor wanted him to get some tests done. He was a bit shaken, nervous, but said that he felt fine and was sure it was nothing. It scared her, but what could she do? It made her think about what would happen if something happened to him. When would she find out? How would she find out?

Would someone call her? Or would he just disappear, and she would never know? Her chest gave a squeeze, and her eyes burned, a lump rose in her throat at the thought that he could be ill or injured and she wouldn't even know, that something terrible could happen and she wouldn't ever get the chance to tell him she loved him or tell him goodbye.

She knew it was time, she had to. When she let herself feel, really feel, the love she had for him, tears came to her eyes. She was so grateful for him. She wanted him to know. Even if they would never be together again.

He arrived in town, and she met him in the hotel lobby. She had decided to stay at home instead of the hotel, so she would drive back and forth. He looked great, so sexy, as always, and he told her how great she looked, as always. He sat down with her on the couch, sitting closely, and she turned toward him with her arm up on the back of the couch, her legs curled up, so that she was fully turned toward him, giving him her full attention.

"So what's been going on? Did you have a good day today?" he asked, with his usual chuckle and smile.

"I am just so psyched to see you, so happy you're here. Makes my day, my week," she laughed, smiling. "Did you have a good trip up north?"

"Yep, it was pretty uneventful. Nice to be back in warm weather, thaw out for a while." He laughed.

"Well, I could certainly help you thaw out…" she said. "Ready to go get something to eat, some drinks?"

"Sure! Let's go!" he said.

She didn't really want to go, didn't want to put any distance between them.

They walked to a nearby restaurant, talking all the way about work, new clients, old clients, laughing, casual, totally comfortable. She so wanted to hold his hand, kiss him, but she tried to respect where he was. If he wanted her, he knew how to come and get her. They ate, had too many beers, listened to some music in the bar. Finally, he asked her again about the bartender, what was going on with him, which opened the topic; or rather, she thought it would.

"Nothing going on. We're done. He was just too negative, no real connection. I didn't want to be around him anymore," she said, not looking at Cam.

"So, anyone else? Looking?" he asked.

"I don't really want to talk about that with you, OK?" she said, and tried to smile to soften her tone. She was trying to be a bit mysterious, not really wanting him to know that she was alone, that it was too hard to motivate herself to go looking when she was in love with him. And it also served to help her figure out if he was jealous, how he would react.

"Want to talk about you and Mary Beth? What's going on?" she posed.

"Things are OK," he said, looking away. He offered nothing more.

"Don't want to talk about it?" she pressed. He didn't answer, didn't look at her. She let him off the hook.

"Ready to go then? I know you need to get up early," she offered. She was a bit drunk, ready for a confrontation if he dared start one.

"Yeah, I guess so. Thanks for understanding."

They were quiet on the way back, but it was only a short walk. She supposed they were both contemplating the end of their evening, each wondering how easy—or difficult—it would be to walk away from each other again. It had to be his move, but she was set on her mission.

"I need to pee," she said when they got back to the lobby. She really did, but she also wanted the excuse to walk in with him, have him wait, so she could hug him goodnight. She used the restroom, checked her hair, her face, took a few deep breaths, and marched back out to say goodnight.

She walked up to him. "Going? Tired?" he asked, smiling.

"Yeah, I think it's time. I had a great evening."

He stood up. "I had a great time, too. Come here," he said, and reached out. She stepped toward him, and his arms went around her. He bent down so they were cheek to cheek. Perfect.

"Night, Cam. I love you," she whispered. She broke the hug, turned, and walked away without looking back. She didn't turn to see if he was staring, mouth agape, or smiling, or already walking away. She supposed she didn't really want to know.

She pushed through the doors, took a few deep breaths, smiled to herself that she had kept her courage, and started toward her car. Tears started leaking down her cheeks. As soon as she was home in bed, she texted him. "The bartender could offer me the moon n stars, but he wouldn't be u…U have no idea how much I want n need u. Meant what I said. LU."

Would he reply? Would he call? Would he acknowledge her at all? He didn't reply. He didn't call. She didn't even know if he'd heard her.

They had their meetings the next day with no time really to have any personal dialogue. She tried to read his demeanor the couple of times she saw him, to see if he was nervous. If he was happy about things, he surely would have taken the time and effort to tell her so. So, he wasn't. Now, time for damage control, and she might not even have the chance to see him before he left for the airport. She texted him again. "Great to see u. Looking forward to a reply."

This time, he did. "Had a great time. Let's talk re messages offline, OK?"

"OK. U tell me when. Miss u already."

And so she waited, again. Four days. Five days. Six days. She finally got an email from him saying he'd been super busy, but he knew they needed to talk.

Why was it so important to talk after hours? With his schedule, that was hard to accomplish. What was the big deal? She was annoyed. Ten minutes later her phone rang.

"Well hey there!" she answered.

"Hey there, you," he replied.

They caught up on work for a few minutes, then, finally, he broke the ice.

"So, are you ready to talk about us?" he asked.

Oh. My. God. She almost burst right into tears, that he had said "us." She couldn't remember Peter ever having wanted to talk about "us." She still wasn't sure he had ever felt there was an "us."

When she and Peter had been living together for more than a year, he wanted to buy a house. They didn't even talk much about it, but when she came home from work one day, he announced that he'd been house shopping with his mother and was going to make an offer. Before she even had the chance to respond, the phone rang, and it was one of his best friends. Peter told him all about the house, all the time saying that "he" was going to buy a house. Jillian sat listening, stunned, that after them being together for two years, living together for more than half of that, he still wasn't thinking in terms of "us." For a few years, once he finally proposed, and they planned the wedding and got married, then had Zach, she almost felt like they were a real couple. Then the distance widened yet again. He would surely have scoffed if she ever brought it up, but she would never forget the day she realized his new "us" was him and Zach, not him and her. She was shut out again.

But Cam had said, "Do you want to talk about us?" Astonishing.

"Yes, please. I hope you haven't been avoiding me because of what I said, Cam."

"No, I haven't been. I'm just worried," he said.

"Worried about what? Cam, do you remember what I said in Las Vegas? About what you mean to me?"

"Yes, I do remember that," he said.

"I meant it. And I meant what I said that night. Cam, you mean a lot to me. I knew it was a risk telling you that, that it might scare you, run you off, but I wanted you to know how important you are to me as a person. I can feel that way about you as a friend, right?" Oh, she was such a coward. What a joke. She was terrified.

"You just said it and walked out, and I didn't get the chance to say anything to you. But that makes me feel a lot better. You mean a lot to me, too. I just thought that we had really gotten to a point where we knew we were just friends," he said.

"Cam, I didn't want to make a big deal out of it. I didn't want to freak you out. We are good friends. Please don't avoid me. If I say something that makes you nervous, or worried, please don't run away. Just ask me about it and let's clear things up, OK? I want you in my life," she said.

"Absolutely. Of course. You mean a lot to me, too."

"So we're OK?"

"Yeah, of course we're OK," he said.

She got an email from him the next day. Totally casual, but there he was again. Back. Again, she did (almost) what she wanted, expecting him to turn away, but he didn't.

She told him she loved him. It took him a few days to process it. But he came back.

43

Three weeks later, Jack asked Jillian to go to Atlanta for a meeting, in his place. They were barely speaking to each other. She passed it off as both being so busy, but there was tension. He knew he'd been put on notice; he was keeping his distance.

She also couldn't help but feel that fate kept arranging these circumstances so she and Cam could be together. They decided to meet for dinner after her meeting. Oh, as soon as he walked into the hotel lobby, where she was anxiously awaiting him, his hands in his jean's pockets, nice button-down shirt, flip-flops, she practically melted into the floor. *Just friends, just friends, just friends.*

As soon as he saw her, his face broke into his glowing, face-softening smile, the one that told her he was happy to see her. She smiled her brightest smile back at him, and tears sprang unbidden into her eyes, making them burn. Sheesh, what was that about? *Control, control, before he sees.*

"Hey there you," he said softly as he neared, and their arms were around each other without another word. He felt so good. She could feel his pecs flexing through his shirt, pressing against her chest. She smelled his cologne, his mouthwash, his hair gel. Intoxicating.

"You feel great," she said, not wanting to let go, but knowing that would be the appropriate just-friends thing to do. But she didn't.

He didn't either. "You do, too. You look amazing, as always," he whispered. They finally pulled away from each other, and he ran his fingers across the back of her hair, then touched her cheek. And then he leaned in and kissed her on the forehead.

"What was that for?" she asked, puzzled.

"I couldn't help myself. And it really wouldn't be the right thing to kiss you on the mouth, like I want to, would it?" He chuckled.

"Certainly not, friend," she said, winking at him. "Ready for some dinner or something?" she asked. Oh, it was going to be a rough night, but she was faking it well so far, she thought.

"How about we just eat here, maybe hang in the bar for a while, get some drinks, talk," he said.

"Sure thing, big guy," she said, smiling again.

They went to the bar and had drinks, and joked and laughed, and talked about work and kids and more work and sports and everything under the sun except Mary Beth, and except "us." They ordered some bar food, laughed some more, talked about music, their parents, their families. Had a couple more drinks.

"Want to go for a walk? I need to stretch," he said.

"Sounds dangerous. Remember the first time we went for a walk?" she teased.

"Uh, yeah, of course I do. Won't ever forget it," he said, not looking at her.

They found their way out, and joked, and teased, and she shoved his arm a couple of times just to touch him, and then he took her hand in his. They stopped joking immediately, and her heart pounded as she wondered what was going on.

They walked for a few minutes in silence, hands clasped together, holding on for dear life, like they were both afraid the other would let go. No, she wouldn't ever let go. Did he know that?

"So, what's going on?" she finally asked quietly, taking advantage of their hand holding and pulling him closer to her. He came, their arms touching, and then he stopped walking, pulling her gently to a halt, as well. She turned to look at him. He was just standing there, staring at her, not smiling, just looking at her, right into her eyes. She stepped closer to him, closer, so they were toe-to-toe. She took his other hand in hers, too, never breaking their stare into each other's souls. She could hear his breathing. She thought she could even hear his heart beating too, along with her own.

They stood that way for what seemed an eternity, until, ever so slowly, he leaned down into her, closed his eyes, and gently kissed her lips, once, twice, three times.

He pulled back, opened his eyes to look at her. Then quickly dropped her hands and took her face in his hands and kissed her again, not so gently. She kissed him back, not so gently. She wrapped her arms around him and pulled him tightly to her as his tongue pushed its way into her mouth and his hands slid down her arms, then wrapped around her, and she reached hers up around his neck to pull him into her even further.

She finally pulled back from him. "Will you come upstairs with me?" she asked. She wanted him so badly. All of him.

He nodded and kissed her again. She took his hand, and they rushed back into the lobby, into the elevator where they kissed some more, and then down the hall to her room, where they tore each other's clothes off at the speed of light and enjoyed each other's bodies the way bodies were meant to be enjoyed.

Wrapped up in each other afterward was pure torture to her. Her head was on his chest, his thumb stroking her arm, and she wondered what he was thinking. If the guilt had taken over already.

"Are you OK?" she asked quietly.

"Yep," he said.

"Don't sound like it," she said, without moving.

"I just don't know what to do," he said. He sounded tortured.

She moved to sit up, turning around to look at him.

"What? Don't you go anywhere!" he smiled, tugging at her to lie back down with him.

"Cam, do you think you can stand to hear it from me face to face?" Her heart was aching for him, and for herself.

He looked at her but didn't say a word.

"Cam, I love you. And I don't just mean as a friend. I am totally in love with you," she said. Tears filled her eyes.

He sat up. "Jilly, I'm sorry. I am messed up. I am so fucked up. I don't know what to do! I don't know what the right thing is anymore. I need to go. I shouldn't be here! But I want to be! More than anything. I just couldn't resist you tonight. I so wanted to be with you, you mean so much to me, but I don't want to hurt you!" he said.

"What do you want from me?" she asked. Here we go again. She got up and put her T-shirt and panties back on. "Cam, I can't take this anymore. I can't take the push and pull, the on-again, off-again. I know you are struggling, but you are not being true or fair to anyone here, including yourself. If you want to make your marriage work, if you love Mary Beth and want a life with her because you love her, then walk away from me and never come back. I cannot make this decision for you; you are the only one who can change your situation, and you make the choice every day to stay with her. I love you, Cam. I am so in love with you. When I allow myself to fully feel it, I can barely breathe."

She choked on her words, the hot tears overflowing and streaming down her face. The lump in her throat was so big she didn't know what would come out when she tried to continue, but she knew she had to. She had to get it all out while she had the nerve. It was time to throw the dice, time to risk it all and let fate take them where she may. She would die if this went on another day.

He hadn't moved.

"I have never met a man like you, a man who seems to love me for just who I am, and who I want to be beside for the rest of my life. But the choice is not mine! And thinking about you with her is breaking my heart! I can't stand imagining you looking at her the way you look at me, kissing her, loving her, the way you love me; living your life every day with a woman who is not me! You have everything, Cam! Your life is full—your family, your home, your job—and you have your cake and you're eating it, too, by staying with her and taking me and leaving me at your will with no consequence. But my life is not full. It's just full of holes. I am alone, and so lonely, because I can't imagine being with anyone but you. I feel like I'm being untrue to you if I even have dinner with another man. Isn't that the most ridiculous thing you've ever heard? How could I feel like I'm cheating on you, when you're the one going home to your wife every night, cheating with me?"

He was still sitting in bed, just staring at her, his face, his eyes, looking more and more concerned, sadder, defeated.

"I deserve more than you're giving me, Cam. I deserve to have the man I love, the man who loves me, beside me every day, committed to me, loving only me, living his life with me, and no other. I can't stand the thought of having to let you go, but I am not sure that I have ever really had you to begin with. You've never really been mine to give up."

Tears were streaming down his face, too. She had never seen him cry. She so wanted to go back, to tell him she was wrong. *Never mind, just hold me, kiss me, tell me you love me, let's just forget this and leave things the way they were, I can't let go, I can't let go…*

But she continued, "I know I have been selfish. I know I have been greedy, and jealous. I have wanted you to break her heart, to leave her, so you could be with me. I know I have been wrong. I know I have asked for too much. But I couldn't help it. I truly believe, for the first time in my pitiful little misbegotten mistake of a life that I have found a soul mate in you. But you choose not to be mine," her tears were slowing. She was beginning to steady, regain control. Or maybe she was shutting down, becoming numb.

She sat down in the chair. She was exhausted.

"And now, I will let you go, showing you how true my love is for you by setting you free, so that you can lead the life you've chosen without the lure, the temptation of another woman torturing your soul. I must move on, Cam. I'm so sorry that I can't hold on to you, or let you hold on to me, like we promised each other we could—not anymore. This has got to end and, since you can't seem to call it, I must, before too much of my life passes me by and I look back and wonder what happened to it."

She wasn't sure this was the right thing to do to live, if that was truly her goal; her heart was being torn out of her chest, every pore, every cell of her being was screaming to stop. It was too hard. Her soul was being ripped in half and lit on fire, or downing, dying a painful death either way. Her whole body was shaking, her skin was on fire, her limbs felt detached, like vapor, numb, dead.

He still hadn't said a word. He had barely moved. The only way she knew he heard her was from the tears streaming down his face. He stood up, still silently staring at her, his huge green eyes red from crying. He didn't reach out to her. He didn't argue. He didn't beg or plead. But when she did finally close her mouth to take a deep breath to steady herself before she suffocated, he opened his.

"Jilly, I love you," he said. He got dressed and, without another word from either one of them, walked out. Without even kissing her goodbye.

She cried all night, until she was sick, even throwing up once. She cried until nothing more came out, her eyes swollen, her nose so full she couldn't breathe.

She tried to decide if she was being true to herself, or if it had all just been a power play, an ultimatum, to find out if he did love her, wanted her, if he would ever choose her.

What did she truly want? What did her heart, her soul, want from this wound?

She wanted Cam to know that she truly cared about him and to lock that away inside of him somewhere, as she had, and keep it safe, knowing that there was someone else out there who wanted the best for him, and was cheering him on, and wanted him to have every happiness, even knowing she had nothing to do with affecting any of that for him, but was always hopeful.

She wanted him to know how in love with him she was. That it was with her constantly, and more every day, every time she saw him, heard his voice.

She wanted him to know that she saw so much in him that she admired, that she respected. They had so many things in common. They were kindred spirits.

But she crushed herself with those thoughts. She couldn't let go. Why? Why couldn't she just walk away? The paradox of being a human being with a heart and a brain is having feelings, although those feelings frequently had no relevance at all to what you knew in your head to be reality.

Your heart refused to acknowledge that it just didn't make any sense, refused to align itself with what your head said it should do or feel.

Her heart knew why she loved him and refused to let go. It just couldn't make her head understand any of it. And her head was unable to talk her heart into changing its mind.

44

At nine the next morning, she was just getting out of the shower when there was a knock at the door, probably the cleaning lady. "Just a minute!" she yelled, grabbing a robe.

She looked through the peephole. Flowers. All she could see was flowers. She opened the door. It was a bellman with a huge vase of gorgeous flowers (not yellow roses). "For the lady?" he said, motioning to bring them in.

"Yes, thank you," she said, puzzled. As soon as he left, she grabbed the card. "Please don't let go. I love you, Jillian. — Cameron"

She messaged him. "You nut. What did u do? Call me."

Her phone rang immediately. "Cam, they're beautiful. Why did you do that? I sent you packing!"

"Can we talk?"

"I thought that was what we were doing," she chuckled, but without feeling any mirth.

"No, in person, I mean. Will you open the door?" and she heard a light rapping.

"You're here?" she shook her head, opening the door.

"Well, you are not dressed yet, young lady!" he said, and they both clicked their phones off.

"Cam…" she started, not really knowing where to start.

"Jilly, stop," he said. "I owe you a really big apology. First, please don't think that I am using you or taking advantage of you, I just…" He stared at her pleadingly.

"Let me bail you out again," she started.

He sighed.

"You've never made me any promises, Cam. And I have never asked you for any. Tonight, you will be home, I will be home, I will be alone again, and the truth will come crashing in on me like a fifty-foot tidal wave. But I know where you are. I'm a grown woman. I make my own decisions. I don't want anyone making my choices for me, including you. But you have made yours. And I have made mine. This can't go on, I'm sorry. If you can't choose me, I have to let go." She went to him and wrapped her arms around him, kissing him on the lips. He kissed her back and held her.

"I love you, Jilly," he whispered.

"I love you, too, Cam. Goodbye."

45

On her first day back from Atlanta, Tom from HR called her and asked if she could come down to his office.

"What's up?" she asked, trying to get a read on him. He had never called her down to his office.

"I need to talk to you about some things. Can you come now?"

"Sure. Be right there," she said. She grabbed a notepad and pen, checked her makeup and hair, and put a mint in her mouth so she'd have something to do.

When she arrived, he was at his conference table, and he motioned for her to take a seat.

"What's going on?" she asked, alerted.

"Jack and I are concerned about you," he started, leaning in on the table.

"We have heard some rumors that you have been personally involved with a couple people from upstairs and that it may be presenting a conflict for you," he said, all business.

"What…"

He held up his hand for her to stop. *What the hell?*

"You aren't here being interviewed. Your personal life is not our business. But Jack and I have discussed it, and we think it might be best for everyone if you leave the firm," he said.

"I…"

He stopped her again.

"Don't say anything, Jillian. Just trust me. Just go," he said.

She did. She went to her office and packed one box of stuff, not caring about the rest. And she left.

She texted Monica and Tempe and asked them to come over to her place as soon as they were able—it was important. They both arrived shortly after five o'clock. She told them what Tom said, and that she had left.

"You know this is about your warning shots to Jack, don't you?" Monica asked.

"What do you mean?" Jillian asked. She was still reeling and in shock but hadn't freaked out yet. She hadn't thought through the reasoning and didn't know what to do. All she knew was that she wanted out, and they had opened the door.

"Well, I'm sure Jack and Tom have both been worried about you, but not the way you think. They have been worried you were going to file a sexual harassment lawsuit, so they tried to find a reason to get rid of you before you could do that, and they did."

"But how do they know about Ethan, or Cam, or both of them? If they know?" Jillian asked, reeling.

"Maybe someone told them. Who else knows?" Tempe asked.

"Well, I don't know who all knows about Ethan, but I didn't tell anyone other than you two, and Cam. And Cam, well, only you two and Kayla know, but only about that first night...I think," she said, going over conversations in her mind to see what might have slipped out. "It had to be Kayla. It certainly wasn't one of you two, right?"

"Right!" they said in unison.

"And it sure wasn't Cam. He wouldn't risk it for fear of his wife finding out. It would be too easy for me to make a call to Mary Beth and out him. And what would be his motive? Anyway, I know Cam, and he wouldn't do that."

"I agree. There's no reason Cam would have told anyone. Too much of a risk. But, Kayla, really?" Monica said, trying to reason it out.

"Who else? She was there that first night with Cam. And we had kind of talked about Ethan at the bar. She asked me about Cam a couple of times. Remember she wanted to go to the Vegas conference? And what she asked me about after? If I'd had any fun? Then almost immediately, Jack asked me the same thing? Then those questions about where Cam worked, and was it with Ethan, and was he helping with Delta? It had to be her. She set me up because she's against Delta, or she wants my job, or something. Who else could it be?"

"That makes sense to me. That little bitch. Some people just aren't who you think they are. But I don't think it's about sexual harassment," Tempe said. "I think they think you have a conflict of interest, especially in regard to Delta and making referrals. Maybe they think you're making inappropriate referrals in their favor, if you have a personal relationship with them," Tempe said.

"No way," Monica said. "Jack knows Jillian, and he knows she wouldn't do that. She spurned him, and he's used to getting what he wants. He didn't even talk to her; they didn't even ask her for a response!" she said, defending Jillian.

"Yeah, that's pretty crappy. You didn't sign anything, did you? Did Tom give you an agreement or anything?"

"No," Jillian answered, all of it spinning through her mind. She couldn't believe Jack would do that to her, after everything. Just kick her to the curb like yesterday's trash. Without even talking to her. Without asking her a single question.

"Well, what are we going to do?" Monica asked.

"I'll tell you," Jillian said. "I essentially already left. I packed a box and walked out. I'm going to turn in my resignation and put all of this behind me—Jack, Delta, Ethan, even Cam—and enjoy this second liberation," she said, starting to feel more hurt and betrayal, but also some relief that she wouldn't have to walk in there tomorrow, or ever again. No months of trying to figure out what to do, of questioning her own motives, of waiting and wondering if it would ever be over, of the limbo she was in while she was trying to get divorced. This bandage came off in one quick rip. Maybe it was better that way after all.

"And do what?" they asked in unison.

"I don't know yet." She smiled.

46

She had found no Elysium, no utopia, no Eden; the happiness and fulfillment she sought still eluded her. Was it to be an odyssey to which there would be no end, no conclusion? She finally left the man she no longer felt anything for, plunged into complete infatuation with an unavailable, uninterested man she had one inane incident with, then fell completely, madly in love with her soul mate, who happened to be married to someone else. Would Ethan ever be back? Would she ever give him another moment of her time? Doubtful, on both counts. He felt completely gone from her world, vaporized. Their lives were entwined, but never joined.

Maybe she should have stayed with Peter. Perhaps she should have taken the path that so many others have taken—that Cam had taken—and stayed for Zach's sake, found the courage to be who she wanted to be despite Peter's response. At least she would be with Zach every day. But, even so, he was still such a smart, happy, well-adjusted kid. She couldn't ask for a more wonderful child, and she certainly enjoyed being his mom, though she missed him so much at times she thought her heart would stop.

If she had stayed, she would have shut Peter out completely, for sure. She could have just had an affair, or a string of them, hoping to never be discovered, but gaining some measure of satisfaction for herself. Would it have worked? How would that have affected Zach? What kind of behaviors would he have learned from that? What lessons that might have negatively influenced his own behavior, his life?

And maybe all the crap with Jack would never have happened, either, if she had stayed. Maybe she would still be enjoying her career and enjoying trying to change things for the better. Just a couple of years earlier the thought of working somewhere else never crossed her mind, was inimaginable. She loved that place once, it was hers.

She did gain her independence, though. She gained the freedom to be the kind of mother to Zach that she wanted to be, to make the kind of home she wanted to have, to be the person she wanted and needed to be. But she certainly hadn't gained all she had hoped to by leaving Peter.

She did find Cam. She found a man who left an indelible mark on her heart and soul, who totally changed her. She just met him too late. Maybe she would have been better off never knowing he was out there. But that didn't matter, because she did know, and she could not go back in time and erase him, erase their time together, erase knowing him and her feelings for him.

She was tired of saying she was sorry. She said she was sorry to Peter. She said she was sorry to Ethan. She even apologized to Cam, more than once. She had been offering the Universe recompense for her involvement with Ethan and Cam. It finally dawned on her that Kate might not be answering her because her father had an affair. She would have told Kate she was sorry, too, if that was why she stopped answering her. Maybe what she was doing was unforgivable to Kate, and therefore Jillian would have to let go of the thought of her, too, as she had to let go of so many other precious hopes, dreams, gifts.

Such a short time ago, it seemed, and yet forever ago, she knew that Ethan was flawed, that they would never be right together, and yet she yearned for him so badly because of the fantasy she had created and because she had buried what she knew to be true. She fantasized about inserting herself into his perfect life. She wondered how it would feel to be in the same room with him. If she saw him, would she flash back to the time she thought he was perfect? Or would he look different now that she recognized the illusion?

And how long would it take to recognize the signs regarding Cam that she ignored, that will smack her in the face later, when she found perspective? What will happen that will make her realize she made it all up, that the connection with Cam was imagined, only desired so strongly that she created it in her mind—again nurturing, nourishing a one-sided emotional affair? With Cam, she fantasized about him joining her in her life, being beside her every day, here, where she was and continued trying to convince herself to continue this journey. She allowed herself to believe that she would be happier, stronger, with him next to her, cheering her on.

She wanted to be with the right person, and she wanted to be able to tell the world about it. She just didn't know if that was ever going to happen. She was just so sick of wasting time! It seemed her life was passing her by, and she wanted the man that she wanted to spend the rest of her life with to be by her side, living it with her. She cried every day that they missed being together.

Was she wrong to love Cam? It shouldn't ever be wrong to love someone, to feel love toward a person, should it? How could it be? Isn't love the most precious emotion, the most precious connection, the most desired link between two people? No, loving someone can't be wrong. But the actions taken in the name of that love can be described as right or wrong, acceptable or not, healthy or insane.

So yes, she loved Peter, right or wrong. It faded away like the color on a rosebud left to dry out in a vase, slowly dying and drying because they failed to learn how to take care of each other. She loved the illusion of Ethan, right or wrong, whether it was really Ethan whom she fell for, or just the yearning for a genuine symbiotic relationship. And she loved Cam, right or wrong. Even when her love for Peter was at its strongest, she never felt him in her soul the way she did Cam. She wasn't even sure she had a soul before she met Cam.

She didn't know what would happen tomorrow; no one does. Maybe Zach would decide he wanted to spend more time with her, and Peter would let him. Maybe leaving the agency would be the best thing that ever happened to her.

Her love for Cam changed her, gave her hope that maybe she was meant to be born, that he was, too, and that they were meant to eventually find each other, and connect, and support each other, even if it was never as more than what was already in the past. And she did know that she loved him, that he was her miracle, and that she would hold him closely in her heart, but that she would let go and move on. She was not afraid. And she was not sorry.

EPILOGUE

Jillian's phone rang, no caller ID and not a number she recognized, but it was local, so she answered it.

"Hi, Jillian? This is Drew, Zach's classmate Joey's dad? We met at school a couple of weeks ago?"

"Yes, yes, hi Drew, I remember. How are you?" She did remember him. He was quite yummy. They had said hello while they were filling out emergency contact forms.

"I'm good! I was just wondering, though…Is this a good time? Are you busy?" he asked.

"No, sure. What's up?" she asked.

"Well, I just thought maybe we could get the boys together sometime," he said.

"Sure, of course. That'd be fun. Any time in particular? Zach is with his dad sometimes, but he'll be home this weekend," she said.

"OK, can we maybe meet somewhere for dinner Friday then, with the boys?" he asked.

"Sure!"

They met at the neighborhood pizzeria that had tons of video games and TVs. They sat among the chaos while the boys ran back and forth getting quarters, and Jillian and Drew talked.

The waitress came for drink orders.

"Um, a Diet Coke," he ordered. "For you?" He looked at Jillian.

"Same for me." She smiled at the waitress.

"No beers? It's Friday night!" Jillian asked.

"Oh, I don't drink anymore. But you can if you'd like!"

"Oh, I don't drink anymore, either. Not good for the health."

"Agreed!"

He was quite attractive, that was for sure. Flawless olive complexion, black hair, dark eyes. Must be Hispanic. Very well built, strong, lean. He was divorced from Joey's mom. He had a brace on his knee from some recent surgery. They talked and laughed and joked.

Another mom from school suddenly sat down next to Jillian, opposite Drew.

"Hi! What's up, girlie?" she asked in her usual jovial tone.

"Hey! Having some eats, boys are playing. You?"

"Yeah, we're over at the other end. Spotted you when I was coming out of the ladies' room," she said. Then she leaned in and whispered, "Are you two on a date? That is so cute!"

Jillian looked at her, puzzled. Oh my gosh, was this a date? No wonder she had been so at ease; she hadn't thought of it that way. If she had, she would have been completely tense and nervous.

"Um, I'm not sure exactly," she said in honesty.

"OK, well, enjoy! See ya!" And she winked at Jillian as she got up.

Jillian looked back at Drew. He looked at her and smiled, then leaned down to rub his knee.

"Sucks getting old. Not even fifty yet, but close, and falling apart," he said.

"Oh, yeah? How soon?" she asked.

"March." March was Cam's birthday: he'd be forty. Her heart starting hammering.

"March what?" she asked.

"Twenty-seventh. Why?" he asked, smiling. She almost fell out of her chair. Her head lifted off her body momentarily as the blood must have rushed to it in shock or excitement, or maybe just to get her attention. Cam's birthday. Exactly ten years apart. So attractive. Single. And here with her. With his son, who was Zach's classmate. Who lived in the same ZIP code. Who had asked her out.

"Just curious. So, what do you do?" she managed and smiled, suddenly very intrigued by this man who had so suddenly alighted on her little pond, out of nowhere, unbidden, unanticipated.

"I'm a career Marine, but trying to retire. How about you?" he asked, looking her in the eye, and smiling the most gorgeous, white-toothed smile she had ever seen.

"I left my advertising job a few months ago and am starting my own business," she replied, smiling.

"Oh, yeah? Wow! Good for you!" he said.

When he asked if she and Zach would come over to their house to set off some backyard fireworks after they all ate, she said sure. Drew drove the boys in his truck, and she drove by herself, following them to a nice home less than a mile from the condo. And the boys played and lit fireworks and had a blast. She told Drew that the next day was her own birthday. "It is? Oh my gosh! Well, these fireworks, then, are all for you! Happy birthday, Jillian!" And he gave her a quick kiss on her cheek as the boys jumped around, looking up into the night sky. *Happy birthday, indeed.*

ABOUT THE AUTHOR

Traci Tucker lives in Tampa, Florida, with her son and rescue Lab.

www.ingramcontent.com/pod-product-compliance
Lightning Source LLC
Chambersburg PA
CBHW071307140726
47996CB00005B/1668